RED SQUARE

A NOAH WOLF THRILLER

Prologue

John Wilkerson put away his broom and sat down in the little janitorial office. Most janitors found their offices in the basement, but John, head janitor for the U.S. Embassy in Moscow, had an office on the very top floor. The reason for this was simple; John Wilkerson was a janitor only when he was not performing his less official function of being a very special agent of the CIA.

On this particular morning, less than a week before he would have been celebrating his birthday if he were back home, John put on headphones connected to what appeared to be a small portable stereo while he powered up the computer on the desk. When it came to life and he saw the icon on the screen that indicated he was secure and free of any electronic eavesdropping or surveillance, he clicked on a game icon and entered a password.

The game opened up on the screen, showing what appeared to be a three-dimensional city. John scrolled down the screen to the image of a small island in a digital ocean and clicked on what appeared to be nothing but a rock. An internal messaging system opened up on the screen, and he saw that there were eleven messages waiting for him. He clicked on the first one and saw that it was from Vasily Jovovich.

Michael,

There's a rumor that someone in the highest levels is greatly dissatisfied with events in the Kremlin. This could be a terrific opportunity, but I can tell you that there's also great risk involved. I would advise extreme caution, but it might be prudent to explore the possibility of arranging a channel for defection. I'll provide more information as I get it.

Vasily was one of John's most valuable recruits. He was a low-level clerk in the Russian government, but one of his duties was to act as messenger for various government figures and agencies. As a result, he was known by just about everyone and could move around the Kremlin almost completely unnoticed.

He was also very good at spotting opportunities. It was Vasily who had orchestrated the defection of a *Politsiya* supervisor eight months earlier. The information and insights gained from that defection had completely revolutionized espionage within Moscow, by providing details about Russian police procedures and activities that had previously been shrouded in mystery.

If he had come across someone in the higher levels of government who might be open to either cooperation or defection, John was going to have to pursue that possibility.

He went through the rest of the messages, most of which were of only minor importance, but the last one was another from Vasily.

Michael,

My earlier message has some serious potential. Anton Kalashnikov, currently the First Deputy Minister of Defense, is prepared to defect to the United States. He has some conditions that must be met before he can do so. I've extremely high confidence in this, as I've placed my own listening devices in his offices and have found no evidence that this is anything other than a genuine dissatisfaction with the Kremlin. I await your instructions on setting up a meeting.

Kalashnikov would be an incredible source of information. John sent a quick response telling Vasily to proceed, then left his little office to go and speak to his supervisor, Albert Duke.

"Hey, John," Duke said as he entered. "How is it going?"

"Might have something major coming up," John said. "One of my sources has found out that Anton Kalashnikov is interested in getting out of Russia. I told him to set up a meeting, so that I can find out what's going on. Vasily says Kalashnikov has certain conditions that have to be met before he can actually defect, but that he is seriously considering it if we can meet them."

Duke's eyes were about as wide as John had ever seen them. "Kalashnikov? Holy—John, if you pull this off, you'll be looking at a commendation and a medal! Just be as certain as possible that it isn't a trap. Ever since Ryan Fogle, the FSB has been trying their best to bait us into making another big screwup."

John chuckled. "Ryan wasn't even real," he said. "You and I both know that whole thing was nothing but a diversion, something to occupy the Russian press while we made some other move they didn't see coming. I mean, come on, what real spook would walk around with a dimestore spy kit made up of wigs and sunglasses?" He shook his head. "Vasily thinks this is legit, and he has been right on the money so far. I understand the risks, but if we can get someone like Kalashnikov to roll over, I have to believe it would be worth it."

"I have to agree," Duke said, "but I want to be careful. I can't afford to lose you, John. You've turned more doubles than anybody else I've had. Don't take any chances, okay?"

"Al, don't make me laugh," John said seriously. "Our lives are all about taking chances. I'll let you know what I find out, but as always, if anything happens to me..."

"Don't worry," Duke said. "I'll see that Liz is taken care of."

It was two days later before John heard back from Vasily, and the message was blunt and to the point.

Michael,

Kalashnikov is ready to meet. Vorontsovski Park, in front of the manor house, at lunchtime. He has already arranged for security to be nonexistent at that time. He will be wearing the uniform of a maintenance worker for the park.

Vorontsovski Park. The exact place where that idiot Fogle was arrested for trying to bribe Russian intelligence officers. John couldn't help wondering if that was a bad omen of some kind.

Lunch time was less than an hour away and it was a thirty-minute drive to the park. John shut down his computer and headed for the elevator. After a quick stop at Duke's office to let his supervisor know where he was going, he left the building and got into his embassy-assigned Lada Priora, and arrived at the park with twenty minutes to spare.

He parked the car at one of the smaller entrances and strolled in, stopping once at a concession stand to get a soft drink. As Vasily had said, there did not appear to be any security in sight, so he finally made his way to the manor house. This had once been the home of a Russian noble, but it was simply a tourist attraction now.

Like most of the espionage agents in the embassy, John was quite familiar with the appearance of most of the ministers and their deputies. He spotted Kalashnikov quickly, as the man walked along and picked up trash. Tourists had a tendency to be litter bugs, John thought to himself. He walked across the grounds at an angle that would let him intercept Kalashnikov when he reached a stand of trees.

"Tourists are pigs," he said in English when he got close enough. Kalashnikov turned and looked at him for a moment, then nodded.

"It's always so," he said. "Do I know you?"

"We have a mutual friend," John said. "He suggested I might drop by here today."

"Then let us speak clearly and quickly. I do not have a lot of time today. Our mutual friend has suggested I might be happier if I relocated, and I think there may be truth in that."

"Just tell me how I can help," John said. "I'll be happy to do whatever I can."

Kalashnikov nodded. "I've a lot of information that your people would want, and there's so much corruption in the Kremlin today that I'm prepared to cooperate. It is, in my opinion, the only way we will avoid a global conflict that will destroy much of the world. There is, however, a problem. Should I suddenly disappear, my family would suffer. My wife and children must go with me, but it must be in such a way that the Kremlin will believe we're dead. Can this be arranged?"

John was surprised, but he didn't let it show on his face. To make an entire family appear to be dead could be quite a daunting task. "I'm certain it can," he said. "I would have to explore the options to see what would be involved and how quickly it could be done. You have a timetable?"

"If it's to happen, it must be no later than the end of this month. After that, I'll not be in a position to have any freedom from observation for a long time. It's even possible that my superior will be changing positions, in which case I would be forced to accept his job. At that point, it would be impossible to accomplish this."

"All right. I'll get on this immediately, and I'll send our mutual friend to let you know what can be done." John strolled away without another word, giving the apparent maintenance worker only a friendly wave goodbye.

All the way back to his car, John expected FSB officers to leap out from behind a bush or tree, but he made it back with no interference. A quick glance at the car failed to show that it had been tampered with, so he got in and started it up. He drove back to the embassy by a convoluted route and finally arrived more than an hour later.

Duke looked up as John entered his office. "How did it go?"

"Kalashnikov wants to defect, and he says he will happily cooperate with our intelligence services in order to avoid World War III. The only problem is that he wants to take his wife and children with him, and he wants us to make it look like they're dead. Has to be done before the end of the month, or we will never get another chance, he says. I told him I thought we could arrange that, but that I would have to find out for sure. What do you think, Al? Could we do it?"

Duke scoffed. "Not us," he said. "That's beyond our immediate capabilities, especially having to do it so quick." He leaned back in his chair and steepled his fingers under his chin. "There are specialists who handle this kind of thing, though. I could send a message off to Langley and see what they can come up with. Somebody there would answer back as soon as they can figure something out."

"The sooner the better," John said. "This is an awfully big fish, and I would hate to have him slip off the hook."

"Okay, let's think this through before I send off a request. If we've got to make the Russian government believe the whole family is dead, we're probably going to need a lot of information. Get hold of your guy and tell them we need as much information about this family as possible. Names, dates of birth, photographs, descriptions, their clothing sizes, medical records, anything else you can think of. We'll need it all, if there's any hope of the right people pulling this off."

John nodded and got to his feet. "I'll get on it right now." He left Duke's office and headed back to his own, where he sent a message off to Vasily. The software in the game encrypted the message and inserted it into Vasily's message inbox, and John Wilkerson sat back to wait.

The following morning, John found a reply waiting for him.

It will take me several hours to gather up all this information. Meet me tonight, 9 PM LavkaLavka. You can buy me dinner.

John sent off a response confirming the appointment, then spent the rest of the day taking care of other duties. He handled the couple of message drops that always seemed to be part of his day, recovering the scribbled notes and thumb drives that his various double agents used to give information to him. He ended up working until after seven that night, just pulling information off the thumb drives and scanning the notes to be sent to the main data analysis groups back in Langley.

That part of his job often frustrated him, because he didn't understand how someone sitting in a cushy desk back in the States could understand the nuances of what was happening in Moscow better than he could. He had been living there for almost a year and a half now and had become quite familiar with the way the city and its people operated.

He arrived at the restaurant a few minutes late, his skin two shades darker than usual, brown contacts obscuring his normally blue eyes, and his blond hair dyed midnight black. He looked for all the world like someone from the Ural Mountains, and that was his intent. Vasily was from that area, and John Wilkerson had carefully cultivated this appearance so that he could pass as the cousin Vasily would claim him to be if they were questioned.

"Vasily," he called as he spotted his friend. "It's me, Nikolai."

Vasily smiled and stood, shaking his hand as if seeing him for the first time in years. "You've gotten fat, old friend," he said. The seemingly friendly insult was a code indicating that they were unlikely to be observed. "Your wife is feeding you too well, I see."

"At least I have a wife," John said. "I take it you're still single?"

Vasily invited him to sit at his table and the two of them kept up the small talk for quite some time. They ordered dinner and continued while they ate, and then John insisted on picking up the check. An observer would have seen two old friends enjoying a dinner together, and then laughing about some private joke as they left the restaurant and went their separate ways.

John drove back to the embassy by a circuitous route that took him more than half the night. It was 3 o'clock in the morning by the time he got back into his office and plugged the disposable cell phone that had been stuck with chewing gum under his side of the table into his computer.

Hidden in its memory chips was almost 50 MB of data. Everything they could possibly need to know about Anton Kalashnikov and his family was there, and he carefully encrypted the information and sent it to Duke's computer.

Six hours later, Albert Duke downloaded it to a secure data chip that was then inserted into a diplomatic pouch. It was carried under armed guard to the airport and passed directly to the courier, who never left the plane.

Fifteen hours later, it was in the hands of Nick Weber, Deputy Director of Analysis for the CIA. The cover letter that accompanied it explained Kalashnikov's desire to defect and his insistence on bringing his family with him, and all that it would entail. Nick thought about it for a total of five minutes, then repackaged it and got it ready to send out again.

CHAPTER ONE

Allison Peterson sat at her desk and looked at the encrypted message that had opened up on her computer screen. The CIA was requesting her assistance in arranging the defection of a high-level Russian Deputy Minister. The problem was that, in order to bring him in, he insisted on bringing his family along, but he wanted the Russian government to believe that they were all dead.

This was not an unusual request, and it had been necessary in the past for E & E to fake deaths this way, but it was usually only a single individual. This particular man had a wife and two children, teenagers, a boy and a girl. It would be impossible to substitute bodies, because even the families of Russian officials had their DNA recorded. The only scenario that could work would be for the bodies to be absolutely unidentifiable, but for the family to appear to meet its end in such a way that it wouldn't be doubted. The death scene would have to be highly visible and dramatic, leaving convincing evidence that there were no survivors.

There were ways to accomplish this, of course. The family could be in an airplane that crashed into the sea, or perhaps on a sinking ship. As long as there could be no doubt the family was present at the time of the disaster, and the entire disaster witnessed to the point that it could not be doubted, there was potential for making it work. The only problem was how to get the family safely out of the crashing airplane or the sinking vessel before they really did die.

How to accomplish it wasn't Allison's problem; whether to even try, unfortunately, was. The request from CIA was loaded with fancy words like "incredible opportunity," "absolute necessity," "avoid global conflict," and "gold mine of information." In Allison's mind, all of that translated to, "Please, please, please make this happen!"

Even worse, the request was endorsed by the president himself. While he could not order Allison to accept a particular mission, his endorsement indicated just how serious the need to pull this off really was. There was just no way in the world she could refuse and still be able to keep everybody happy, but before she would agree to such a difficult mission, she had to have more opinions than just her own.

She picked up the phone on her desk and punched in a number. "Donald? Find Molly and get your butts in here. We've got us a puzzler."

She hung up the phone and sat back, but it was only a couple of minutes before Donald Jefferson and Molly Hansen entered the room. Jefferson was her second in command at E & E, and Molly was a brilliant data analyst who could almost predict the future from bits of data anyone else would overlook. She let them take their seats and get comfortable, then briefed them on the request.

When she finished, Jefferson was staring at her with his eyebrows almost meeting in the middle. Molly, on the other hand, was looking up at the ceiling with her eyes open wide, a sure sign that she was running various scenarios through her computer-like mind and evaluating their chances of success. Allison watched both of them, waiting to see which would speak first.

Molly suddenly locked her eyes on Allison's. "A plane crash is possible," she said, "but it would be extremely difficult to make it happen in such a way that the wreckage and bodies couldn't be recovered. We could try a car crash, with fire and explosions, but it's virtually impossible to destroy all the DNA and prevent identification with the limited kind of heat that would generate. Besides, not being able to retrieve any DNA at all from the bodies might seem suspicious. I think most governments would automatically assume there was something fishy about it, don't you?"

"I would have to agree," Jefferson said. "The problem is that I can't think of another scenario that might work." He turned to Molly. "You?"

"Oh, I can think of a few. Have their car crash into a tanker truck full of diesel fuel; that would create a fire hot enough to destroy DNA, at least to the point that it can't be used to confirm identity. Same for a jet plane crash, which would be plenty hot enough from the fuel exploding. The trick is to get them out alive without anyone seeing it."

"What do you mean?" Allison asked. "Surely they wouldn't be in the crash, right? That would defeat the purpose."

"Of course we don't want them to be in the crash," Molly said. "At the same time, it's necessary for witnesses to be absolutely certain that they are. There's got to be incontrovertible evidence that the family was present in the explosion or fire, that's the only way to circumvent the problem of nonviable DNA. I'm sure Wally's people could come up with an idea."

Allison turned to Jefferson. "Donald, what do you think?"

He shrugged. "I'm sure we could arrange some kind of a fire," he said. "But even if we're certain DNA will be destroyed, wouldn't we still need some sort of corpses?"

"Yes, there would have to be bodies," Molly said. "Fire would leave pieces of bone and teeth, but even so, there shouldn't be any viable DNA. Anything over about four hundred and fifty degrees Fahrenheit will completely destroy DNA beyond any possibility of identification. As long as any bodies that are recovered match gender and size, and if we can produce witnesses to the event, there shouldn't be very much doubt that the family is dead."

Allison leaned back in her chair and chewed on her bottom lip for a moment, then nodded. "All right," she said at last, "let's work up a plan. We need to create a scenario that will leave no doubt the family is dead, and some way to get them out of the country and onto American soil. Molly, I'm going to put you in charge of planning. You'll be working with Team Cinderella on this, so prepare yourself for Jenny and her particular idiosyncrasies."

Molly smiled. "I've actually gotten to know her a little bit," she said. "I think she might be perfectly suited to this mission. Of course, you do realize we're going to have to produce the requisite corpses. Is there any particular way you want us to handle that?"

"Well," Allison said with a suspicious grin, "we don't want to go killing off innocent people. I might suggest you talk to Wally. He should be able to provide whatever you need in that regard."

Molly's eyebrows shot upward. "Corpses? He actually has corpses?"

"We collect quite a number of them, because occasionally we need one for a purpose like this. However, we also have bodies that are physically alive even though they're completely brain-dead. They can be kept that way all the way to moments before the death event, so there's no discrepancy that might indicate they were physically dead prior to that event."

Molly stared at her for a moment. "Wow," she said after a few seconds. "Gruesome but cool."

She turned and left Allison's office and went to her own, just down the hall. She shut the door behind her and sat down at her desk, then picked up her phone and dialed out to R&D.

"Lawson Research Group," said a cheerful receptionist. "How may I direct your call?" The ruse was just in case of an actual wrong number, but Molly had been expecting it.

"Molly Hansen calling for Wally Lawson," she said. Her name was one that every staff member at R&D was familiar with.

"Just a moment, please," said the woman. Soft rock music began to play and then Wally came on the line.

"Molly? Hey, girl, how are you?" Wally asked.

"I'm doing okay, Gruesome. How have you been?"

"Me? I'm awesome, just doing my daily mad scientist routine. What can I do for you?"

"I've got to plan the extraction of a family that's going to be defecting from Russia," Molly said. "It's going to be necessary to make the Russian government believe the entire family has died. Allison said that I should talk to you about how to provide bodies. I'm thinking that we're going to need to burn them, to destroy any viable DNA. Any suggestions?"

"Oh, wow, that's a good one," Wally said, and Molly stifled a giggle. Wally often sounded like a child getting ready to open a Christmas present when he was presented with a new conundrum. "What about switching the DNA of the family? In any relevant databases, I mean? Any possibilities there?"

"Hmm, I have my doubts. The father is apparently a high-ranking Russian official, so it's safe to assume they've got DNA records on file that we wouldn't be able to touch."

"Oh, too bad," Wally said. "Well, what about medical records? Can we get hold of those? If there's any previous surgeries that could be identifying, they can be a problem. If you can get them for me, though, I can produce bodies that would be so close any discrepancy would probably be ignored."

"We've got them, and a ton of other information about them. I can tell you what brand of makeup his wife wears, and that his daughter, who is only fifteen, is already using birth control."

"Oh, excellent. Of course, we'll only provide the bodies as an exercise in caution. The best way to handle this is to kill them all off in a situation that makes recovering the bodies pretty much impossible, anyway. I can think of a few different ways to do that without resorting to fire. Fire, believe it or not, would probably raise more suspicions than it could possibly alleviate, simply because the DNA would be destroyed, like you said. I'm thinking that we need to let dozens, maybe hundreds of witnesses see the family in an obviously fatal situation, but make it essentially impossible to recover enough remains for DNA retrieval."

"Ooh, sounds diabolical. How would we pull that off?"

"These are Russians, you say? How many in the family?"

"Four," Molly replied. "Parents and two teenage kids, a boy and a girl."

"Good. Russians like the water. It shouldn't be too hard for high-ranking officials to get a week's vacation around this time, because they celebrate Victory Day next week. You'll want to get them onto a yacht, maybe a sailboat, even. I would suggest Vladivostok this time of year; there's a lot of people who go there to get in some sailing, but the place isn't really tourist friendly. What you want is to make sure the boat the family is on goes down in the middle of a lot of other boats, maybe with an explosion and fire to cap it off, but within sight of at least a few other boats, or some of the ships that are always going in and out of port."

"Ew," Molly said. "But what if the fire goes out before the bodies are burned enough? It could be obvious it wasn't them, or it could be that they pull DNA out that proves it isn't."

"Oh, but there won't be any bodies," Wally replied. "Sharks, girly. In the last few years, the waters around Vladivostok have become known for sharks, and there have been a lot of recorded shark attacks. You make sure there are plenty of sharks around and nobody's going to expect to find any bodies at all. That's why you want witnesses, of course."

Molly shook her head in confusion. "Wait a minute," she said. "You're saying that I should put them on a boat and let it sink with a school of sharks swimming around. Wally, how am I supposed to accomplish that?"

"Commander Lester Flanagan," Wally said. "Les is my opposite number in the Navy. Works with naval intelligence, he devises gizmos and gadgets for them, and we often swap ideas. I can connect you, and Allison has the authority to commandeer any of their assets in support of a mission. He has got Big Willie."

Molly blinked. "I know I'm going to regret asking, but who is Big Willie?"

"Willie is not a who, it's a what, although there's actually five of them. Big Willie is a stealth submarine designed to look and move like a blue whale. It's a masterpiece of robotics, and it even returns a sonar signature that's identical to that of a living blue whale. Blue whales are very common in that area around Vladivostok, so nobody's going to be surprised to see one. Your defecting family can be sealed into canisters and dropped overboard, and Big Willie can pick them up. Then the yacht goes boom and sinks, the bodies float to the surface and the sharks go into a feeding frenzy—Big Willie can be dumping chum into the water to draw the sharks, then release the corpses in the middle of their feast—and everything's done. Dozens of shocked people on nearby boats or ships can testify to the fact that the sharks were having a smorgasbord on the family, and your people are home free."

Molly's mouth opened and closed two or three times before she managed to speak. "Wally, are you serious? There really is such a thing as Big Willie?"

"Oh, yes," Wally said. "Some of his software was actually developed right here. Les and I always help each other out when we can."

"Okay, but what about risk? We're talking about bringing in a Russian defector. What happens if he decides to go back to Russia one day and tells the Kremlin about Big Willie? I mean, it's gotta be top-secret, right?"

"That's why you put your people into the canisters. They're sealed in, they can't see or hear anything outside. They get dropped over the side or out the bottom of the yacht, and then Big Willie swims by and opens his mouth. Once they're all inside, Willie swims back to his mother, which looks for all the world like a container ship. He gets taken in through the big hatch in the bottom, crewmen remove the canisters and carry them up into one of the containers that's set up like a living area. They let them out of the canisters but lock them into the container, so nobody knows they're even there. When it gets back to the U.S., it's offloaded onto a truck and disappears onto the highway. All they have to do is sit around and watch movies or play video games for about two weeks, and then their new lives begin."

Molly's eyes were wide but she was smiling. "Wally, how soon can you confirm that Willie is available? This actually sounds like it could work, and it's crazy enough nobody would ever figure it out."

"Hang on a minute," Wally said. He put Molly on hold and was gone for almost five minutes, then came back with a chuckle. "You couldn't be any more lucky if you were a four-leaf clover. Big Willie three can be at Vladivostok within a week. His mother ship, the *Hyperion*, carries lots of different cargo that can go just about anywhere. Les can modify a few shipping documents and deliver fifty containers of rolled steel for the Russian auto manufacturers there. It will take the ship about two days to clear port, and then you could stage your little accident while the *Hyperion* is heading out."

"Wally, you're awesome! Let me get back to you, but I think this might work."

Molly called Allison and asked if she could come right down to discuss a possible plan, and Allison invited her to lunch, instead. The two of them met down in the parking garage and Allison drove them to the Assassin's Club, where they could discuss sensitive information while they ate.

Once they were seated and their orders placed, Molly went over the plan Wally had come up with. Allison nodded in all the right places, raised her eyebrows a couple of times and finally gave Molly her blessing.

"It sounds like it ought to work," Allison said. "I'll put in a request for assistance from the Navy as soon as I get back to my office, and you can start working the plan up today. As soon as we confirm the availability of the *Hyperion* and Willie, you can begin briefing Team Cinderella."

"HOW DO YOU FEEL ABOUT sailing?" John Wilkerson, once again in disguise, asked his passenger. John was driving a taxi cab, and his passenger was Anton Kalashnikov.

Kalashnikov looked into the rearview mirror, focusing on the driver's eyes. "I find it enjoyable," he said. "Of course, I don't get to do as much of it as I would like. My work keeps me very busy."

John shrugged, trying to affect an air of nonchalance. "That's too bad," he said. "I understand there's quite an experience next week near Vladivostok. I've a cousin who would be happy to rent you his yacht. Let me give you his card."

He pulled a small envelope from his pocket and passed it back to Kalashnikov. Inside, there was a business card for a small yacht rental service in Vladivostok, along with a miniature electronic tablet with a two-inch video screen, like the ones used in cell phones. Kalashnikov tucked the envelope into his own pocket, showing no signs of the excitement he felt. Somewhere inside it, he knew, would be the plan for getting him and his family out of Russia forever.

The taxi made it to its destination and Kalashnikov paid the fare and got out. He was having lunch with another deputy minister, this one from education, but he was early. He went to the men's room and into a stall, lowered his trousers and sat down on the commode, and then opened the envelope. The little tablet confused him for a second, but then he found the power button on the side.

The screen lit up and Kalashnikov spent five minutes reading the plan. He was to call and rent a sailing boat for the following weekend, then take his entire family out to join the whale watchers. Some hours afterward, while they were in international waters, the FSB would be alerted to a planned assassination attempt and would send agents from Vladivostok to try to warn him. Those agents, in a helicopter hovering overhead, would themselves become witnesses when the yacht exploded.

Kalashnikov and family, of course, would no longer be on the vessel. Each of them would be locked into a coffin-like device that would be dropped into the water when the explosion took place, and then retrieved by some kind of undetectable submarine. They were then to be transported to a ship and taken to Japan, where they would be placed on a diplomatic flight to the United States. The plan was so detailed that it even described the video games and movies that would be provided for them to enjoy for the hours they would be on the ship.

Kalashnikov committed the general details to memory, then dropped the tablet into the toilet. It was designed to be flushed, and the memory chip inside would be instantly wiped on contact with the water. Even if it were recovered somehow, there was no possibility that anyone could recover the data.

Three hours later, when Vasily stopped by to drop off some papers, Kalashnikov looked up at him and smiled, then said, "I think I'm taking the family out whale watching this weekend. Would you like to come along?"

Vasily declined, but later that evening he reported to John Wilkerson that Kalashnikov had agreed.

CHAPTER TWO

J enny's phone rang, and she rolled over to pick it up from the nightstand. "It's Allison," she said, and then she hit the button to answer. "Hello?"

"My office, 10 A.M. Briefing for your next mission." The line went dead.

She glanced at the time and saw that it was only seven thirty, then dropped the phone back on the nightstand and rolled over. She snuggled up against Neil and pulled him close. "I've got a mission," she said. "Allie wants me at the office by ten for briefing." Her hand played with the sparse hair on his chest, and then started moving lower.

An hour later, freshly showered and dressed, the two of them got into Jenny's Jaguar and drove the 300 yards to Noah's house. Ever since Jenny had given up her apartment and moved into Neil's trailer with him, they had gotten into the habit of having breakfast with Noah and Sarah. Usually, that meant that Jenny and Sarah would make eggs and sausage or waffles and syrup or some other breakfast combination, but occasionally they would simply go down to Charlie's. Charlie's was a restaurant not far from the headquarters offices, and breakfast was their specialty.

This particular morning called for waffles, and Sarah was already in the kitchen preparing them. Neil sat down at the table while Jenny poured coffee for each of them. She added sugar to Neil's cup, stirred it carefully, and set it in front of him. "Here you go," she said. "Is it okay?"

Neil took a sip and smiled. "Perfect, like always," he said. "Good girl."

Jenny beamed as she got her own cup and sat down beside him.

Noah came in a moment later and poured his own coffee, then sat down at the table with them. "Any idea where you're going?" he asked, but Jenny shook her head.

"Not yet," she said. "You know better than to ask, Allie never gives out any details over the phone."

"True," Noah said. "I heard a rumor yesterday that there's a mission coming up in Russia, but nobody knows any details yet. If that's it, just be careful over there."

"I'll find out soon enough." She turned to Neil. "I'm gonna miss you," she said, putting a pout into her voice.

"Ditto," Neil said. "Like Noah said, you just be careful. I don't want anything happening to you."

Jenny smiled, her entire face getting in on the act. "I'll be careful," she said.

Sarah dished up the waffles and set them on the table along with butter and syrup, and the four of them sat down to eat. Without any details of the mission, they simply made small talk. Noah noticed that Sarah kept grinning at Jenny, but he'd already grown accustomed to it. She found Jenny's natural submissiveness entertaining, even though it only manifested itself when she was with Neil. At any other time, Jenny was as controlling and ruthless as Noah himself. The only difference was that she could be quite emotional at the same time.

Noah couldn't. After witnessing the traumatic deaths of his parents when he was a child, Noah suffered from a form of PTSD known as histrionic affect disorder, which meant that he lacked the ability to feel normal emotions. Without emotion, he was also without conscience, and it was this reputed handicap that made him the most effective assassin the United States government had ever known. He could kill his target without feeling any guilt or recriminations, but only if his own internal logic agreed that the death was necessary.

Jenny, on the other hand, was classed as a highly functioning psychopath. After carefully plotting and executing revenge against New York City gang members for murdering her sister, Jenny had discovered that she enjoyed killing. Unfortunately, she had been arrested for those murders and was looking at the death penalty when Allison Peterson, the director of the organization known as E & E, found her. Allison paid her a visit and she gratefully accepted the opportunity to become an assassin rather than keep her own date with the Grim Reaper. It was only when she was at home with Neil that she could relax and be the submissive she had always wanted to be, and Neil's natural dominance suited her perfectly.

When breakfast was over, Jenny kissed Neil goodbye and hurried out to her car. Neil sat at the table, his long legs stretched out under it, and listened as the Jaguar drove away.

"She'll be back," Sarah said.

Neil looked at her. "I had a bad dream last night," he said. "I dreamed she went out on a mission and wasn't coming home ever again." The look on his face was one of total despair, and Sarah reached across the table to lay her hand on his.

Noah didn't believe in premonitions, but he was fully aware that all of the teams were under a constant risk when they were on mission. Just being in a foreign country with the intent of committing an assassination that would manipulate political factions was considered an act of espionage, and possibly even of war if it could be proven they were agents of the United States government. This was the reason that they were automatically disavowed by the State Department if they were captured. Each and every one of them was expendable, and they knew it.

JENNY ARRIVED AT THE headquarters building and parked the car in the underground garage, then rode the elevator up to the top floor. That's where Allison's office was located, inside a dummy corporation known as Brigadoon Investments. As she entered the executive offices, Allison's secretary smiled and told her to go on into the conference room.

Allison, Donald Jefferson, Molly Hansen, and three men were already there, and Jenny waved and smiled at all of them as she got herself a cup of coffee and sat down at the conference table. The men were Jim Marino, the intelligence specialist for Team Cinderella; David Lange, the transportation specialist; and Randy Crow, the backup muscle.

Randy Crow had, until a few months earlier, been known as Randy Mitchell, but he had been blackmailed into complicity with an unknown person, at the time thought to be a CIA mole, who was manipulating agents and agencies all over the world. He had been forced to provide that person with information about Noah, but his complicity had been compromised by that point. Instead of divulging true information, he passed off a fabricated file that concealed much of the truth about Team Camelot and its leader.

The mole had then ordered Noah to eliminate Randy. In order to keep him from being actually murdered, Noah had used a risky drug that made him appear to be dead so convincingly that a death certificate had been issued. In reality, however, he had been given a new face and a new identity and sent right back to work with Jenny.

As Jenny took her seat, Allison looked sternly at all of them. "You're about to embark on a mission that's very different from anything you've done before," she said. "This time, you'll be doing everything possible to keep your targets alive while convincing the entire world, including the Russian government, that they're dead. A general plan has already been put together, and Molly will brief you on it, but I'm sending you because you have the ability to adapt. The objective of the mission is to bring out Deputy Defense Minister Anton Kalashnikov and his family, so that they can defect to the United States. Kalashnikov has absolutely invaluable information, and confidence in his intentions is very, very high."

Jenny scowled. "You mean I don't get to kill anybody this time?"

"If I know you," Jefferson said, "an opportunity will probably present itself. You're authorized to kill only in the furtherance of the mission, however. Don't go off the reservation, Jenny."

She shrugged. "Sorry, but I was looking forward to it," she said. "I've been stuck at home for almost two months, now."

Allison stared into her eyes for a moment and Jenny subsided. A moment later, Allison raised a finger and pointed at Molly, and everyone turned their attention to her.

"As Allison says," Molly began, "the objective of the mission is to bring this family out safely. We put together the scenario that will allow that to happen, but there are going to be some very tricky aspects of it. Some of those," she said, looking pointedly at Jenny, "may provide an opportunity for you to utilize your particular talents."

She squeezed a clicker and the face of Anton Kalashnikov appeared on the screen behind her. "This is Minister Kalashnikov. For almost a year, now, he has been carefully providing information to a Russian double agent who has been forwarding it to one of our operatives. Some of that information has helped us avert some terrible tragedies in former parts of the old Soviet Union, as the Russian government tries to reassert itself in certain areas."

She squeezed the clicker again. "Here is Kalashnikov with his wife and children. His wife's name is Ivana, his fourteen-year-old son is Piotr and his fifteen-year-old daughter is Olga. As far as we know, the family has no idea they're about to become Americans, but Kalashnikov refuses to leave them behind. He is afraid that, should it ever become known that he defected, they would be murdered in retaliation. Considering that the FSB employs many of the same agents and tactics of the old KGB, he is probably correct."

A new picture appeared, of a sailboat. "In a few days, Kalashnikov and family will board this boat at Vladivostok and sail out into the ocean to watch the passing of blue whales. This is something that only happens rarely in that area, but it happens to play directly into our plans. The boat will be rigged with explosives, and hidden in its hull are four escape pods. An American agent who lives in Vladivostok will be posing as the captain of the boat, and it will be his job to get the family into those escape pods when the time comes.

"Shortly after the boat leaves port, we're arranging for the FSB to be notified that there's a planned assassination attempt against Kalashnikov, and that the boat will be blown up. The idea is for the FSB to send a helicopter to try to warn Kalashnikov, and it's at that moment that the explosion will take place. The FSB agents in the helicopter will witness the explosion, which we hope will eliminate any doubt that Kalashnikov and family have perished. When it goes off, the escape pods will be dropped into the ocean..."

She squeezed the clicker again and an unusual image appeared. It looked like the outline of a whale, but the inside resembled blueprints of a ship.

"Meet Big Willie. I know, I know, I was just as surprised when I found out about this as you are. Big Willie is actually a submarine, but it's designed to look and move like a blue whale. His mechanisms are all controlled by a computer, and a single operator steers it. It's literally capable of doing everything a blue whale can do, even to the way they jump out of the water and splash back down. When the explosion happens, Big Willie will be close by, and the four escape pods will be taken inside and carried away."

"Are we changing Kalashnikov's name to Jonah?" Marino quipped.

"I'll take that under advisement," Allison said with a grin.

Molly grinned also, then went on. "Big Willie can swim about 300 miles at a time, so his mother ship, the *Hyperion*, will be stationed about 80 miles away. Since there will be other blue whales in the area, no one is going to pay attention as they continue on their journey, and the Hyperion will be sitting right in their path. When they get there, Willie will simply be drawn up into a hidden compartment in the hull, the escape pods will be taken out and carried to a shipping container on the deck that's been fitted up like a luxurious state room, and the family will be released. The ship will head for Niigata, Japan, where the container will be offloaded onto a truck. It will be carried to the U.S. Embassy in Tokyo, where the family will be placed on a diplomatic flight to Washington DC."

Jenny held up her hand. "Question," she said. "What happens to the agent running the boat? How is he supposed to get off the sailboat?"

"He will be the only one to be rescued," Molly said. "Ironically, it will probably be the FSB who rescues him, but he is well known in Vladivostok and shouldn't have any problems. Since the FSB will already believe the explosion is part of the assassination attempt, he will probably be questioned for a while, but he shouldn't be in any danger."

Jenny looked at Allison. "It sounds to me like this is already worked out," she said. "What do you need us over there for?"

"Mostly just to ensure the plan comes off without any problems," Allison said. "You'll be posing as American tourists who are also there for the whale watch. You'll spend Friday night in the same hotel as the minister and his family, and you'll be on another sailboat close by when everything happens. Once Big Willie picks up the escape pods, you'll receive a brief radio signal telling you that phase of the mission is complete, and then you'll just go back to port with everyone else. You'll undoubtedly be questioned about what you saw, but I doubt you'll be detained more than a couple of hours. You'll stay in the hotel again that night and come home the following day."

"Bor-ing!" Jenny said, making everyone chuckle. "Doesn't sound to me like I'm going to get the chance to kill anybody."

"Actually, you might. It's common practice for high-ranking officials in Russia to be under regular surveillance. The reason you'll be at the hotel is to look for that surveillance and eliminate it. That will actually fit in with the information we provide the following day about an assassination attempt, because the surveillance agents would be seen by most assassins as a form of security that needed to be out of the way."

"Oh, goody," Jenny said, "at least I can look forward to a possibility, right? This surveillance, it would probably be somebody bad, right?"

Allison gave her a wicked grin. "Probably," she said. "I suppose you can enjoy yourself if the opportunity arises."

Jenny broke out into a big smile.

"You'll be leaving today," Molly went on. "We have our own agent in Vladivostok, and he will provide weapons and such when you get there. Other than normal tourist clothing, the only thing you're taking with you is the special receiver you'll need when the mission goes down. Wally will have that for you when you go to R&D to pick up your bags."

"And I have your ID kits," Jefferson said. "Jenny, your name is Patricia Stewart, and you're married to Jack Stewart, which is Randy. Jim, you'll be going under the name of Arthur Hickman, and Dave, your name is Charlie Ross. Arthur and Charlie are old friends of Jack and Patricia, and records have been established as showing that the four of you travel quite a lot together. Your passports all bear the same stamps, and you'll have lots of photos showing you in different locations around the world. Wally has all of that stuff ready, as well."

Allison looked at the team. "Any other questions?"

Since there weren't any, the four of them left the conference room and headed straight out to R&D. An hour later, they were all in Dave Lange's Cadillac Escalade and on the way to the Denver airport.

CHAPTER THREE

The flight made two stops, one at Los Angeles and the other at Seoul, South Korea. They arrived in Vladivostok at just after two in the afternoon on Thursday and took a shuttle directly to their hotel. Kalashnikov and his family would not arrive until the following day, so the itinerary called for Jenny and the men to act like tourists until then.

The shuttle driver turned out to be one of the American agents, and they discovered that they had an extra suitcase when they arrived at the hotel. Jenny opened it quickly in her room and was delighted to find a number of weapons, including her personal favorites: a simple Beretta 9 mm pistol and a 9 inch stiletto knife.

After such a long flight, however, Jenny decided that it wouldn't be out of character for them to simply rest. Once they were checked in, they went to their rooms—she and Randy shared one, while Dave and Jim were in the adjacent room—and relaxed until dinnertime. The hotel had a five-star restaurant, so they lay down to nap until it was time to meet for dinner at seven.

The next morning, they rose early and rented a car. Jim had looked at tourist attractions and they decided to visit the Vladivostok fortress. The fortress had been one of the most advanced of its day, built before World War I as the most impregnable fortress in the world. It was claimed that the fortress' existence was the reason Japan chose not to ally themselves with Germany against Russia. Vladivostok was too close to Japan and was capable of defending its fleet of ships. Those ships could have wreaked havoc on the small island nation, and so Japan refused to engage Russia.

They spent the morning going through the fortress, seeing the underground barracks and tunnels that led from one section to the other. Although it was completed before 1918, the fortress had electricity in every part of it and underground communication cables kept every section in touch with the rest.

Jenny and the men took a lot of photos and even encouraged other tourists to take pictures of the four of them posing together. They were laughing and having an obvious good time, and Jenny was confident that they were accepted as only what they appeared to be.

They went to a restaurant called Zuma for lunch, and Jenny joined a few other American tourists in complaining when a surcharge was added to their checks because they were American. Randy played his part well, obviously trying to calm down his wife without ending up in the doghouse himself. When they finally left, Jenny couldn't help laughing at him.

"You need to find somebody and get married," she said. "You've got the henpecked husband routine down to a science, buddy."

"It's called acting ability," Randy said. "I have to play my part, right? Just chill, this ought to be one of our easiest missions yet."

In the afternoon, they visited Primorski Aquarium. The Aquarium was a major tourist attraction for Vladivostok and known for its underwater exhibits. Transparent walls allowed visitors to go down below the water level and watch many types of marine life in their natural environments. They all thought it was fascinating, but then they got to go and watch the dolphin shows. Trained dolphins performed a number of tricks, similar to what a tourist might see at Sea World or Marine Land parks in America.

They got back to the hotel at six and it was Dave who first spotted Kalashnikov. He and his family were checking in, and Jenny signaled the men to watch for the expected surveillance. It took them only minutes to spot it; two men, doing their best to go unnoticed, were carefully watching everything Kalashnikov did. As soon as the Minister and his family were checked in and got into the elevator, both men stepped up to the desk to claim the rooms they had already reserved.

Randy and Jenny stood close behind them, apparently waiting to check with the desk for any messages. Randy, who spoke fluent Russian, managed to pick up the room numbers the two were assigned, so after they were told there were no messages waiting for them, they headed on up to their own room. Dave and Jim were already there and waiting for them when they arrived.

"One of them," Jenny said, "is right below this room. I'll call him Demetri. The other one, call him Khrushchev, is in the room next door to the one the Kalashnikovs are occupying." She opened the window that led out to a balcony and stepped outside, looking over the rail. "I could get to the one underneath me this way," she said. "I'll need some rope. Jim, what about video security in the building?"

"I checked it out last night," he replied. "It's a pretty simple system, and I can get into it to shut off any cameras you want, or just erase a section of video."

Jenny nodded. "Okay, then I'll take them out tonight. Dave, I need you to go find me some rope somewhere. There's a lot of scuba diving around here, so they probably have rope in any of the dive shops. Jim, I want you to keep an eye on the targets. Let me know if they go anywhere, and what they're doing. I don't know if Kalashnikov is aware of their presence, but I want them out of the picture before morning."

Randy snickered. "Yeah, and you want to let the monster out of its cage. I feel a little bit sorry for these guys."

"Why?" Jenny asked. "These guys are killers themselves, they probably deserve everything I'm going to do to them."

"So what? I know that look in your eyes, you're planning to enjoy yourself. We all know you get off on killing people, that's just part of who you are."

Jenny smiled sweetly at him. "That's true," she said. "And I'm very frustrated, so unless you want to help solve that problem by becoming my next victim, shut your mouth and do your job."

Randy burst out laughing. Jenny's threats sounded a lot worse than they really were. Well, usually, anyway.

Dave returned an hour later with the rope, just as Jim reported that the Kalashnikovs were headed down for dinner. Both of the surveillance officers left their rooms a moment later, also headed for the restaurant.

"Well, we might as well join the party," Jenny said. The four of them left the room and rode the elevator down to the main floor, then entered the restaurant a moment later. The maître d' seated them right next to the Kalashnikovs, by pure coincidence. Jenny noticed that Olga, the teenage daughter, was paying close attention to Jim Marino and quietly encouraged him to flirt a bit. That opened the door for some friendly banter between the two tables, which caught the attention of the surveillance officers.

"Demetri thinks you're hot," Randy whispered to Jenny.

"I doubt that," Jenny said just as softly. "He's probably just wondering why they're talking to us at all."

Jim chuckled. "Art's right," he said. "The dude is spending more time thinking about getting into your pants than he is watching his assignment."

Jenny pretended to ignore what was said for a moment, then turned and looked directly at Demetri. She let her eyes rove over him, as if she were appraising his physique, and saw the little smile he gave her in return. His own eyes bounced down and back up, as he made it clear that he liked what he saw.

Jenny winked at him. She hoped he got the idea that she wanted to meet up later for some fun, because that was exactly what she had in mind. Of course, it wouldn't be the kind of fun he was hoping for.

She went back to pretending to be a happy little wife, but made a point of glancing back at him every once in a while.

The Kalashnikov family finished their dinner first and left the restaurant with Khrushchev following them out. They would be leaving the hotel at 6 A.M. to go and board the boat, and Jenny and the boys would be right behind them. They stayed in the restaurant for another fifteen minutes, then Randy paid the check and they headed back to their rooms. Jenny gave Demetri one more wink as she left the restaurant and smiled shyly when she saw him lick his lips.

He followed them out of the restaurant and into the elevator, avoiding Jenny as he punched the button for his floor. He spoke politely to Randy, but in Russian, and Randy pretended not to understand. A moment later, the elevator door opened and Demetri waved to all of them as he walked down the hall.

"What did he say?" Jenny asked.

"Cocky jerk asked me if I was going to get upset about him taking you to bed." Randy grinned. "You don't know how tempted I was to tell him he was the one who was going to be upset."

"We can forget the rope," Jenny said when they got back upstairs. "Demetri will happily let me in. Jim, make sure you kill the security cameras on that floor. I'm going to head down to see him in a few minutes. As soon as I'm done, I'll go take care of Khrushchev, too."

"I'm killing the one in the elevator, too," Jim said. "I don't think they have anybody actually monitoring the cameras; they just keep them recording so they can look at it later if they need to."

Jenny went into the bathroom and changed into a simple dress, then took advantage of the moment to use the facilities. She found in the past that it was best to do her killing with an empty bladder, because the excitement could cause it to become slightly overactive. She didn't want to have to make another stop before she got to Khrushchev.

"How do I look?" She twirled around once as she stepped out of the bathroom, and all three of the men gave her an appreciative nod. She went to her purse and took out a small tube that was labeled as hand sanitizer, squeezed some into her palm and rubbed it into both hands, including the fingertips. It seemed to dry almost instantly, but it was in reality a liquefied plastic that was better than wearing gloves. As long as it was on her hands, she could not leave a fingerprint anywhere. "Wait up for me. I shouldn't be long."

With the knife tucked into the top of her left stocking, Jenny gave the men a finger wave and stepped out the door. She went to the elevator and found it waiting, then pushed the button for the floor below. When the doors opened, she turned and walked down the hall and then knocked on Demetri's door.

He opened the door cautiously, and she saw that he had one hand behind his back. A smile broke across his face, though, and he immediately stepped back to let her in. As soon as she was inside, he turned to keep the hidden hand behind him as he pulled open a drawer and dropped something heavy into it.

Jenny smiled. "Do you even speak English at all?"

"Quite fluently," he said. "Your husband didn't understand what I said, did he?"

She laughed. "No, he doesn't speak any Russian. Neither do I, for that matter, so what was it you said?"

Demetri smiled and took her into his arms, looking directly into her eyes. "I told him he was a very fortunate man," he said. "I told him he was fortunate because he is married to such a beautiful woman."

Jenny laughed with delight and then slipped her arms around his neck. She leaned her face toward him and felt his lips touch her own for only a second before her knee came up and ruined his day.

Demetri doubled over, but his instinct for survival made him turn and grasp at the drawer where he had dropped his gun. He managed to get it open, but then Jenny caught his hair and yanked him backward, driving her other knee into his kidneys as hard as she could.

"Don't you know it's not nice to flirt with a married woman?" she hissed at him. "It's also not nice to lie, you son of a bitch. You didn't tell him I was beautiful, you said you wanted to boink me!"

Demetri looked up into her eyes, his own eyes wide and staring. The thin blade in her hand caught his attention, and he tried to raise an arm to ward it off, but she was too fast. It sliced across his right carotid artery and jugular so quickly that he didn't even feel it, and he continued to try to struggle for almost forty seconds more before the lack of blood flow to the brain stole his consciousness.

Jenny looked down at him as she let him fall, then reached down and wiped the blade on his shirt. "You weren't half as much fun as I wanted you to be," she said. "Maybe your friend will do better."

Demetri had fallen between the bed and the dresser, out of sight of the door to the room. She checked herself carefully to make sure no blood had gotten on her dress, then slipped the knife back into her stocking and walked out the door. She put the do not disturb sign on the door, pulled it shut behind herself, and walked with a smile to the elevator.

The Kalashnikovs were on the top floor, and Jenny rode the elevator up. She walked down to Khrushchev's room and tapped on the door, and wasn't surprised when he opened the door just as cautiously as Demetri had done.

"Oh, I'm sorry," she said quickly. "I was looking for the other man who was with you. Do you know where I can find him?"

Khrushchev gave her an odd smile, one that seemed almost predatory. "He is three floors down," he said. "If you wish, however, I could have him come up and we could all enjoy ourselves together."

Jenny threw him a shocked smile, as if the thought excited her at the same time it seemed shameful. "Oh, my goodness," she said. "I—I—do you think he would?"

Khrushchev chuckled and stepped back, allowing her to enter the room. Unlike Demetri, he didn't even bother trying to hide the gun. He simply laid it on the bed as he turned to the hotel room phone.

"Wait, don't be in such a hurry," Jenny said. "Couldn't we have a little fun without him, first?"

She had walked to the other end of the room, twirling around as she did so to give the impression that she was nervous. Khrushchev grinned and replaced the receiver, then took a couple of steps toward her. Jenny reached up and unbuttoned the top two buttons of her dress, allowing her cleavage to show as she spread her arms to invite him in.

Khrushchev took the bait, pulling her close to him and burying his face in her cleavage. He was kissing the tops of her breasts as he began pulling the dress down over her shoulders, and Jenny squealed delightfully as she yanked up the dress and snatched out the knife.

Khrushchev froze as the point of the knife touched his left temple. He slowly raised his eyes to look into her face, and then his expression turned to one of terror.

"Let me tell you a secret," Jenny whispered. "Your friend is a whole lot better looking than you are. Well, he was."

Khrushchev continued to stare into her face. "He is dead?"

"Very. The problem is, he didn't tell me what I want to know."

"You're Americans?" Khrushchev asked.

"Oh, goodness, whatever would make you think that? We are actually from a small town in China, but it's amazing what they can do with plastic surgery these days, isn't it? Now, tell me. Why are you so interested in following that family around?"

Khrushchev moved back slowly and allowed himself to sit on the corner of the bed just behind him. Jenny kept the knife point at his temple, exerting just enough pressure to convince him that she could plunge it into his brain without any warning.

"He is an important man," he said. "It is our job to watch over him."

"Really? You don't seem very good at it. Your friend was spending more time trying to flirt with me than paying attention to what they were doing. Do you think he's in some kind of danger?"

He shrugged. "Important men are often in danger. That's why we were assigned to watch over him. If some danger approaches him, we will be there."

Jenny nodded. "Okay, that's pretty much what I thought." She grinned at him. "I bet right now you're wishing you had called in sick, aren't you?"

Khrushchev moved suddenly, whipping his left hand up and around and slapping her hand and the knife away from his head. He was up in a split second, turned and lunged for the gun that was laying on the other bed, but Jenny caught the back of his shirt collar. Instead of using it to pull back on him, however, she only used it to help her move forward more quickly. The knife flashed downward and sliced across the back of his right thigh, and Khrushchev fell face first onto the floor with Jenny on top of him.

"Dammit," she said, "you got blood on my dress." She hopped upward and brought her knee down in the middle of his back, then used the knife to slice quickly down the back of his right arm. The sensitive skin and tissues there caused him to grunt in pain, but she was impressed when he didn't scream. She put the knife against his temple once again, this time on the other side as his head lay on the floor. "Well, you just ruined all my fun. I was really planning to make this last a few minutes, but you had to go and be stupid."

She yanked the knife away from his head and quickly sliced his throat. She kept her knee in his back until his feeble struggling stopped, then got up and looked down at herself.

There was an obviously wet blood stain on her dress, just above her right knee. She shook her head in disgust, then stepped over to his open suitcase. She selected one of his button-down shirts, then took off the dress and rolled it up with the bloodstain inside. A moment later, she had the shirt on and the rolled- up dress tucked under her arm as she left the room. The sign on the door said the occupant did not want to be disturbed.

All three of the men looked up questioningly as she reentered her room, but she simply shook out the dress to explain. "I couldn't exactly wear that through the halls, now, could I?" she asked. "People will pay less attention to a girl wearing a man's shirt than they will to a girl with a bloodied dress, trust me."

CHAPTER FOUR

"Before the boat launch," said the Russian guide in badly accented English, "you must know these two things. Number one, there must be no noise. Nothing can be done to disturb the whales. Number two, do not throw thing into water. Nothing, throw no thing into water. Whales do not eat food like you and me. Do not feed the whales."

Jenny had laughed, at first, about having to take an hour-long class before being allowed to sail out on the whale watch, but she was finally beginning to understand. Blue whales had been hunted almost to extinction during the nineteenth and early twentieth centuries, and were almost wiped out. Now, after three decades of being protected under law, blue whales were beginning to regain their population.

For more than fifty years, however, they had not been seen in the Sea of Japan. That had only changed over the last couple of years, when three pods of blue whales had begun appearing there during their feeding season migrations in the summer months. The total numbers of all three pods was less than a hundred whales, but they were rather predictable in their travels. The pod they would be watching on this particular day was moving very slowly, covering only about fifteen miles a day as they hunted the krill that made up their diet. The guide explained that all of these tourists were very lucky to even get the opportunity to see these magnificent animals in their migratory journeys.

"That's our boat," Randy said. "The one with the picture of the mermaid on the mainsail."

"You guys do know how to sail, right?" Jenny asked. "I've always wanted to learn, but I never had the chance."

"I grew up on the water," Dave said. "That's only a thirty-five footer, I could handle that in my sleep."

The Kalashnikovs were boarding a slightly larger boat just a few slips down. Randy helped Jenny step aboard, then watched as Dave started the small diesel engine and then prepared to move out of the bay. Randy and Jim cast off the lines and the boat slowly began moving backward out of its slip. When it was clear, Dave spun the wheel and shifted the transmission into forward, then eased the throttle ahead. They had to keep it under three knots inside the bay, to avoid wakes that could cause problems for any other vessels.

Jenny kept an eye on the Kalashnikovs' yacht, which was just beginning to leave the dock. It was apparently a more agile vessel than theirs, because it seemed to turn completely around right after it came out of its own slip, and it was moving alongside them only a moment later. Jenny saw Kalashnikov look over and recognize her, and gave him a cheerful wave.

"We're going to watch the whales," she shouted, and she saw him nod. She wasn't sure if he actually heard her or not, but she gave him another wave and turned her attention towards the water ahead.

It took almost an hour for the boats to get far enough out to raise their sails, but finally they were moving along with the wind powering them. Dave sat at the helm, as perfectly at home controlling the seagoing vessel as he would have been behind the wheel of a Lamborghini.

The journey out to see the whales would last only about two and a half hours, due to the fact that the whales, following the krill, tended to stay close to the Russian shoreline. The current pod was only about twenty miles off the coast and the boats were averaging seven knots, or slightly over eight miles per hour.

Despite the sunshine, the air was rather cool. Jenny kept a jacket on as she sat beside Dave at the stern, watching him handle the helm deftly. They chatted a bit, and Dave explained quite a few things about sailing to her, but the boat they were on was a fairly new one. Almost everything on it, including the sails, were primarily controlled by a computer. About the only thing David really needed to do was pay attention to the compass and keep the boat pointed in the right direction, but he could easily have turned on the autopilot for that.

Up at the bow, Randy and Jim were relaxing in their own way, drinking beer and watching some of the girls on other boats nearby. Jim speculated that Russian girls must not feel the chill in the air, because several of them were stripped down to bikinis and laying out in the sun on the decks.

"Wish Jenny would try that," Randy said. "She is a sight to behold when she is wearing a bikini."

"Don't get yourself all twisted up," Jim replied. "She and Neil have something pretty special, I think. Have you seen the two of them together yet?"

"Yeah, more than I want to. Blows my mind, seeing her acting like—like a lovesick schoolgirl. What she sees in him, I'll never know."

Jim was quiet for a moment, then looked over at his friend. "She sees a man who can accept her for who she is," he said, "and one that will let her feel safe when she's at home with him. Considering how messed up our lives are, I figure she's entitled to any kind of happiness she can get."

Randy puffed up his cheeks and blew out the air. "Yeah, yeah, and I agree. I just can't figure out what it could be about him that caught her attention. Good grief, he's a foot and a half taller than she is. You think it would be impossible for them to—you know."

Jim chuckled. "Where there's a will," he said, "I guarantee you there's a way."

The easy banter continued for the rest of the ride out to the pod, but finally the word came through the radios that it was time to reduce their speed. They were within a mile of the whale pod, and it was time to cut the noise level down.

And a few minutes later, the first whales were sighted. Dave turned on the autopilot so that he and Jenny could go up to the bow, as well, and the view turned out to be every bit as magnificent as its advertising had suggested.

More than two dozen big blue whales were continually breaching the surface, and Jenny let out an uncontrollable squeal of delight when one of them breached right between their own boat and that of the Kalashnikovs. Its huge snout rose several feet out of the water before plunging back in, and its broad back was visible for several seconds before the tail flukes rose a dozen feet or more into the air. Jenny braced herself for a splash, expecting the tail to slam down onto the water as she'd seen in YouTube videos, but it sliced the waves cleanly.

That was when she saw the fins in the water, and realized that the whale was being followed by what looked like a massive school of sharks. Moments later, the same whale appeared again, and it suddenly struck Jenny that this one, along with its toothy followers, was actually keeping pace with the boats. The next time it breached, she looked very closely and then nodded her head. She was absolutely convinced that she was looking at Big Willie.

Everything was set for the mission, and Jenny quietly told the men to prepare. Her guess proved correct when the sound of a helicopter reached their ears, and they looked back to see one approaching at high speed. It seemed to hunt around for a few moments, then zeroed in on the boat with the Kalashnikovs.

The biggest difference between their boat and that of the Kalashnikovs was the forward cabin. Where Jenny and the men had to stand out in the weather to watch the whales, the Minister and his family were able to stay inside and watch through clear viewports. They were already inside when the helicopter appeared, and by the time it began hovering overhead, Jenny knew that they were probably inside the escape pods and waiting nervously for what was coming next.

IN THE KALASHNIKOV'S yacht, Anton Kalashnikov saw the whale that was staying close to the boat and knew that it was time. That was the signal he had been told to watch for and he cleared his throat noisily.

"My family," he said, "there is something I must tell you. We are about to embark on a great new adventure."

His wife, who was aware of the plan to defect to the west, looked at him nervously. "It is time?" she asked.

He nodded. "Yes," he said. He turned to his children, Piotr and Olga. "You must both do exactly as I say. We are not returning to our home, children, because we are leaving today for a new life in the United States of America. There are things happening in Russia that endanger us all, and I want both of you to grow up safe and in freedom."

Piotr stared at him while Olga started to cry. "Father, in America?" Piotr asked. "Why would you do this to us?"

"I will explain everything later," Kalashnikov said, "but this is not the time. Right now we must go below the deck. Come, we must go now."

With Olga still crying, Kalashnikov led his family into the belly of the vessel. There were four objects attached to the inside of the hull, and it took him a moment to find the catch that caused one of them to open. When he succeeded, he showed it to the rest of them.

"We get inside these," he said. "In a short while, there will be an explosion and we will be released into the water. A special submarine will pick us up and take us to a ship, and from there we will be taken to America. All you have to do is get inside. When it is opened again, we will be on the ship."

"But I do not wish to leave Russia," Piotr said. "My school, my friends, I do not wish to leave them."

"Piotr, listen to me. You know that I have a high position in the Russian Federation. I have become aware of plans that will leave Russia open to war, and such a war as we have not seen before. If it happens, Moscow will be utterly destroyed, and that would mean that our family would die. I have spoken with Americans who are willing to see to it that we live very well in their country, and the information that I will give them may help to prevent that war from ever happening. Is giving up our home too great a price to save the world?"

"Mother," Olga cried, "don't make me do this! If we go into those things, we could die, we could be lost in the sea and die there!"

Ivana wrapped an arm around her daughter and pulled her close. "Do not be afraid, Olga," she said. "This has all been carefully prepared so that we will all be safe. Trust your father. He has not done this lightly, but only when he was certain that it is the only way to keep us all safe and together."

Piotr argued and Olga wept, but both of them got into the canisters, and then Kalashnikov helped his wife get into her own. He smiled as he closed it tight and then climbed into the last of them.

As soon as it latched shut, a small screen in front of his face lit up and a message appeared, written in Russian.

Please relax and remain calm. You are perfectly safe and there is more than enough air in this unit. You will not be in it for more than a few hours.

Kalashnikov suddenly wished he had thought to use the toilet before getting into the canister. At his age, holding his water was not always an easy thing to do.

Suddenly it didn't matter, as a massive explosion seemed to throw the entire yacht upward. It crashed back down a moment later and he was thankful for the foam padding that kept him cradled and safe from being bashed about. There was a moment of calm and quiet and then a sudden lurch as the bottom of the boat came apart and the canisters were dropped into the water.

The churning water tossed the canister around and for a moment Kalashnikov felt that he was almost upside down. It righted itself after a few seconds and then seemed to be slowly sinking. He fought down his rising panic, thinking of what his wife and children must be going through at that moment.

Something impacted the canister and bumped it, then it seemed to come to rest for a moment. Seconds later, it was sloshing in water once again, but then there was another moment of calm. This happened a couple of more times and then the canister settled onto something slightly off level so that he was leaning gently on his right side. The padding still cushioned him and he was able to steady his breathing after a few minutes.

There was still a sense of motion, but it was very gentle. The canister seemed to be moving up and down, sometimes with his head upward and other times with it angled downward slightly. The motion was actually quite soothing and reminded him of the sensation of floating on an inflatable raft in ocean waves. He couldn't quite relax enough to drift off to sleep, but there were moments when he felt he might.

How long it lasted, he had no idea. The gentle, wavelike motions seemed to make time unimportant, so it may have been only an hour, or could have been several. Finally, the motion stopped and he felt as if he might be rising, but then there was a solid clank and all motion ceased.

LIEUTENANT BUTCH ALDERMAN carefully dropped Big Willie back behind the yacht, descending under the waves and using the powerful, hydraulically-operated tail to keep the boat in sight. The video screen in front of him showed a very clear view, constructed of input from cameras mounted in Willie's eyes and sonar echoes. The soundwaves the big artificial whale emanated were unlike any sonar used elsewhere, but the software that translated it worked flawlessly. No one who heard it would have any idea that it was part of an underwater echolocation system, so Butch didn't worry about being detected.

The explosion occurred only moments later, right on schedule. Butch waited until the turbulence generated settled down, knowing that this was when the canisters would be released. Each of them was designed to be only partially buoyant, reaching neutral buoyancy at about fifty feet below the surface. Small, computer-controlled ballast tanks would see to that.

The first one appeared, its faint transponder putting out a signal that could only be detected underwater and within three hundred meters. Butch accelerated slightly and opened Willie's mouth as he approached it, letting it drift inside. It lodged itself against the inner padding that was designed to look like living tissue, and then Butch spotted and caught the second, the third, and the fourth. When they were all inside, he closed the big mouth and pumped out the excess water. The canisters settled and Butch steered the disguised vessel out to sea.

He kept close to the pod of whales for about an hour until there were no ships close by, then veered off alone. The *Hyperion*, his mother ship, was moving at its normal slow pace toward his rendezvous point, and it would take him a couple of hours to reach it. Until then, there was little for him to do but pay attention to his heading and listen to the music that was playing in his headphones.

When he got to the ship, cruising along the surface, he dived under and came up below it amidships. Then and only then did he use the short-range transmitter to let the *Hyperion* know that he was there. A large pair of doors in the bottom of the ship slowly opened, and Butch brought Willie up slowly until it was surfaced in the moon pool near the keel of the ship. The big doors closed and Willie settled onto the cradle that they formed.

Butch shut down the electronics, pulled the lever that opened the escape hatch above his cramped pilot's quarters, and began to climb the ladder. The noise in the bay assaulted him as soon as it opened and got even louder as his head popped up into the air.

"*Heeeerre's Jonah!*" That was Commander Wilson, Big Willie's crew chief, who always announced Butch's arrival that way. "How did it go?"

"I got them all," Butch called back. "No problems."

A gangway was lowered and he stepped onto it as the service crew stepped off. The big charging cables lowered from the bulkhead above them and one of the technicians grabbed it and opened the charging port to plug it in. Willie's batteries could have gone a few hours longer, but he was always treated to a full charge when he came back from a mission.

Another technician climbed into the cockpit to open Willie's mouth. The big lower jaw forced the head upward, making it possible to run a gangplank into the mouth. Men were lined up and waiting to rush inside and pick up the canisters, then carry them quickly up into the cargo container that was awaiting them.

Butch stood on the catwalk over the bay and looked down at Big Willie. As he always did after taking Willie out, he whispered a quiet prayer of thanks for the opportunity to see the ocean through Willie's eyes. He felt there was something special about his assignment, that it gave him a point of view few other men would ever understand.

FOR A FEW MOMENTS, nothing happened. Kalashnikov laid in his canister and waited for some sign that it was about to open, but then it felt as if it were lifted and carried away by several people. He couldn't hear anything, but he got the impression that he was being carried in the same way a coffin might be carried. That mental image did nothing to help him stay calm, and he began to feel panic rising once again.

The canister was set onto something and then it was opened. He looked up into the bearded faces of some rough-looking men, and then one of them extended a hand to help him get out of the canister and onto his feet. It was at that moment that he realized he had pissed himself during the ordeal, but he refused to allow himself to feel shame. He suspected that many people would have done the same in such circumstances.

"Welcome aboard, Mr. Stanislav," said one of the men. "These will be your quarters until we reach Japan. It shouldn't take terribly long, but there are new clothes for you and your family, plenty of snacks and drinks and things to do, and there is a shower and toilet toward the back."

"Stanislav?" Kalashnikov asked.

"Yes, sir," the man said. "You'll find your new identification cards and passports on the table over there. Your name is Yakov Stanislav, now. I don't remember what your family's names are, but you'll find them over there."

Kalashnikov—or Yakov—looked around and saw his wife and children being helped out of their own canisters. They were on the way to freedom, on the way to new lives that he fervently hoped would keep them safe.

"Listen," the man said, and Yakov turned to look at him. "I hate to do it, but I have to lock you folks in here. When we get to Japan, this whole container will be lifted off the ship and carried to somewhere else, and then you'll be released and taken to the airplane that will take you to your new home. Everything you need should be here for now, so I wish you the best of luck in the future." He held out a hand and Yakov shook it.

A moment later, he and his family were alone and the container was closed and sealed. They went to the table and looked at their new identities, and then sat down to read the back stories that had been created for each of them.

"This will be an incredible opportunity," he said to his family. "To live in a world without the threat of the SVR hanging over our heads. This is a gift, and we must do all in our power to treat it as one."

"Is it?" Piotr asked. "You have turned us all into traitors. We have betrayed our country, what kind of gift would that be?"

"It was our country that was betraying us," Yakov said. "The things that our government is planning will turn most of the world against us over the months to come. Within a year, perhaps two, we will be at war, and I do not believe such a war can happen in this new world without employing nuclear weapons. With our home in Moscow, there is almost no possibility we could survive an attack on that city, and it is inevitable if the war comes. It is my hope that by working with the Americans, I can prevent that war from ever taking place. If I am successful, then perhaps one day we can return to Russia, but for now it is my decision that I want to keep my family safe. If that means living as an American, so be it."

"But you cannot know that," Piotr insisted. "You cannot know that such a war will come."

"Are you not aware of my position? Do you not understand that part of my job is to prepare us for such war? Our prime minister seeks to return to the days of the Soviet Union, to return to the Cold War. Do you believe that the Americans or the British or the Chinese will allow that to happen? The United Nations will sanction us, we will be threatened with trade embargoes that will force us to fight for every drop of petroleum, every morsel of food. The new Soviet Union will seek to build an empire, just to ensure that our own people are safe and secure, but that empire is what will lead to war. This cannot happen. If I must be branded a traitor to prevent it, then I shall be branded a traitor. In my heart, I know that I am loyal to Mother Russia."

"But, father..."

"That is enough," Ivana said. "You will respect your father. He is giving up everything for the chance to keep us safe, my son. You have no right to question his decision."

Piotr glared at both of his parents, then sat down and picked up the passport that had his photo in it. His name was now Peter, and his sister would be called Olivia.

He put his elbows on the table, laid his face in his hands and wept. After a moment, his sister sat down beside him and put an arm around his shoulders as their parents whispered quietly some distance away.

"It will be all right," she said softly. "We have talked about what it would be like to live in America. Now we will get to find out."

"As traitors," Peter said. "I shall undoubtedly die of shame, one day, knowing that I did nothing to resist what our father has done. If only I had seen the signs, if only I had known that this was coming. I could have run away, I could have stayed."

"But then I would be alone. I need you, Piotr. How can I face this new life without my big brother?"

"Hmpf," Peter said. "You should be fine. You always wanted to be able to go to American shopping malls, to go to the parties and schools that you see on the American television programs. You will fit in perfectly there, but I will not. I will be almost a prisoner, because our father will be afraid of what I might say or do."

"No, he would not treat you that way. Still, would you really tell anyone about this? Would you truly want anyone to know about it? If you are so ashamed, it will be in your own best interest to keep the secret. You can learn to be an American boy, and you have always told me that American girls are much sexier." She grinned, because she saw the barest hint of a grin on his own face. "They are certainly going to be interested in you, with your mysterious Russian accent. I expect you will have your pick of them."

"The only reason I will not tell anyone about this is because it could hurt you. I have always been your protector, I will not fail you now. As for the American girls—at least there might be some compensation for my silence." He sighed deeply. "Perhaps we won't live in such a big city. I might be able to have an automobile, that would be good. And you, you might be able to achieve your dream."

She squinted at him. "What dream?"

Her brother laughed, and she felt as if a weight had been lifted from her shoulders. He was one of the great joys in her life and had always been there when she needed him. Seeing him laugh and smile again was important to her.

"Do you think I don't hear you when you sing to yourself at night? Do you think I never hear you singing in the bath? Olga, you have the voice of an angel. Perhaps, in America, you can become famous for your singing."

"Oh," she said, her face turning bright red. "That dream. I wasn't aware that you knew about it."

Peter shook his head, smiling at her. "That's because I always kept quiet, so that I could listen to you sing."

JENNY AND HER TEAM didn't have to wait long. They saw the captain speak into a microphone and then start into the cabin, but then the entire front of the boat disintegrated in an explosion. The sharks seemed to scatter for a moment, but then the fins regrouped and headed toward the stricken yacht.

Jenny stood at the rail, watching the events unfold. Her eyes were wide and her mouth was hanging open, so disastrous did the scene appear, but then she saw the captain struggling back up out of the cabin and onto the stern. He grabbed the microphone and shouted something into it, then threw it down and picked up something that looked like a duffel bag. They watched as he pulled something out of it, and then the entire bag burst open and became an inflatable life raft. He held onto it as the yacht began to sink, then threw himself into it just before the stern went under the water.

The earbuds Jenny was wearing suddenly stopped playing the music from her iPod, and a voice came through. "Glass Slipper, this is Jonah. All four birds are in the nest."

The music resumed instantly and Jenny breathed a sigh of relief. The sharks were having an obvious feeding frenzy, and she could hear the occupants of other boats screaming about sharks eating people in the water. She looked closely and saw a body in the water, bloodied and obviously dead, just before three sharks began ripping it to shreds.

As planned, only the captain would be listed as a survivor. Since the Russian government had been notified that Kalashnikov was going to be assassinated, the explosion would almost certainly be accepted as the evidence that the plan had succeeded. Unless a major error were to occur, the Kalashnikovs were home free.

The message came through a short time later that the whale watch was being cut short. The explosion had frightened the pod, they were told, and it was necessary to abort and head back to Vladivostok Port. Dave turned the boat around and followed the rest as they all did as they were told.

It wasn't long before they were passed by a half-dozen high-speed boats, all racing out to the scene. The sharks would have done their job long before any potential rescuers could arrive, and there would be nothing to recover as far as remains. While sharks might leave a leg or an arm behind in movies, a true feeding frenzy would leave nothing uneaten. Some of those sharks were big enough to swallow a human head whole, so Jenny was looking forward to returning home the following day. Kalashnikov was no longer her problem.

The day had begun early, but it had ended much earlier than expected. As a result, they were back in port by one o'clock in the afternoon, but then they had to wait their turns to be questioned by the police about the explosion. They all told exactly what they'd seen and were finally released at just about two thirty.

They made it back to the hotel an hour later. The news of the disaster had preceded them and a number of people in the lobby were talking about it. Jenny and Randy spoke of having actually witnessed the explosion and sinking and made a point of telling everyone that it had ruined their entire vacation. They would be going home the following day, they said, and hoped never to return to Vladivostok.

This was precisely the behavior the locals would expect from "entitled" Americans, so no one paid much attention. They were ignored as they got into the elevator, and were completely unprepared when they stepped into Jenny's room to find four FSB agents waiting for them.

All four men had guns drawn and aimed at them, and six more appeared from adjacent rooms. Jenny and the men were hustled inside and forced to sit on the beds, while an FSB Captain took a chair from the table and sat in it, facing them.

"My name is Captain Evgeny Dimitrovitch," the captain said. "I'm with the Federal Security Service. Our Deputy Defense Minister has been assassinated. What do you know of this?"

Randy, since he was supposed to be the only married man in the group, shook his head. "Defense minister? What are you talking about? We're not from around here, why would we know anything about that?"

Dimitrovitch grinned at him. "I suppose you also know nothing of the deaths of his security detail? Two men were brutally murdered in this hotel sometime last night, men who were assigned with the task of protecting the minister. The security cameras on both of those floors were mysteriously malfunctioning at the time, so we were not able to get any footage showing who entered or left their rooms, but there are some guests in this hotel that you Americans would refer to as 'nosy neighbors.' One of them happened to look out her door last night and saw a beautiful young blonde woman walking through the hallways wearing only a man's shirt. She had something under her arm, as well, but we're not sure what that might have been. All we know is that when the nosy woman was shown photographs of other women who were guests of the hotel, she pointed to the photo of your wife." He looked pointedly at Jenny. "She says there is no doubt in her mind that this was the woman she saw leaving the room. On the basis of this information, we obtained authorization to search your rooms. During the search, we found a number of pistols and an interesting knife, along with the computer that seems to have the capability of accessing the security network of this hotel."

One of the other agents in the room said something in Russian to the captain, and then he turned back to Randy. "Mr. Stewart," he said, "it gives me no pleasure to inform you that an American spy has just been arrested. You see, when you came under suspicion, we began looking at everyone with whom you've had contact since you arrived in Vladivostok. Your driver, the man who brought you to the hotel yesterday, is an agent of the American CIA. We know this, because the regular driver confessed that he had accepted money in return for allowing another man to use his shuttle. He was able to identify that man from the lineup of photographs we presented to him, and so we've arrested Anthony VanHorn. Mr. VanHorn was, until today, employed in the public affairs division of the U.S. Consulate General's office here in Vladivostok."

Dimitrovitch held up a photo of VanHorn. "This is Mr. Van-Horn. Do you recognize him?"

Randy screwed up his face, staring at the picture as if confused. "Never seen the guy, far as I know. Why? What is this all about?"

Dimitrovitch grimaced. "You see, Mr. Stewart, while the video was not working on the upper floors last night, the security video in the lobby was working just fine when you arrived yesterday. It was working so well, in fact, that we were able to get a clear image of all of you getting out of the shuttle, and of Mr. VanHorn posing as your driver as he helped you unload your luggage."

"So? Do you think we pay attention to every cab driver? I'll bet if you ask every guest in his hotel, not one in ten would be able to recognize a picture of the driver who brought them here. Human nature, Captain. We don't pay attention to people who are not personally important to us, you know?"

Dimitrovitch nodded. "And of course, you failed to pay attention to the fact that you left the shuttle with one more piece of luggage than you had when you entered it at the airport. Yes, the security cameras were working just fine, there. The four of you checked a total of nine bags on the aircraft, and we found footage of you picking up nine bags when you arrived. Nine bags were loaded into the shuttle, and yet, somehow, ten bags were unloaded when you arrived at the hotel. Now, considering the fact that we've found weapons that could not possibly have come with you on your flight, it's not difficult for us to imagine that those weapons were in the tenth bag. Can you follow my logic?"

Randy shook his head. "Not really," he said. "I don't know anything about a tenth bag, and I certainly don't know anything about any weapons. If you found any kind of weapons in my room, I've got to believe somebody planted them there. Or is that what this is all about? You Russian cops like to plant evidence on Americans, so you can lock us up? I've heard stories about that kind of thing, but I didn't believe it until now."

Dimitrovitch stared into his eyes for several seconds, then turned his gaze on Jenny. "Mrs. Stewart," he said. "You have been awfully quiet. Do you deny that you went to visit another room last night? A room on the top floor of the hotel?"

Jenny cut her eyes to Randy for a second, then turned them back to Dimitrovitch. "I certainly did not," she said. "I'm a respectable married woman. I certainly wouldn't be going to some other man's room, especially with my husband here with me."

Dimitrovitch burst out laughing. "Oh, forgive me," he said, "but this is becoming rather comical. I already have enough evidence to arrest the four of you for the assassination of Anton Kalashnikov, and the collateral murders of his wife and children, and the charges against you will include espionage. This is inevitable, since you were seen in the company of a known American spy who provided you with weapons. Such charges will only result in the death penalty, but you can spare yourself that fate by confessing."

Suddenly, one of the other agents swung his fist, striking Dave Lange on his right ear. Dave fell onto the floor, and began retching. The agent kicked him twice, and Jenny saw him spit blood onto the carpet.

"Stop it," she shouted, but two of the other men grabbed her as she tried to get to her feet. Randy reached out for one of them, but then a fist connected with the back of his own head and he pitched forward onto the floor.

"Enough," Dimitrovitch said, and the agents backed off. Jenny pushed herself back up to a sitting position and glared at him.

"The famous Russian torture? I've read all the stories about how Americans get tortured when they're arrested here. Is that what we've got to look forward to?"

"Ah, Mrs. Stewart," Dimitrovitch said with a grin. "Does every respectable married woman in America have so much fire?" His grin faded away. "You are foreign agents, and your assassination of Minister Kalashnikov can be construed as an act of war against Russia. That is not up to me, however. I am only going to place the four of you under arrest, and you will be transported to Moscow for interrogation."

He rose to his feet and twirled a finger in the air. "Bring them all," he said. The other agents forced them all onto their feet, two of them supporting Randy, and Dimitrovitch led the way to the elevator.

When the doors opened again, Jenny saw that they were in the basement of the building. They were led toward the rear of the structure, where a flight of stairs led up to an alley. An FSB van was waiting there and they were shoved inside. Four of the agents climbed in with them while the others shut the doors. The engine started and the truck began moving only a moment later.

Jenny sat close to Randy, holding him as his head lay on her shoulder. "It'll be okay, honey," she said. "It will all be okay. They'll figure out what's going on, don't worry. They'll probably let us go tomorrow, and we'll go straight home, okay?"

He grunted, but said nothing else.

CHAPTER FIVE

"Noah! Noah, get up!" Neil's voice rang through Noah's bedroom window, and Noah woke and was out of bed instantly.

"Front door," he called out. As Sarah stirred and leaned up on an elbow, Noah pulled his pants on and hurried into the hallway. He snapped open the front door and Neil rushed through it, grabbed him by the shoulders and looked into his face. Noah saw tears, and grabbed the boy and led him to the kitchen table. "What's going on, Neil?" As he got Neil into a chair, he glanced at the clock on the coffeemaker and saw that it was one A.M.

"I couldn't sleep," Neil said, "so I was just surfing the Internet, playing around, and I came across the news. Noah, Jenny's been arrested as a spy and assassin in Russia, the whole team has been arrested."

Anyone else would have expressed doubt, would have tried to claim that there was an error, but Noah was not anyone else. "Stay here," he said, and he rushed back to his bedroom. Sarah was wrapping herself in a bathrobe as he grabbed his phone.

"What's going on?" Sarah asked.

"Team Cinderella has been arrested in Russia," Noah replied, and then he hurried back to the kitchen. He had dialed Allison's direct line on the way and was holding the phone up to his ear when he got there.

"How the hell did you find out already?" Allison asked as she answered the phone.

"Neil. He found it on the Internet and came to wake me up. What's the situation?"

Allison sighed deeply. "He probably knows as much as I do, maybe more. I don't know the whole situation, but Jenny and the team were arrested on a charge of conspiring to assassinate Kalashnikov, carrying out the assassination, a total of four charges of espionage and at least three charges of murder. I've got the State Department looking into it, but—Noah, they can only do so much. The Secretary of State has no choice but to disavow them. How is the kid holding up?"

Noah looked at Neil. "Not well," he said. "What else can we do?"

The sigh came again. "Nothing," she said. "I hate it, Noah, but this is one of the risks of our business."

Neil could hear her voice through the phone, and he reached out and tried to snatch it away from Noah. Noah kept it out of reach, but Neil started shouting. "We have to go after them," he yelled. "We have to go get them, Noah. You tell her, you tell that bitch we're going after them!"

"Oh, God, Noah," Allison said. "Maybe it was a mistake to allow romantic relationships in the teams. It's bad enough we're going to lose Jenny and her guys, but I don't know if Neil will survive it."

Noah's mind was bouncing back and forth between Allison and Neil, considering both of their points of view. "What about a rescue mission? Let me take my team and go get them."

"Noah, there's no way. State says they'll be transported to Lefortovo prison, that's where all suspected spies are taken. The place is about as impregnable as it can get."

"It's not," Neil said. "Tell her it's not impregnable, I can find a way in. I can get us in, we can get them out. Tell her, Noah."

Sarah came into the kitchen and sat down beside Neil, wrapping an arm around his shoulders. Noah looked at her for a moment, then spoke again to Allison.

"We can do it," he said confidently. "I trust Neil to find the weakness in the building, and if we can't get them out that way, we'll find another way."

"Noah, I could never get approval. There's no way the president would ever..."

"You don't need his approval," Noah said. "You told me that the first day we met. As director of E & E, you're autonomous. Let me take my team and go rescue them."

"Noah, this isn't like you. Of all people, I'd expect you to understand the logical necessity of disavowals."

"I do," Noah said. "At the same time, I know the value of these assets, and that the organization can't afford to lose them. I believe that my team can successfully bring them out. If I didn't believe that, I wouldn't ask for the mission."

He heard her take a deep breath and let it out slowly. "Talk to me after I know more," she said. "Understand this: even if I agree, it may be necessary for me to simply look the other way. Do you understand?"

"I understand."

"High noon, my office. God, we're working on Saturday!" The line went dead.

Noah dropped the phone onto the table and looked at Neil. "She won't give me an answer right now," he said. "We're supposed to be at her office at noon."

Neil put his head in his hands, shaking it from side to side. "I can't leave her there, Noah," he said. "You went back for Sarah, you went after her more than once. I can't leave Jenny there."

Noah looked at Sarah, who was staring into his face. "We're not going to leave her there," he said. "With or without authorization, we're going to rescue them, but that means being at the top of our game. For that, we need rest. Neil, Sarah and I are going back to bed.

You can stay here if you want, just use the couch. Try to sleep." He reached out for Sarah's hand and led her back toward the bedroom.

"Maybe I should stay up with him," Sarah said as they got down the hall.

"No," Noah said. "If he's going to be of any use to us, he has to get himself under control. The best thing for him right now is to stay quiet, force himself to think. If he believes we're sleeping, he'll do that."

Sarah followed him into the bedroom and they got undressed and back under the covers. A minute later, she heard Noah's breathing slow as he drifted off to sleep once again. She envied him the ability to sleep at will, but she was surprised to realize that she was also falling asleep only a dozen minutes later.

Neil was asleep on the couch when they rose at seven, and they left him there as they made coffee. Sarah started breakfast a few minutes later, and the aroma of bacon woke him. He came walking into the kitchen a moment later, poured himself a cup of coffee and sat down at the table beside Noah.

"I slept a little bit," he said. "I couldn't decide whether to stay here or go back home, but I figured you had a reason for wanting me here. I need to go get my computer, though."

"Drink your coffee first," Noah said. "You look a little shaky."

"Just my nerves," Neil said, trying to force a grin. "Noah, man, I don't know what I'll do if we can't pull this off."

Noah only nodded. A moment later, Sarah set a plate of bacon and eggs in front of Neil and he began eating. She gave Noah a plate and then made her own before sitting down with them.

They ate in silence, and Neil left half his food on the plate. He got up without a word and walked out the door, but was back ten minutes later with his laptop. He set it on the table and powered it on, scanning for any further news stories about the arrested team.

"They're being flown to Moscow today," he said. "Actually, they're already on the way. Vladivostok is seventeen hours ahead of us, so it's already past midnight, there."

"That's in Vladivostok," Noah said. "Moscow is only ten hours ahead of us. Takes about nine hours to fly from Vladivostok to Moscow, so they may have already arrived."

Neil rubbed his hands vigorously through his hair. "I can't hang on until noon, Noah," he said. "Can't we call her now? She's bound to know something."

"She said noon," Noah said. "That's when we'll go. In the meantime, I want you to start looking at how we can get to them inside that prison. It will help if we have a basic plan ready to present."

Neil sighed and started working on the computer. Noah and Sarah watched him silently for several minutes, but then he turned the computer around so they could see the monitor.

"This is what Lefortovo looks like from the outside," he said. "It was built in the late eighteen hundreds, and it's been used by the KGB and every other version of the Russian Secret Police. It will be a very tough nut to crack, but nothing is impossible."

"Can you get any idea of where they would be held inside it?" Noah asked.

"There's a section of the prison that's devoted to spies," Neil said. "It's on the second floor, and it's probably the most secure part of the whole facility. I haven't found blueprints of the building yet, but give me time and I will."

Noah nodded. "Give me all the information you can on staff, as well. I want to know how many guards we're looking at, what kind of office staff they have, everything. Look at every possible entrance and exit, no matter how small. I'm going to drag Wally in on this, and every gadget we can get our hands on to help us."

"You were serious, then?" Neil asked. "What you said last night, about going in no matter what the Dragon Lady says?"

"I'm serious. The one thing we've always said is that we don't leave anyone behind, because we're a family. Jenny is family. We're going to get them out."

Tears started to run down Neil's cheeks again, but he brushed them away and turned back to his computer. "I'll get every bit of information I can," he said. He started tapping on the keyboard, and Noah turned to Sarah.

"You can stay home on this one..."

"Don't even think about it," Sarah said, cutting him off. "Where you go, I go. Besides, you're going to need a driver. I can handle Moscow, and we may have to move awfully fast."

Noah nodded, then pulled his phone out of his pocket and dialed Marco. The call was answered on the third ring.

"Hey, Noah," Marco said. "What's shakin'?"

"Have you heard the news? Team Cinderella was captured yesterday, in Russia."

Marco whistled. "Holy crap," he said. "When do we leave?"

JENNY AND THE MEN HAD been placed in sparse holding cells, small, bare concrete rooms with nothing in them. A hole in the floor, they were told, would serve as their toilets, but there wasn't even a pad to lay on. Jenny spent her hours in the cell sitting on the floor and leaning back against the wall. She managed to sleep, but only fitfully, for a few minutes at a time. Still, she knew she would need whatever rest she could manage.

Between the darkness and the intermittent sleep, she had no idea what time it might be when the cell door suddenly opened. Light flooded into the room and four men rushed inside. She was yanked up onto her feet, her hands were cuffed behind her and a black bag was pulled down over her head. With one man holding each arm, she was marched out the door and through the hallway, and then the echoes of their footsteps told her that she was in a large enclosed area, like a big garage.

It probably was a garage, because she was pushed into the backseat of a car a moment later. The doors slammed and the engine started, and she heard several other vehicles close by. More car doors slammed, more engines fired up, and then they started moving.

The ride lasted quite some time, but she couldn't quite say how long. She had just decided to guess that they had been moving for an hour when they made a turn and the vehicle began to slow. It stopped a few minutes later and her door was yanked open once more. Rough hands grabbed hold of her arm and dragged her out, almost causing her to fall. She was pulled back upright and then marched ahead, but her captors stopped her after only a couple of minutes. One of them said something to her in Russian, and then reached down to grab her right leg and lifted it slightly.

She felt a step under her foot, and realized that they were boarding an airplane. She moved up the steps carefully, one step at a time, and another pair of hands was waiting at the top. She was walked into what seemed to be a fairly large aircraft and pushed into a seat. Her hands were left cuffed behind her and the bag was still in place as seatbelts were fastened around her.

She heard others being brought onto the plane and called out once, but someone slapped her head. She didn't need an interpreter to know that it was an order to be quiet, so she closed her mouth and sat there. She tried counting seconds and realized that about fifteen minutes had passed by the time the aircraft's door was closed and locked and the engines began to whine.

The bag over her head seemed to be made of some heavy fabric, because she couldn't even see light through it. She could breathe easily, though, so she leaned her head back and relaxed. As the plane climbed up to its cruising altitude, Jenny managed to drift off to sleep.

This time, she slept fairly well. She woke refreshed some hours later, when someone lifted the bag enough to put the mouth of a water bottle to her lips. She took a grateful drink, swirling it around in her mouth to moisturize the dry tissues, then swallowed as much as she could before it was taken away.

It seemed to her that a couple of hours passed after that, before the plane suddenly began to descend. She was fairly certain they were coming into a landing at Moscow, and finally allowed herself to wonder if anyone back home in Neverland was aware of her arrest, yet. Her heart ached for Neil, because she knew that he was incredibly attached to her.

Suddenly, her anger at being arrested turned into guilt, because she blamed herself for letting it happen. She had been so anxious to let her demons out that she had been less than cautious. Killing the two surveillance agents had been stupid, especially since she knew that the Russian government was going to be notified of a planned assassination of the very person they were assigned to watch.

Now, because of her stupidity, she and her entire team were going to die. Despite knowing full well that death was a risk in her profession, Jenny had a strong love for life, and it had gotten a lot stronger since she had grown close to Neil. Tears began to run down her cheeks as she thought of the suffering he would endure after she was executed, and even more when she thought about the future she had allowed herself to dream of having with him. She had even spoken to Allison, very privately, about the possibility of having a child.

Allison had been blunt. While she would not order a pregnancy to be terminated, becoming a mother would not remove Jenny from her position with E & E. Should she become pregnant, Allison would urge her to consider placing the child up for adoption, but Jenny knew she could never do that. She had planned to talk to Sarah about it, to see if she and Noah had given any thought to parenthood, but she didn't get the chance.

Now, it wouldn't matter.

After the plane touched down, Jenny was the first one to be led off. She was once again put into the back seat of a car, and waited again while others were brought down and put into different vehicles. She was sure she heard at least half a dozen different cars, which meant that she and her team weren't the only prisoners being brought to Moscow. One of them was probably VanHorn, but she didn't have any idea who else there might be.

This time, the ride lasted just over half an hour. When the car stopped again, Jenny was taken out and walked quickly into a building and put into a chair. The bag was finally taken off her head, and she blinked several times as her eyes adjusted to the light in the room.

She was sitting on a hard wooden chair at the side of what looked like a roomful of clerks. There were armed guards standing around the room, including one that was only a few feet from her and keeping his eyes locked on her at all times.

One at a time, the others were brought in and placed in chairs close by. As each bag was lifted, she recognized Randy, Dave and Jim, and then VanHorn, whose picture she had been shown by Dimitrovitch. Two more men were brought in after him, but she had no idea who they might be.

The way they were being watched, she figured it wouldn't be a good idea to try to talk. She sat and waited, and it was only about fifteen minutes later that she was ordered onto her feet once again. The cuffs were removed from her wrists and she was escorted by two men into another room.

"You will change," one of them said in broken English. He pointed to the table, where stacks of rough clothing were waiting. Jenny walked over and picked out a pair of pants and a shirt that looked small enough for her, then looked around.

"Bathroom?"

"Change," the man said. Jenny stared at him for a moment, then shrugged. While both men watched closely, she stripped down to her underwear and put on the clothes she had chosen. The ones she had removed were picked up and thrown into a trash bin, and then she was led through another door.

That door opened into a long hallway, and she saw cell doors on either side. She was allowed to go almost all the way to the other end before the man who had spoken told her to stop. He opened a door on her left with a massive key and pointed, and she stepped inside.

The cell was a definite improvement over the last one. There was a steel bunk with a fairly thick mattress on it, and there were sheets, pillow and blankets stacked neatly on it. There was also a toilet, which she quickly and gratefully used, and a table containing a pad and several short pencils.

She moved the blankets and pillow to the table and started assembling the bed. With nothing else to do, she thought she might as well try to get a little bit more sleep.

CHAPTER SIX

Noah, Sarah, Neil and Marco walked into the conference room with two minutes to go before noon, but Allison, Donald Jefferson and Molly were there waiting for them. For once, Neil walked past the doughnuts without even noticing them and took his seat at the conference table.

"First things first," Allison said. "Neil, I'm so sorry this is happened. Please understand that this is a risk every team faces in the field."

"I know that," Neil said. "I just don't understand how we could just leave them there, walk away from them."

"It's because of something called plausible deniability," Jefferson said. "Every intelligence agent we have, of any kind, is fully aware that the Secretary of State will disavow any knowledge of them or their actions if they're captured. To do anything else would mean that sending them into the country to complete their mission would be an act of war."

"I don't," Neil said immediately, "have any issue with that. My issue is with the fact that this organization is capable of pulling off a rescue, so that's what I want us to do."

"Unfortunately," Allison went on, "rescue is not always possible. In fact, I've had to order the deaths of American agents in the past, when they had information that simply could not be allowed to fall into enemy hands. Everyone eventually cracks under torture, Neil. Everyone." She cleared her throat. "In this case, however, the only thing Jenny and her team could reveal is our existence. The Russians are already fully aware that we exist, and they even know more than I like about Noah and Team Camelot, so I'm not in that position. For that very reason, we're going to discuss the possibility of a rescue mission, but I have to caution you that what we talk about cannot leave this room without my explicit authorization. Is that understood?"

They all agreed that they understood and would obey, and Allison nodded once.

"All right. State has been advised that Jenny and the others are being charged as spies, as well as assassins. What that means to us is that the State Department can do absolutely nothing to try to secure their release. They will be going before a Russian court about forty hours from now, and will almost certainly be convicted and sentenced to death. A conviction for assassination or espionage is not appealed in Russia. If they're sentenced to death, which they will be, the executions will be scheduled for four days later. That means we've less than five days to figure out how to get them back. Any ideas?"

Noah leaned forward. "Neil has located blueprints of the building they're being held in," he said. "With some help from Wally's department, I believe Marco and I can get into the building and eliminate any opposition long enough to find them and get them out. The hardest part will be getting away from the prison itself and out of the country. My plan is to have Sarah waiting with a van, something big enough for all of us to fit into for the drive to the airport. Since Jenny and her team can't be acknowledged officially, we can't risk putting them into a diplomatic aircraft, so my plan is to bring them out as cargo, instead."

Allison looked at Molly. "What do you think?"

Molly scowled. "He had me until he mentioned a cargo flight. Russian cargo jets are searched several times before takeoff, usually with sniffer dogs. I'm pretty sure they would catch the scent of people hiding inside the plane."

"Alternatives?" Jefferson asked.

Molly shook her head. "I'm afraid I can't think of any," she said. "We're talking about Moscow. I have trouble imagining any way to get them out of the country."

"Just give us some new IDs for them," Neil said. "We can take some clean clothes to them, give them wigs and colored contact lenses and whatever else it takes to change their appearance. With a passport that seems to match, they should be able to walk right onto any commercial flight, right?"

"I'm afraid not," Molly said. "Russian airports use some very sophisticated facial recognition technology, now. They would be spotted, no matter how well disguised they might be. The software uses things like facial bone structure, things that can't be changed with a simple disguise."

"Oh, come on," Sarah said, "there's got to be a way. There just has to be."

"I might have an idea," Jefferson said softly. "It's going to sound crazy at first, but it just might have a chance of success."

Allison looked at him with a grin. "Well, don't keep us in suspense," she said. "Spit it out, man."

Jefferson licked his lips and turned to Noah. "When you got Sarah back from the Chinese, you had to steal a plane and fly it yourself, right?"

Noah nodded. "That's correct. I flew a Cessna 195 under the radar to Vietnam."

"I'm thinking of a similar stunt," Jefferson said. "If arrangements can be made to get them to a plane, it's not all that far from Moscow to Warsaw. Our embassy there could have a diplomatic plane ready to go when they arrive, to bring them back home."

Allison looked at Noah. "What do you think?"

"It would depend on the plane," Noah said. "My grandfather taught me to fly in his Cessna 310 when I was a kid, and I remember it clearly enough. The 195 was a fairly easy plane to fly, but I don't know that we'd find one in Moscow. If I have to fly under the radar again, I want something similar."

Molly turned to the computer beside her and started tapping on the keys. A moment later she looked up and smiled. "There's a tour service with a 1976 model Cessna 310 for sale in Moscow right now, and it has its own private airfield. We've got seven dummy corporations set up in Moscow at the moment, and I can arrange for any one of them to purchase it today."

Allison looked at Noah, who nodded again. "I can fly it," he said. "It's got plenty of range for the trip, and it could fly under radar if necessary. It was only designed to carry up to six people, but we could squeeze all eight of us in there. The plane certainly has enough power to get us off the ground, and the fuel capacity to compensate for any loss of range from extra load."

Allison chewed her bottom lip for a moment as she stared at him, then turned to Molly. "Buy it," she said. "Do whatever is necessary as far as registration, insurance, all that, then get it checked out mechanically. I want it ready to fly when Noah gets to it, fully fueled and everything."

She turned back to Noah. "Get out to Wally and pick up whatever you need. If there's something you can't carry into the country, make sure he gets it on a diplomatic flight today. I'm authorizing this mission, but there's one thing I want all of you to understand. I cannot afford to lose both teams. If at any time you decide the mission cannot succeed, abort and come home. Is that understood?"

"Understood," Noah said without hesitation. Neil, Sarah and Marco nodded their agreement, but Allison could see the reservation in their faces.

"All right, then," she said. "As soon as Wally provides you with mission IDs, Donald will make arrangements for your flight to Moscow. Remember that you only have a matter of days to pull this off, so move as quickly as you can."

Allison got up and left the room, and Noah and his team followed. They had arrived in Neil's Hummer, and climbed into it as soon as they got to the garage and headed directly out to R&D.

Allison had called ahead, so Wally was waiting for them when they arrived. As soon as they stepped into the foyer of the building, Wally reached out and grabbed Neil's hand and pressed it between his own. "Allie told me," he said. "Don't you worry, Neil, Noah will get her back for you. He is the best, the absolute best."

Neil mumbled his thanks as Wally turned to Noah. "Okay, Noah, tell me what you need. Allie says you've got *carte blanche* out here, you can have anything you want."

"Good. Remember the guns that make people freeze where they're standing? The ones with scopolamine gas in those little capsules?"

Wally broke out into a smile. "Yes, of course."

"I need four of them loaded onto a diplomatic flight today, headed for Moscow. Can you do that?"

"Consider it done, and I'll send along plenty of the antidote gum. We'll have to put the ammunition inside a pressurized container, though. I'm afraid they would all burst when the plane reaches altitude. Wouldn't do to have the whole crew go to sleep all of a sudden, now would it? What else?"

"Send along the tools we used that time, too. I don't know that we'll actually use them, but I prefer to have them if we need them."

"Okay, no problem," Wally said. "What else?"

"The iPhone, the one with the backscatter detection system. I may need to see through walls now and then, and it works."

Wally motioned for them to follow him, and led them to one of the many workshops. He had a quick word with the technician inside, and a fully functional iPhone was quickly activated and programmed. Wally handed it to Noah, and then smiled.

"One of our girls here had a couple of bright ideas about backscatter," he said. "Check it out, try it on the wall over there."

Noah put the phone against the wall and activated the backscatter detection system. Backscatter radiation can be collected and analyzed digitally to render an image of what might be behind a solid object, like a wall. Noah had used it before, and had found it to be incredibly useful. The image was monochromatic and grainy, but it was clear enough to allow him to determine how many people might be on the other side of a wall and a general idea of the type of weapons they might be carrying.

The screen lit up and Noah's eyebrows rose a quarter inch. Instead of the grainy, black-and-white image he was used to, the screen showed a view of the room on the other side of the wall that was as good as an old black-and-white TV image. He looked around at Wally.

"How did you manage this?"

Wally pointed at the girl who had programmed the phone. "That's Holly," he said. "Holly came up with the idea of combining backscatter detection with sonic echo impulses. The phone emits a sound wave in such a high frequency that only electronics can detect it, then reads the echo and combines it with an analysis of the backscatter radiation. The result is a view that's much clearer than anything we've had before." He giggled. "The only problem was creating the computer circuitry that would be small enough to stuff inside that case. Don't let anybody measure that phone, because it's three millimeters thicker than normal iPhones."

Noah looked the phone over, then looked up at Wally again. "I really don't think anyone will notice," he said. "Now, we need IDs for the mission."

"Got 'em ready," Wally said. "Follow me."

They went to another room, where they were each handed an ID kit. Noah would be operating under the name of Samuel Winston and Sarah would be his wife, Marcia. Neil's ID said Dennis Lampley, and Marco's read Harold Locksley. Wally explained quickly that all four were listed as employees of Valkyrie Communications, a high-tech company based in Seattle that had contracts with the government. Each of them had a drivers license, passport, and wallet full of photos and the odds and ends that are normally accumulated there, while Sarah received a purse that Marco joked could be used as a carry-on bag.

"Donnie Jefferson has your flight ready to go," Wally said. "You'll be leaving from Kirtland airport by helicopter, rather than driving all the way to Denver. We took the liberty of packing you some luggage to save time, so you can head for the airport right now. Let's face it, you don't have a lot of time to waste."

Noah shook his hand. "Thank you, Wally," he said. "Don't forget to send my toys."

"Oh, don't worry," Wally said. "They'll go to Denver with you, but the diplomatic flight that's picking them up will actually arrive in Moscow before you do. One of our people will have them waiting for you when you get there." He shook hands with the rest of them, wished them the best of luck and then turned to go back to his office.

Noah looked at his team. "Anybody need to make any stops?" No one did, so they loaded their new luggage into the back of the Hummer and climbed in. They got to the Kirtland airport in only twenty minutes and were directed to a spot on the tarmac where a helicopter was just starting up. Eight minutes later, they were in the air and on the way to Denver.

The flight to Moscow departed Denver at just after four that Saturday afternoon and made two stops along the way. The first was in Reykjavík, Iceland, where they changed planes for the second leg of the flight to Stockholm, Sweden. From Stockholm, they flew directly to Moscow, arriving at Sheremetyevo Airport at eight P.M. on Sunday evening, even though it was only eighteen hours after departing Denver.

As they left the baggage claim area forty-five minutes later, Sarah tapped Noah on the arm and pointed at a man who was holding a sign. Written on cardboard with a marker was the name "Samuel Winston," and Noah instantly recognized Larry Carson, E & E's man in Moscow.

Sarah broke into a smile. Carson had been instrumental in saving Noah's life the last time they had seen him, after Noah had been severely wounded in a confrontation with Nicolaich Andropov, a former FSB senior officer who had gone rogue. Andropov had captured Sarah and used her as bait to draw Noah into the trap that almost killed him. Working together, Noah and Sarah had escaped, but not before a bullet had nicked the artery in Noah's leg. But for Carson's quick action, Noah would have bled out before he could have gotten any other kind of medical attention, but the U.S. Embassy in Moscow had its own small but efficient clinic.

"Mr. Winston," Carson said as they approached. "I'm Larry Carson, from the U.S. Embassy. I hope you had a pleasant flight, but I'm sure glad to see you. Our phone system has been acting screwy for weeks."

Noah gave him a friendly smile. "Well, we'll see if we can't get it straightened out," he said, staying in character. "I've brought my A team. This is my wife, Marcia, and these two gentlemen are Dennis and Harold. I don't think it will take us long to sort things out."

"Glad to hear it. Shall we go? I've got a car waiting out front right now."

Since the cover story for the team was that they were coming in to straighten out a phone service problem at the embassy, Carson made no attempt to conceal his destination. As soon as they were in the car and away from the airport, he looked at Noah with a grin.

"Good to see you again, Camelot," he said. "When all this broke a few days ago, I actually let myself hope they would send you in. My orders are to give you any assistance we can, and I've got a box of Christmas presents for you sitting in my office. It came in about two hours ago, just before I left to come pick you up."

Noah nodded. "Good. The tall, skinny guy is my intel man. He'll need access to anything you got on Lefortovo, and I want to talk to anybody who knows anything about that place. Have you heard any update on our people there?"

Carson scowled. "They'll be tried today, but it's really just a formality. They've already been convicted as far as the Kremlin is concerned. Now it's just a matter of putting the rubber stamp on it and sentencing them. Word we got is that they will be executed publicly, hanged in Red Square three days from now."

"Oh, shit," Neil muttered, but Noah ignored him.

"That doesn't give us a lot of time, then. I'm going to need a package van, something that can't be traced back to the embassy. Can you handle that?"

"I will," Carson said. "There are a few dozen quiet assets in Moscow, deep cover agents. This mission has high enough priority that I can call on any of them, and I'm sure there's a van available somewhere among them." He started to say something else, but then stopped.

Noah looked at him. "What is it?"

Carson grimaced, then let out a sigh. "When I got the communiqué yesterday, telling me you were coming, I talked to our Colonel Towers. He was an army colonel from the Corps of Engineers and our resident expert on buildings and architecture. He claims there's no way in the world to get into Lefortovo's secure detention areas, even if you had an entire platoon to back you up. The place is literally designed to go into a physical lockdown in the event of an attack, and it's built to withstand multiple hits by artillery. Any explosive powerful enough to break into it would destroy it and everyone in it."

"That's what Dennis said, too. That's why you got that Christmas box, it contains the things I need to get in and out before anyone can react."

They arrived at the embassy a couple of minutes later and Carson took them inside. Noah was introduced to Towers, who took them all into his office to begin discussing the details surrounding Lefortovo prison.

"I've got blueprints of the building," Towers said, "but I've got to say there's no way I can imagine that you're going to get in and out of that place. It's one of the most advanced prisons in the world, controlled by a computer system more than by staff. There are sensors inside the building that can detect an unauthorized presence and lock the whole place down instantly. If you did manage to get inside, you'd only find yourself sealed into an area you can't escape from."

"I'm not exactly planning to break in," Noah said. "I intend to walk right in through the front door, and I've got some interesting little weapons to help me accomplish that. Instead of bullets, they use compressed air to shoot gel capsules that burst on impact and release a gas that instantly inhibits initiative. All somebody has to do is get a whiff of it and they just stop wherever they are and do nothing. We can walk right past them, take keys away, whatever. I'm hoping that will let us get in and out without setting off any of those defenses."

Towers shook his head. "I don't think there's much chance," he said. "The system is designed to keep track of all authorized personnel, and just detecting one additional body inside is enough to set it off. Once that happens, it requires a manual override from a control booth on the top floor of the building. The officers in that booth can release a poison gas anywhere in the building, and they're trained to be absolutely certain the situation is under control before they give the override command. If that means they have to kill everyone in a particular section, they'll do it."

"He's right," Neil said. He was sitting at a table in the room, looking at the screen on his computer. Towers had given him access to the embassy's intranet so that he could look at every bit of intelligence they had on Lefortovo. "Noah, there's no way in the world we can get them out of the prison itself. We'd all die in the process, so I'm looking at other possibilities." The tremor in his voice told Noah just how serious he was as he looked up at Towers. "As far as I can tell, the only point of vulnerability on this place is its garage. Now, the garage itself is secure, but what I'm thinking of is when they bring them out for the execution. Larry says that will be in Red Square, is that right?"

Towers nodded. "Yes. They'll have the gallows up by tomorrow, most likely, but I'm gonna correct your guy, there. That garage is every bit as hard as the rest of the prison, and if you tried anything inside it, you'd end up with a hundred heavily armed guards suddenly up your ass."

"Then we need to know exactly when they'll be bringing our people out of that garage, and the route they'll take. How do I get that information?"

"I don't know that we can," Towers said. "One thing about the Russians, they don't like to do anything on a computer they can do on paper. Lefortovo is still in the 1950s as far as digital information is concerned. All of their execution plans are done on paper, and we've never managed to find anything on them electronically."

"Where would they keep it?" Noah asked. "The execution itinerary, where would it be kept?"

Towers turned to a print-out of the prison layout that he had tacked to his wall and pointed to a section just inside the front entrance. "Here," he said. "That's the operations office. The execution plan would be in a file cabinet in that office."

"Is that section part of the automatic lockdown?"

The colonel made a face. "No, but it's pretty secure. There are probably a dozen people in that section, and security watches over it through hidden cameras. You'd have one hell of a time getting in there, let alone finding the itinerary for a particular execution."

Noah glanced at Neil, who was watching and hoping. "If our only chance to rescue our people is while they're being transported to Red Square, then I don't think we have much choice. Neil, start planning it for me. I need to know the best possible time to hit them, and the most likely place to find that execution plan."

Neil nodded and turned back to the computer. "I'm on it," he said.

Towers scowled. "This sounds like total stupidity to me," he said. "You need a much better plan than this, if you want to have even the lightest chance of success. All you're going to do with this one is get yourselves killed."

Noah looked at him for several seconds, then nodded once. "You may be right," he said. "Luckily, I've just thought of one." He turned to Carson. "Larry, I want you to send all my Christmas presents back to Santa. Is there any way you can get me Tasers, instead?"

Carson squinted at him as he nodded. "We've got a pretty good batch of them, and I could get you a few. What have you got in mind?"

Noah looked at Neil, who was suddenly watching him closely. "I think our best bet might be to get me and Marco inside with Jenny and the others. If we're captured while trying to steal the execution itinerary, they'll automatically connect us to them, so we ought to be taken to the same area, right?"

Towers grimaced. "Probably, but all that means is you'll be locked into cells. Under the way things work here, you can automatically be adjudged part of their crimes, so all they'd do is add a couple more gallows and execute you right along with them."

Noah nodded. "That's what I'm counting on," he said.

CHAPTER SEVEN

"**T**his scares me," Sarah said. She and Noah were in the room they had rented at the Moscow Marriott Hotel, just a short distance from the embassy. "If you were going in to get them out, that would be one thing, I could understand the risk, but..."

"We can't do that," Noah said. "The place is just too secure for that kind of rescue operation, so we had no choice but to rework the plan. We need the Russians to think we plan to take them while they're being transported to Red Square, and in order to do that I'd need to know the schedule for that day. That's what makes this ploy believable."

"But Now you'll be captured, too, and if even one thing goes wrong with the rest of your plan, we lose all of you at the same time. Noah, I'm scared. If anything happens to you, I don't know what I would do."

Noah put his arms around her and pulled her close. "If anything were to happen to me," he said, "I want you to get out of the country as fast as you can. You'll be at the embassy while this goes down, so Larry can put you on a diplomatic flight. You take Neil and you go home, that's all you can do."

Sarah clung to him and let out a sigh. "Don't even talk like that," she said. "I understand you have to do this, but you come back to me. Promise me."

Noah held her in silence for another moment, then tilted his head back to look into her eyes. "I promise you that I'll do everything in my power to come back to you safely. That's the best I can do. Other than that, we stick to the plan."

Sarah stared at him for a moment, then nodded her head. He pulled her close again and held her for another minute, then let her go and turned to Marco, sitting on the bed.

"Let's go," he said.

Marco stood. Like Noah, he was dressed in black and wearing a long, light trenchcoat, which was also black. Sarah followed as the two of them walked out the door, and all three rode the elevator down to the main floor. It was close to midnight, but the few people in the lobby ignored them as they walked out the front door and turned to the right.

The car Carson had arranged was sitting where they had left it, a four-door sedan that looked like a million others in the city. Sarah got behind the wheel as Noah took the shotgun seat and Marco slid into the back. She started the car and put it in gear, following the directions she had memorized to Lefortovo prison.

The plan was simple. Sarah would park the car just out of range of the prison security cameras and Noah and Marco would walk the rest of the way. Each of them carried two of the powerful Taser stun guns, special ones made for use by clandestine services like the CIA; a single jolt from one of them would instantly render the biggest man unconscious. They would pound on the front door until someone paid attention, then use the stun guns to immobilize whoever answered, then threaten the rest with the pistols they had tucked into their belts. Hopefully, nobody would try to play hero, because Noah wanted to pull this off without casualties on either side.

As soon as the room was under control, they would enter the office and start searching for the schedule. Towers had given them his best guesses on where to look, so they would start there. If they didn't find it, they would keep looking, shooting the people in the room again if they began to stir.

Sarah pulled up at the spot they had chosen and the two men got out. She would wait in the car, where security officers would later assume she was ready to race forward and pick them up as soon as they came out. Each of them was wearing a Bluetooth-style communication headset, with Neil using a fourth to keep track of what was happening from the embassy.

"They're moving," Sarah said. "Keep your fingers crossed, Neil."

"I've got my fingers crossed," he replied, "my toes are crossed, my eyes are even crossed."

A light, apparently on a proximity sensor, suddenly came on over the prison entrance doorway. Sarah leaned forward onto the steering wheel, trying to get a better look, and saw the door open as Noah and Marco drew near. There was a sudden flurry of motion, and then the two men rushed inside the building and out of her line of sight.

"They got in," she said. "Now all we can do is wait."

Inside the imposing building, Noah and Marco were surprised to find only a half-dozen people present. Four of them were guards, and they froze instantly when the guns were aimed at them, and went down under the stun guns a few seconds later. The other two were clerks, and unarmed. Noah stunned one of them, then grabbed the other by the arm and spun the man to face him.

"Do you speak English?"

The clerk, obviously terrified, nodded his head. "Yes, but not good," he said.

"Where can I find the schedule for the execution of the spies from America?"

The clerk stared into his face for a moment, then slowly pointed at a double-doored cabinet. Noah nodded to Marco, who snatched it open and began looking at the papers inside. There were a dozen narrow shelves, and it took him a couple of minutes to find what he was looking for.

"Got it," he said. He turned back to Noah, triumphantly holding a sheaf of papers in his hand.

Noah turned to the clerk again. "Do you want to live?" he asked. The man nodded vigorously, and Noah hit him with the stun gun.

He dropped to the floor instantly, and Noah turned to where Marco was hurriedly photographing the papers with a cell phone.

Noah stood patiently while Marco put the papers back where he had gotten them. They turned toward the door and Marco grabbed the knob, but then he stopped. He turned to Noah with a sickly look on his face and said, "It's locked."

"Stay exactly where you are," said a voice from speakers in the ceiling. "Put down your weapons or I will be forced to kill you where you stand."

Noah looked around the room quickly, but there were no windows or other means of escape. He hesitated for only a few seconds, then dropped the stun guns and his pistol as he raised his hands. Marco let out a sigh and did the same, and Noah whispered the word, "Abort," as security guards came rushing into the room to arrest them.

Sarah, out in the car, wiped the tears from her eyes as she put the car into gear and drove away. She made sure to speed past the security cameras as she did so.

LARRY CARSON WAS WAITING when she arrived back at the embassy and took her directly to the room where Neil was still staring at his computer screen. He looked up at her as she entered and Sarah saw the tracks of his own tears, then she hurried over and threw her arms around him. The two of them wept together for a couple of minutes, and then Sarah forced herself to get her tears under control.

She turned to Carson. "What do we do now?" she asked.

Carson shook his head sadly. "There's nothing we can do," he said. "Camelot knew it was a high-risk mission, but now there's no way we can get them out. My orders are to put the two of you on the next diplomatic flight, tomorrow afternoon. You'll be going back to Neverland for reassignment to another team."

Sarah stared at him. "No way," she said. "Get Allison on the phone, let me talk to her."

Carson started to protest, but the look on her face made him think better of it. He went to the desk in the room and picked up the receiver, then punched a series of buttons. It took almost a minute for the call to go through, but then he held the receiver out to Sarah.

"Allison? It's Sarah," she said.

"Oh, shit," Allison said. "Give me the situation."

"Noah tried to get the execution schedule, but he and Marco were caught. I need to talk to you about what we're going to do to get them back."

"Sarah, they were there to try to rescue Cinderella. As I told you all before you left, there's nothing more we can do. The Secretary of State will have to disavow Noah and Marco as soon as we're officially notified of their capture, probably before tomorrow morning. I left orders for you and Neil to be returned here if this should happen."

"Screw your orders," Sarah said. "I'm not coming back without Noah and the rest. Now, tell me what I can do."

"There's nothing you can do," Allison said firmly. "I cannot commit any more assets, and there's no way you could manage any kind of rescue on your own. You'll return to Neverland on the next available diplomatic flight and wait for reassignment. Those are your orders, Mrs. Wolf, and I expect you to obey them."

Sarah slammed the receiver down and turned to Neil. "She says there's nothing we can do. We're supposed to go back tomorrow." She looked at Carson. "Could we have a few minutes alone, please?"

Carson started to speak, but then simply nodded and left the room. Sarah immediately went to Neil and put her arms around him, as she whispered into his ear.

"Okay, you're doing great," she whispered into his ear. "Stay focused, because we are not going back without them. We work the plan Noah came up with; I don't know how we're going to survive this, but we're sticking to the plan. Are you with me?"

"Absolutely," Neil whispered back. "I can't really think clearly right now, so you're in charge. What do we do next?"

"We get the hell out of here, that's what. Let's go."

Neil grabbed his computer and tucked it under his arm while Sarah opened the door and peeked out into the hallway. There was no one in sight, so she motioned for him to follow and headed toward the rear door. She had parked the car back there, but Carson hadn't taken the key from her.

They walked confidently, as if they knew exactly where they were going, and the few people who saw them paid no attention. The back door was not locked because it was inside the embassy perimeter, so they walked out without any difficulty. The Toyota she had been driving was right where she had left it, and they got into it quickly.

Sarah started it up and headed for the gate, where the security guard recognized the car. His job was to keep unauthorized vehicles out, and it never occurred to him that this one should not be leaving. He raised the crossbar and waved as they drove through, and Sarah waved back with a smile.

She drove directly to the hotel and left the car running with Neil in it as she hurried up to the room and grabbed their bags. A bellman politely provided a baggage cart and pushed it down for her, then helped her load the bags into the trunk and back seat of the small car. She thanked him profusely, shoving a wad of Russian currency into his hand, then got behind the wheel and drove away. They were away from the hotel for less than six minutes before the first Embassy security officer arrived there looking for them.

"You know we're on our own, right?" Neil asked. "The Dragon Lady is going to have our hides. They'll have alerts out for us within an hour, and let's face it, they know what we're driving."

"Not for long," Sarah said. She whipped the car into a parking lot outside a shopping center, told Neil to wait and got out. He watched her walking along the line of cars for a minute, but then she got into a Lifan sedan. She fumbled with it for a few seconds, then backed it out of its parking spot and drove back to the Toyota.

Neil grabbed the bags from the back seat while Sarah got the ones out of the trunk. They stuffed them into the Lifan and drove out of the dark parking lot as quickly as they could without drawing attention to themselves.

"This will help for a few hours," Sarah said. "What we've got to do now is get a place to operate from, but they can track our mission credit cards. Do you have any Russian currency? I used what I had to tip the bellman back there."

Neil shook his head. "No, but that isn't that big a problem." He opened up his computer and busied himself for a couple of minutes. When he looked up again, it was with a smile. "One of the perks of being a hacker is knowing some of the nasty little tricks the banks don't want you to know. I just reassigned our card numbers to a bank account that isn't going to be noticed. Neverland won't be notified of any transactions, because the money isn't coming out of their accounts. Since nothing will show up there, I don't believe anyone will think to check any deeper."

Sarah laughed. "Smooth," she said. "Still, I think we should hit some ATMs and get cash. We need a room, someplace to base ourselves out of while we figure out what to do."

"I can solve that problem, too," Neil said. "There are a dozen different companies that lease fully furnished houses through the Internet here in Moscow. I can get us one now, and it will give me the code we need to get the key out of the lockbox on the house. And don't worry, I'll charge them off to Amazon or some other big company. It will be at least a month before they notice, so that'll give us plenty of time."

"Do it, then. We need to get started working on the plan."

Fifteen minutes later, Neil gave her an address. She punched it into the navigation app on her phone, then followed the directions. After only a few minutes more, they pulled up in front of a small bungalow and Neil retrieved the key from the lockbox and opened the door. The two of them carried in the bags, and then Sarah put the car behind the house.

"What about our phones? Can they track us with them?"

Neil grinned. "Not anymore," he said. "I thought of that when I thought about the credit cards. I got into the system and changed the electronic serial numbers, then assigned new phone numbers to them. It's almost the same numbers we had, but I added fourteen to the last two digits. It'd take days for anyone to figure it out, so we can use the phones for now."

"Good. Why don't you lay down and get some rest, I've got a couple of calls to make." She sat down in the living room chair while Neil laid on the sofa, then took out her phone and took a deep breath before she dialed a number.

A woman answered in a very sleepy voice. "Hello?"

"I'm probably the last person in the world you ever expected to get a call from," Sarah said, "but I need your help."

The woman seemed to be making an effort to wake herself. "Who is this?"

"Mrs. Camelot," Sarah said. "Hello, Monique."

Monica Lord, formerly known as Monique in political circles, gave a soft chuckle. "Well, you're right," she said. "I certainly never expected you to call me. Show up at my door and blow my head off, maybe, but a phone call is a definite surprise. May I ask what prompted it?"

"That's pretty simple," Sarah said. "Camelot has been captured, and you're going to help me get him back."

"Hold on," Monica said. "My husband is sleeping, let me go into another room so we can speak more clearly." Sarah waited for about a minute, and then she came back on the line. "Okay, tell me everything you can about what's going on."

Sarah quickly explained about the mission to rescue Team Cinderella, and how they had planned to snatch them when they were being transported to Red Square for execution. She told about the plan to steal the execution schedule and how it had proved impossible, and then she confessed that she had defied orders to try to pull off the unlikely rescue plan Noah had concocted.

"Well," Monica said when she was finished. "You have definitely got yourself in a mess. The question is, what do you expect me to do?"

"Look, we know you have contacts in Russia," Sarah said. "I need you to get me men and equipment, I need information, I need anything and everything you can possibly do to help me save my husband and the rest of them. Maybe you've forgotten that Noah was supposed to kill you, that it was him who convinced Allison that you're more valuable alive. Don't you think you owe him something for that?"

"I owe him my life," Monica said. "On the other hand, you seem to have forgotten that your bosses monitor everything I do. Do you think they'll miss this phone call?"

"I can take care of that," Sarah said. "Neil is here with me, and I'm pretty sure he can get in and delete this part of the recording before anybody sees it. I know he's done that before, so I think he can do it again."

Neil sat up suddenly at the mention of his name, smiled at Sarah and nodded. He pulled his computer closer on the coffee table and started typing.

"He's already working on that now," Sarah said. "Everything we talk about and everything you do for me will be under the table. Now, can I count on you?"

Monica was quiet for a moment, then she sighed. "Can your whiz kid just turn the monitor off for a while? Just a few days, that's all I'm asking for. Yes, I'm willing to help you, but I can't do it with them looking over my shoulder, and I can't do it from here."

Sarah told her to wait, then muted the phone and repeated the question to Neil, and he looked at her. "I can do it," he said, "but can we trust her?"

"I don't think we have any choice," Sarah said. "Like Noah said, she's the only person we can get to who has the kind of connections we're going to need."

Neil looked at his computer for a moment, then typed something into it. His hand hovered over the enter key for a moment, and then pressed it decisively. He looked up at Sarah. "Done," he said. "I've turned it completely off for the next seven days. I also locked it to an encrypted password, so it would take them more than that to undo it in any case."

Sarah unmuted the phone. "You're off the leash for seven days," she said. "Now, what can you do for me?"

"You're in Moscow?" Monica asked.

"Yes."

"I have a distributorship there for my beauty products. If I move quickly, I can be there within twelve hours. Is this number on my caller ID valid?"

"Yes, it is," Sarah said. "But why do you need to come here?"

"Because somebody has got to keep the two of you from getting yourselves killed," Monica said. "Get some sleep, I'll call you as soon as I arrive."

"All right," Sarah said. "Don't disappoint me, Monique. I'm quite capable of putting that bullet into your head if you do."

"Get some sleep, Sarah. I'll talk to you tomorrow." The line went dead and Sarah put the phone on the coffee table.

"She's coming here," Sarah said to Neil. "I'm just as nervous about trusting her as you are, but there's nobody else we can turn to. I'm going to get some sleep, and I suggest you do the same."

She got up from the chair and went to one of the two bedrooms, stripped out of her clothes and climbed under the covers. Her mind raced for several minutes, thinking of imaginative, probably far-fetched ways to effect a rescue, but at last she drifted off to sleep.

NOAH AND MARCO HAD been taken into an interrogation room and questioned for almost an hour, but neither of them would give any answers. An FSB captain named Fedorov finally got tired of looking into their blank faces and they were escorted deeper into the prison. They were forced to change clothes and then placed into cells.

Noah laid down and went to sleep, but Marco was too over-stressed. He sat on the bunk in his cell, just thinking, and it was only after his mind began to slow down that he heard the noise.

At first, he thought there was an animal in his cell, but then he realized that the noise seemed to have a rhythm to it. It came and went, a series of taps and scratches, and it slowly dawned on him that what he was hearing was Morse code. A tap was a dot, which meant a scratch was a dash.

Marco had learned Morse code many years earlier, as a teenager interested in ham radio, but he was pretty rusty. He listened to the sounds closely and used the pad and pencil from the table to write what he thought he was hearing.

Tap, scratch, scratch. That, he thought, was a W.

Four dots. H.

Three dashes. That was an O.

The sequence began to repeat, and Marco realized that someone was asking who had been brought in. Knowing that Jenny and her team were also being held somewhere in the prison, he decided to take the chance and respond. He used the back of the pencil to tap and scratch.

Two dashes, dot dash, dot dash dot, dash dot dash dot, three dashes. MARCO.

A moment later, as the reply started to come in, he realized that it was spelling out "THIS IS JIM."

For the next two hours, Marco and Jim Marino used the code to bring each other up to date.

HERE WITH JENNY DAVE RANDY

HERE WITH NOAH

HOW

RESCUE YOU

WHY

FAMILY

SORRY

NO PROBLEM ANY NEWS

WE HANG THREE DAYS

YES US TOO SOON

SORRY ANY HOPE

ALL PART OF PLAN

WHERE JENNY

TWO CELL OVER

SHE CODE

NO ONLY ME

ANY OTHER TALK

NO GET HURT IF TALK

After two hours, Marco knew that Dave, Jenny and Randy were the next three cells past Jim's, but none of them knew Morse code. He knew that the few attempts they had made to shout to each other had resulted in beatings, so they had stopped. Jim had only taken the chance that whoever came in might know code on a whim, but they were both glad he had done so.

Marco suspected Noah would know Morse code, but there was no response when he tried. He figured Noah was probably getting some sleep, and finally decided that he should do so himself. He lay down on the bunk and closed his eyes, and was amazed at how quickly exhaustion set in.

CHAPTER EIGHT

"Tell me who sent you."

"I told you already. Nobody sent us, we don't work for anybody, we don't have anything to do with anything."

The next sound out of the man's mouth was a scream, as the electrical device sent paroxysms of pain through his body. The scream lasted for half a minute, and then he was simply gasping for breath.

"You are quite amazing, Mr. Stewart," said Captain Fedorov. "Very few men can endure as much pain as I've given you without telling me what I want to hear. Most of them, in fact, will try to tell me anything they think I want to hear, even if it is not true. They will do anything to make the pain stop, but you've obviously been trained to endure it. I'm curious what kind of training it took to accomplish that. Were you subjected to these kinds of torture, to let you build up a tolerance for them?"

"No," Randy said, still trying to catch his breath. "I just—I just had to—get used to listening to—people who are full of bullshit, like you." He managed to chuckle at his own joke.

Fedorov burst out laughing. "Very amazing, truly amazing. Of course, none of this really matters. You have already been sentenced to die, so I'm merely offering you the chance to live without pain for your last hours. Tell me what I wish to know, and all of this will come to an end."

"If I had anything to tell you," Randy said, "maybe I would. You want to know who I work for? I work for that woman I'm married to. I know you checked our backgrounds, so you know I'm telling you the truth. She inherited a fortune from her daddy when he died, including that god-awful matchmaking website. When we're back home, all I do is sit in an office and pretend I give a shit when the customers call in to complain about their latest date."

"Ah, yes, the lovely Mrs. Stewart. Perhaps it's time to tell you that she and I will be spending some time together this afternoon. You don't need to worry, though, we've found that pain is less effective with women. They respond better to rape, in fact. They can usually hold out for the first two or three men, but by the time they've been raped for the fourth or fifth or sixth time, they tend to open up and start talking." He chuckled. "I like to go first, myself."

Randy grinned at him. "Go for it," he said. "That little whore will probably enjoy it. It didn't take me long to figure out that her idea of being married was just having a husband to blame everything on. Being faithful isn't something she is too familiar with."

"Really?" Fedorov asked. "Then perhaps you would like it if I make sure to hang you last, so you can watch her drop through the gallows."

"Suit yourself," Randy said. "If we're all gonna die, I don't think it matters which one of us lives sixty seconds longer."

"Tell me about Samuel Winston," Fedorov said, suddenly changing the subject. "If you don't work for anybody else, why would Mr. Winston have been arrested trying to steal the schedule of events for your executions?"

"I've not the slightest idea who you're talking about. Can you give me a hint?"

"Sure. He is six foot two, blonde hair, blue eyes, and in very good physical condition. Does that ring your bells?"

Holy crap, Randy thought, *Noah's been caught, too.* "Can't say it does."

The questioning went on for a few more hours, with occasional electric shocks to stimulate Randy's memory, but he managed to hold out. The occasional scream he heard muffled in the background told him that he wasn't the only one being tortured, but he hadn't heard anything that sounded like Jenny, yet. A part of him was glad of that, but he knew it was only a matter of time.

Finally, Fedorov motioned to one of the guards and Randy was taken off the chains from which he'd been hanging. His legs wouldn't function, so he was carried back to his cell and dropped unceremoniously on the bunk. The door slammed shut, and a moment later he heard another one open.

The guards ordered someone to step out, and Randy heard a voice he would know anywhere.

"Sure, no problem," Noah said. He walked out of the room and stood while he was handcuffed, then let the guards take him by the arms and walk him through the hallway.

Noah was taken into the same room Randy had just left, and three armed guards kept him covered while his cuffs were removed and he was suspended by his arms from the same chains that had held Randy only moments before. Captain Fedorov, who had questioned him when he had first arrived, stepped into the room and smiled at him.

"Hello again, Mr. Winston," Fedorov said. "I trust you've been comfortable?"

"Not bad," Noah said. "I needed to stretch, though, so this feels pretty good."

"I wonder if you know, Mr. Winston, what the single greatest hardship is for an intelligence agent in the modern world. Would you care to guess?"

Noah made what he considered a facial shrug, a sort of grimace that indicated a complete lack of interest. "Coming up with new lines like that one?"

"No, but that is a nuisance, at times. Actually, I am speaking of digitalization. The very fact that so much information is now stored in computers in digital form, rather than on paper, means that there's always a risk that some foreign agency might be able to get into those

files and corrupt them. Take, for example, fingerprints. Most people believe it was your FBI who first started storing fingerprint information in computers, but it was actually the Japanese. We were
second, and there's actually substantial evidence that your FBI got
the idea from us. However, having such records only in digital form
makes them vulnerable to those despicable creatures known as hackers. These people are able to get past all of our defenses and modify
any record in any database. In our example, fingerprints, this means
that your fingerprints actually tell us nothing at all about who you
are. Since our own hackers have managed to crack the FBI fingerprint
database, we were able to run yours against it, and all it told us is that
you're supposedly one Samuel Winston."

"I coulda saved you a lot of trouble," Noah said. "If you had asked
me, I would've told you that's who I am."

"But we both know that you are not," Fedorov replied. "While
I may not know for sure who you are or who you work for, there is
absolutely no doubt that you're an American agent. The electronic
weapons you carried, they speak of American development, and so
do the earpieces you were wearing. Even just the fact that you were
attempting to steal the event schedule for the execution of five other
American agents is enough to confirm what we already know. It appears to me to be obvious that you were planning to attempt to rescue your compatriots as they were being transported to the place of
execution. Am I correct?"

"Dude, what on Earth are you talking about? The stun guns are
something I bought on the black market, because I just don't like to
kill anybody when I rob them, and the earpieces let me and my buddy talk to each other if we got separated, you can buy those at Radio
Shack. The only thing I was trying to steal was money. Word on the
street says there's at least a hundred million rubles in that office somewhere, so we thought we'd try to find it."

Fedorov chuckled. "In order to steal the equivalent of a million American dollars, you decided to break into one of the most secure prisons in the world? Really?" The look on his face was one of incredulity.

Noah smiled. "It does sound kinda stupid now," he said, and then he added a conspiratorial wink, "but if we'd gotten away with it, it would've been awesome. We would've been legendary, you know?"

Fedorov stared at him for a moment, then shook his head. "Well, I had to try this the easy way," he said. "Now we'll do it the hard way." He picked up a device from a table nearby and brandished it at Noah. "This is the latest thing in electronic pain stimulation. It uses over fifty thousand volts of direct-current at less than ten milliamps, which stimulates every pain-sensing nerve in your body but without doing any lasting harm. Now, would you like to tell me the truth about who you are, or should I demonstrate?"

Noah tried to look scared. "Oh, come on, man," he said. "I'm telling you the truth, we're just thieves, That's all. Why the hell don't you believe me?"

The twin prongs of the device brushed lightly against Noah's shoulder, and even through the thick clothing he could feel the jolt that threatened to rip off his skin. He didn't even bother to try holding back the scream.

Fedorov drew it back and looked at him. "Who do you work for, Mr. Winston?"

"I work for myself, man," Noah screamed at him. "Hell, Harold works for me!"

"Harold, yes," Fedorov said. "I'll be talking with Harold a bit later. For now, I'm concentrating on you." The prongs pressed against Noah with more force, this time, and the resulting agony was greatly multiplied. Again Noah screamed, while deep inside, he was forcing his mind to explore and embrace the pain.

Some years earlier, Noah had read a book on pain management that suggested the best way to endure pain was to embrace it, draw it in, make it an absolute part of your inner core being. The author had not been able to explain the concept clearly in words, but Noah thought he could instinctively understand. He had suffered pain in the past, but never truly been tortured until now, so he put the concept into practice the best way he knew how.

While he was screaming on the outside, his mind was analyzing the pain on the inside. He was thinking about different parts of his body and comparing the level of pain in one part to the level in other parts. When he found that it was the muscles in his chest that seemed to be hurting the most, he concentrated on those muscles and focused on the agony they were experiencing, and he was gratified to realize that accepting the pain actually made it bearable.

Each time Fedorov hit him with the device, Noah forced himself to examine and embrace the pain. By the time it had gone on for an hour, Noah had reached the point of being able to ignore most of the agony completely. Where Randy had felt as if he was being torn apart, Noah was able to convince his mind that he felt only a dull ache.

"Tell me who you work for," Fedorov said again.

Noah forced his head up and looked Fedorov in the eye. "I work for no one," he said. "If you want to charge me, charge me. If you want to try me, try me. It won't change anything."

Fedorov gave him a smile that would have frightened any other man. "You were charged the moment you were arrested," he said. "You were tried the moment you first saw my face. You were convicted the first time you lied to me. You were sentenced to die before you ever entered a prison cell. Two days from now, when your friends are taken out to hang, there will not be five nooses on the gallows. There will be seven."

Three hours later, after a session similar to the one Randy had already had that morning, Noah was carried back to his cell and dropped on his bunk. He laid still until the guards had closed his door, then hurriedly got up and rushed over to it. With his ear pressed against it, he could hear voices in the hallway, and it was only a moment later that he caught Jenny's voice as she was taken out of her cell.

He waited until he was sure the guards were out of earshot, then called out. "Marco?"

There was no response at first, and he was about to call out again when a series of soft noises caught his attention. It sounded like someone was tapping on the concrete wall, but then there were scratches, and then more tapping.

Noah's logical mind caught the pattern. Three quick taps, three scratches, and then three more taps. Someone was spelling SOS in Morse code. A memory surfaced of a movie he had seen when he was a child, about prisoners of war using a similar system to communicate with each other. He listened closely and realized the sounds were coming from the wall on the right, which is where the table was placed in his room. He sat down in the chair beside it, picked up the only object he could see that might work, and used the blunt end of the pencil to send:

NOAH HERE

A moment later, the sounds began again. This time, they spelled out MARCO HERE JIM NEXT CELL.

WHERE JENNY

OTHER CELL AND RANDY DAVE ONE MORE

GOOD TOGETHER

ANY NEWS

WE DIE TGTHR

O GOOD NO TRIAL

NO FSB ORDER

SARAH NEIL
NO WORD SAFE EMBSY
PLAN
YES CAN U TELL OTHERS
ONLY JIM CODE

Noah thought for a minute. Jenny and her men were in the same cellblock, but the only one Marco could talk to was Jim Marino. In order for Noah's plan to work properly, he needed to find some way to let Jenny and Randy and Dave know what to expect.

IT WAS ALMOST A QUARTER of one by the time Sarah's phone rang, and she answered it instantly. "*Da?*" she said.

"I have to tell you, your accident is atrocious," Monica said. "Okay, sweetie, I'm in town. Let's get together and see what we can figure out."

"Fine," Sarah said. "Where do you want to meet?"

"Meet? Right here at the damned airport. How long will it take you to get here and pick me up?"

Sarah blinked. "I—probably about a half hour."

"That's fine, I'll grab a bite to eat. JetBlue doesn't always offer an in-flight meal that I like. Call me on this number when you get here and I'll come right out."

The line went dead and Sarah told Neil that she was going to pick Monica up at the airport. He was doing something on his computer and merely nodded in response, so she hurried out the door and got into the Lifan she had stolen the night before. She was just about to back out when Neil came running out the door and caught her attention.

"Hey," he said. "The police are bound to be looking for that car by now, so I rented you one. When you get to the airport, dump that thing in long-term parking and go straight to the Avis Russia office. Just show your Marcia Winston ID and they'll give you a Nissan SUV. That'll be a lot safer than stealing one car after another."

Sarah grinned at him. "That's why we call you the genius," she said, and then she took her foot off the brake and drove away.

Getting to the airport didn't take as long as she had expected, and she was glad to see that the Avis office was actually quite close to the long-term parking area. She parked the Lifan and locked it, then went nervously into the car rental office. When she gave her name, the girl at the counter smiled brightly. Sarah was handed a couple of forms to sign, her driver's license and passport were copied, and then she was taken outside and told to choose the vehicle she wanted. She picked the Nissan Armada and was driving out of the lot only a minute later.

She took out her phone and called Monica as she was approaching the terminal, and spotted the tiny woman waiting at the curb when she got there. She seemed to have only two bags with her, and she tossed them into the back seat before climbing in the front beside Sarah.

The two women looked at each other for a moment, and then Sarah put the vehicle in gear and drove out of the airport. "Blows my mind you had so much power," Sarah said. "You look like a little kid."

"Then I'm sure you know where that power came from," Monica replied. "Look, Sarah, I don't expect you to like me at all, especially after what I did to you, but I'm here to help your husband. He saved my life, so I'll do whatever I can to help you get him back. Okay? Truce?"

"We don't need a truce," Sarah said, "because no matter how I feel about you, we're not enemies. When it comes down to it, you and I are on the same side, now. If I didn't believe that, I couldn't have called you at all."

"Fair enough. Now, tell me the rest of the situation."

Sarah took a deep breath. "Noah and Marco were arrested last night, like I told you. Jenny and her team, three men, were arrested a few days earlier on the charge of assassinating the deputy defense minister."

"The one who defected, right?" Monica asked.

Sarah glanced at her in surprise, unaware that she would have known about something so potentially devastating, but she shrugged it off. "Yes. Jenny and Team Cinderella were sent over here to make sure everything went okay on that mission, but when they were arrested after Kalashnikov was supposedly assassinated, all the suspicion landed on them. We were sent over here to try to rescue them, get them back, but there was no way to break them out of Lefortovo prison. Noah and Neil looked at every possibility, and there was just no way to get it done without starting a war. That made Noah look at the possibility of snatching them while they were being taken to Red Square for hanging, but even that would be pretty much impossible. They bring the prisoners out one at a time, in different vehicles. It would take at least a platoon of soldiers to be able to get them all, and again it just seems impossible to pull it off."

"Wait a minute," Monica said. "If Noah decided it wouldn't work, what was he doing inside the prison to get arrested? Don't look so surprised, I've done my homework. I can get into an awful lot of government computer networks, so I know that's where he and Marco were caught."

Sarah sneered at her for a second, then went on. "They were arrested inside the prison, because that was part of the plan. The only way we can pull off this rescue is to have Noah and Marco on the inside, but that means I have to take care of everything that goes on out here. It also has to be done without any further connection to the United States government, which is why I'm acting as a rogue agent at the moment, and before you ask, no; the Dragon Lady is not aware of what we're doiing, she honestly thinks Noah has been captured." She glanced at Monica one more time. "That's where you come in. Noah said if I could get hold of you and play on the fact that he kept you alive, he was certain you'd be willing to help. Since you got to keep your network of operatives intact, that means you have assets and access to assets that we're going to need."

Monica stared at Sarah. "That little shit," she said. "So, he is inside the prison with Marco. Was he too stupid to realize that he will be tortured in there?"

"He knows that," Sarah said. "They both do. In this case, though, they both consider it a necessary evil they have to put up with in order to be in the right place to make this rescue happen."

"Then, fill me in, honey," Monica said. "The sooner we get this done, the sooner I get back to my kids."

CHAPTER NINE

"So, we still have no idea when they will be taken out of the prison, right?" Monica asked. "Isn't there anybody who would know what the schedule is?"

"We weren't able to find anyone, no," Neil said. "They don't keep any information in computers at that place, which actually makes them a lot smarter than they look, but it still screws me as far as trying to get any intel."

Monica nodded. "But it's supposed to happen on Friday, right? Is that part still correct?"

"As far as we know," Neil said, "they still hang on Friday, yes."

"Okay. We know that each of them will be in a separate vehicle, so trying to grab them on the way to Red Square is probably not going to work. The only time we know for sure they're going to all be together is when they're led up onto the gallows. Geez, I miss the good old days when all I had to do was figure out how to manipulate one country against another."

"Come on, Monica," Sarah said. "You've got to have somebody under your control that can help us pull this off."

"Yeah, well, it would be a lot easier if I didn't have to worry about starting World War III. Let's face it, kids, any action we take to rescue American agents is going to create an international incident. With the way the U.S. has fallen into disfavor with so many other countries lately, it's not entirely outside the realm of possibility that the UN could issue sanctions against us. Just the very fact that these are American agents..."

Sarah and Neil both stared at Monica. "I know that look," Neil said. "That's the look Molly always gets when she has a brainstorm."

"Monica? What is it, what did you think of?"

Monica looked from Sarah to Neil and back again. "The fact that they're Americans," she said. "Right now, everything is based on the fact that they're American agents. Their identification says they're Americans, the way they talk, the way they act, it also is American, right?"

"Yeah," Sarah said. "What are you getting at?"

"Holy..." Neil said. "I see it, I see it."

"Exactly," Monica said. "What we've got to do is eliminate America from the equation. We've got to dump evidence into Russia's lap that says none of these people are genuinely Americans."

Sarah shook her head in confusion. "Do what? How is that going to help anything?"

"Because it removes the spectacle. If they're not American agents, then the Russian government gains nothing by putting on this big public execution. They gain even less if we can show that they're not only not Americans, they're actually Russians."

"Yes!" Neil said, bouncing in his chair. "We hand the Russians their own freaking conspiracy theory, by creating enough evidence that these are Russian agents who were sent to assassinate their own defense minister or whatever, just so that they can justify starting a whole new Cold War. That's freaking brilliant!"

"But that's not the plan!" Sarah shouted at them both. "Noah says we have to snatch them either just before their ride to Red Square or right after they get there. The whole reason he and Marco went inside the prison is so that they can try to get the rest of them ready when the time comes."

"But this plan is better," Monica said. "It will still work the way Noah wanted, but it takes away a lot of the risk. If the execution won't get as many benefits, they're not going to be so all fired excited about doing it that way. If we can move fast enough, we can get the Kremlin to cancel that execution. They'll make some kind of excuse about having to investigate further before the sentence is carried out, something like that, but they'll cancel the public execution."

"But how does that help us?" Sarah asked. "If they don't bring them out for the execution, it's going to be even harder to get to them."

Monica shook her head. "No, it won't. They won't be bringing them out for the execution, but they will need to move them. I've access to a couple of United Nations ambassadors who will do what I tell them. All I've got to do is have them start demanding a UN investigation and the Kremlin is going to want those prisoners moved somewhere else immediately. Somewhere out of sight, somewhere reporters and investigators can't find them, but somewhere safe where they can be produced when they're needed. This is perfect, I'm telling you."

"Sarah, she's right," Neil said. "If we do this the right way, it buys us more time. It will put off the execution for at least several days, maybe as much as months, and that means they won't be stressing over it. No stress, less security."

"Okay, I'm starting to get it," Sarah said. "If we can lower the security on them, we stand a better chance of being able to rescue them, right?"

"Absolutely," Monica said. She turned to Neil. "Can you create some kind of convincing documentation that makes them some sort of Russian agents?"

"Damn right," Neil said. "Amerigrad. There's an old conspiracy theory that says the Russians ran a school back in the eighties to train secret agents to act like regular Americans. They even based a TV show on it a while back, and there were some actual spies like them arrested in 2013. Everybody thought they were Americans, but they were really Russian deep cover agents. In that arrest, they picked up ten of them, but what if there were more? I can create some documentation that could indicate that all of us, both Cinderella and

Camelot, are actually Russian agents who infiltrated the U.S. for the express purpose of creating a problem between the two countries. This whole assassination of Kalashnikov was nothing more than a way for Russia to get away with starting a new Cold War. Make sense?"

Sarah's mouth was partly open as she stared at him. "No," he said, "but I'm not the genius here, you are. As long as it makes sense to you, I'm good with it." She turned to Monica. "What he was saying, will that fit into what you got in mind?"

"Hell, yes," Monica said. "It fits perfectly, because there have been rumors of an underground organization that wants to bring back the Soviet Union for years, now. We can play on those rumors with this and make it even more believable. Get on it, Neil, I need as much as you can give me by tomorrow morning. I've got newspaper and TV reporters in five countries that I can send this to and make them run the story, and I can get an uproar started in the UN by tomorrow night. This is it, kids, this is how we buy ourselves more time and force the Russians to make a mistake we can use against them."

Sarah chewed her bottom lip. "I just wish there was some way to let Noah in on this," she said. "For all we know, he could ruin it if they start questioning him about whatever we put out there."

Monica looked at her thoughtfully. "You have a point," she said. She reached into her bag and took out a pair of cell phones, then dropped one of them back into it. The other was quickly dialed, and she held up a finger to tell both of them be quiet for a moment.

"I have a job for you," she said to whoever answered. "I'm very interested in the alleged American spies that are being held in Lefortovo prison. Can you arrange to see them?"

She listened for a moment, then grinned. "I'm going to have a package delivered to you today. Inside, you'll find a number of sealed envelopes. I want you to visit these spies and give one to each of them secretly. Do not try to read the notes inside. I'll know if you do, and you don't want that." She listened again. "Your position gives you all the authority you need. No one in the FSB is going to be stupid enough to question you, or to check whether you actually have permission to visit them. Is this too difficult for you? Good, because I would not like to think that you're no longer of use to me."

She disconnected and dropped the phone back into her purse, then turned to Neil. "Write up a very brief description of the plan and make a total of six copies. The man I just spoke to is a crisis advisor in the president's office who was stupid enough to allow me to get video of him indulging a rather perverted fantasy. He's exactly the type of man who might be sent to speak to captured spies on the president's behalf, and he doesn't dare refuse to do what I want. As soon as you get them ready, Sarah and I will take a drive. We'll need to pick up some envelopes, and then we'll hire a courier service to deliver them to him as soon as possible."

DONALD JEFFERSON ENTERED Allison's office and sat down in the chair in front of her desk. "So far, we can't find any trace of them. They seem to have gone completely off the grid."

"Well, crap," Allison said. "They surely don't have any money. Aren't they using the credit cards we gave them?"

Jefferson shook his head. "I've had accounting watch those cards, and there have been no new charges on them. Not so much as an ATM withdrawal. Their phones seem to be malfunctioning, too, or else they just turned them completely off. There are no new calls on them and any attempt to call them goes straight to voicemail."

"It's Neil," Allison said. "He is more loyal to Sarah than he is to us. In some cases, I might consider that admirable, but at the moment all it is is a pain in my ass." She threw the pencil she was holding across the room and Jefferson turned his head to watch it bounce off the wall. "Donald, dammit, I would never have believed that Sarah would pull this. There's no way in the world she and Neil are going to be able to pull off a rescue like this, all they're going to do is get themselves killed."

Jefferson shrugged. "That might be exactly what they're trying to do. Sarah wouldn't want to live without Noah, and Neil is just as attached to Jenny. I think they would rather die with them in a suicide mission than live without them."

"You may be right. Maybe I was an idiot to allow the teams to have romantic relationships."

"I don't think so," Jefferson said. "In many ways, Team Camelot has come out much stronger since Noah and Sarah became a couple, and even more so since they were married. Jenny has become a bit more manageable since she has been with Neil, as well."

"What good does that do us, if we end up losing them all?" She started to say something else, but the phone on her desk rang suddenly. She snatched up the receiver. "Yes?"

Her eyes suddenly went wide as she listened to whoever had called. "Well I'll be... Get down here, would you?" She hung up the phone without waiting for a response.

A moment later, Molly Hansen came into the office and took the chair beside Jefferson. Allison looked at her and smiled. "Tell Donald what you just told me on the phone."

Molly turned to Jefferson, her own face solemn. "I went to our monitor server to download the latest reports from Monica Lord's monitor implant," she said, "but there was nothing there. Everything since the last download two days ago is completely gone, and the system has been shut off. I tried to turn it back on, but the code has been rewritten. It will take me at least a few days to find the changes and correct them."

Donald stared at her for a moment, then turned to Allison. "They've recruited her," he said. "Do we have any idea where she is?"

Molly shook her head. "Her JetBlue account was activated yester-day, and she took a flight to New York City, but that's where we lost her. God only knows how many other identities she has, so without us watching over her shoulder, she could be absolutely anywhere."

"She is in Moscow, you can count on it." Allison was grinning. "Neil is probably the only one who could possibly have shut down her monitor well enough that you can't fix it. Sarah must've asked him to do it, so that she could recruit Monica to help in the rescue."

"And Monica still has all of her puppets in place. Allison, they might just pull this off after all."

Allison nodded. "They might. I just wish I knew what the hell it is they're trying to do." She turned to Molly. "Have you checked for activity on Monica's phone?"

"I did. It last registered a GPS location in New York, so I'm as-suming she turned it off and took the battery out after that."

"Smart girl. Besides, she undoubtedly has several more phones. She's not going to let herself be unable to communicate with her as-sets." Allison leaned back in her chair and steepled her fingers. "Don-ald, for once, I think I'm going to sit back and do nothing. These kids have the best chance to save Noah and Jenny, so let's see what they can do. Things certainly can't get any worse than they already are."

Molly bit her lip. "If you honestly think Monica is in Moscow helping Sarah and Neil, then I would suggest we keep a close eye on what's happening in Russia. I'm going to set some people to watch-ing news stories related to our people who were arrested, but also to watching anything else that seems to be affecting the situation." She got to her feet. "May I go?"

Allison waved at her. "Go, get on it. Anything else you can think of, do it. We need to be as aware as possible of what they're up to, and if we can help in any way, then let's make it so." She shook her head as Molly left the room and looked at Jefferson. "Why the hell didn't

I think of trying to recruit Monica for this? Geez, Donald, am I getting old?"

"You'd better not be," he said. "I got ten years on you, and I don't feel all that old."

She looked at him for a long moment, then sat forward again. "Donald, those kids may need some serious firepower before this is over. Any idea who might be close enough to do them some good, somebody who won't turn this into a war?"

Jefferson sat and thought for a moment. "There's nobody actually in Russia," he said. "There's McDermott in Hong Kong, he's our station chief there, and there's Greystone in Belarus. Both of them are private security companies that make up their own small armies. McDermott is ours, and Greystone is tied to the CIA. We could probably get at least a couple of squads out of either of them."

"Get on the horn and find out if either of them has any Russian nationals on their teams. I would really prefer to have any casualties be locals. McDermott, McDermott—didn't Noah work with him once before?"

Jefferson grinned. "It was McDermott's plane that he stole, remember?"

"Yes, I remember now. He sent a squad to help Noah recover Sarah. Get hold of both groups, see what you can put together and how quickly they can get to Moscow."

"Okay, but you've still got the problem of not knowing how to get hold of Sarah and Neil."

"You think so? Neil has so many ways a message can get to him that he couldn't possibly miss them all. Once we have some idea of what they're up to and how we can help, I'm pretty sure I can get him to respond. You just take care of finding out what assets we can provide without going through any official channels. Let me handle these upstart kids. Trust me, mama knows how to spank if necessary."

BORIS PETROSKI LOOKED up as the courier tapped on his office door. "Come," he said in Russian, and the young man stepped inside and passed him a small package. He tipped the courier a thousand rubles, and the young man smiled as he turned to leave.

The package, really just a thick envelope, went into his pocket. Ten minutes later, he stood and told his secretary that he had a matter to attend to and left. He went to the car park and got his car, then drove calmly but quickly out to Lefortovo prison.

It took only a moment for the prison staff to lead him to the meeting room, where prisoners were brought to be interviewed by ranking officials. As a senior clerk and advisor to the president, no one was about to question his appearance there, or in any way impede his desire to speak with the American spies. They even went so far as to let him see them remove the microphones from the room, ensuring that he would have absolute privacy.

The first of the spies was brought to him only a moment later. Introduced as Jack Stewart, this man was obviously in considerable pain. Boris waited until he was seated and his escort had left the room, then smiled at him.

"I see you've experienced Lefortovo's hospitality," he said.

Randy grunted. "Is that what they call it? What do you want?"

Boris reached into the inner pocket of his coat and pulled out the package. He had already torn it open and seen that there were several envelopes inside, just as he had been told there would be. He extracted one and handed it to Randy.

"Open it and read it, and then destroy it. I would personally suggest eating it, since I know they examine what gets flushed in your toilets."

Randy's eyes narrowed but he opened the envelope. Inside was a small sheet of paper that contained a single paragraph.

Friends on outside working on rescue. Steps being taken to convince world press that you're all Russian agents-provocateurs. Your mission was to create a new Cold War. Be prepared for sudden rescue.

Randy read the message several times, then crumpled it up and stuck it in his mouth. The paper was not very big, so he only had to chew for a few seconds to get it wet enough to slide down his throat. The envelope, now empty, he slid back across the table to Boris.

"I do not know what it said," Boris told him, "and I do not wish to know. If you're questioned about my visit, say only that I wanted to ensure you're being treated humanely, and that you assured me this is the case. Do you understand?"

Randy nodded. "No problem," he said.

Boris called the guard, and Randy was taken away. A moment later Jenny was brought into the room, and the entire process was repeated. Jenny was followed by Jim Marino, then Dave Lange, and Noah was brought into the room next. Like the rest, he read the message and chewed up the paper, then was escorted back to his cell. Marco was next, and then VanHorn.

VanHorn, out of all of them, was the only one who seemed completely confused by the message, but he did not hesitate to swallow it. When he was gone, the guards told Boris that he was the last. Boris thanked them and left the prison, grateful to be putting the place behind him.

Noah and Marco discussed the message in code, and Marco relayed comments back and forth between Jim and Noah. They agreed that the "friends outside" must refer to Sarah and Neil, and Noah was personally convinced that they must have successfully recruited Monica. She was probably the only person Noah could think of who would be capable of getting a message to them inside the prison, and he wondered briefly just who the visitor had been.

CHAPTER TEN

Peter McDermott was locking up his office when his phone rang, and he recognized the call as coming from Neverland. "Peter McDermott," he said.

"Peter, this is Donald Jefferson. How have you been?"

"Not too bad, Don. Been a while since I've talked to you, everything going okay back home?"

"Oh, you know, problems crop up every now and then and there's not much you can do about it. Am I calling at a bad time?"

"No, not at all. I was actually just leaving the office, so I'm all by my lonesome and headed for my car. What can I do for you?"

'All by my lonesome' was a code phrase that meant the line was completely secure on McDermott's end. "I've got a situation," Jefferson said. "You heard about our team being captured in Russia?"

"Yeah, that was bad. Any new developments?"

"In a way. Do you remember Camelot?"

"Ha! Like I could ever forget. I had more fun that week than I've had in the past five years. What's he up to, nowadays?"

"He went into Moscow to set up a rescue mission, but it wasn't going according to plan. Somehow, he and one of his team were also arrested, and they're also scheduled for execution day after tomorrow. Do you remember the young woman you helped him rescue?"

"Sarah, sure. She okay?"

"As far as I know, she is. She and Camelot were married not long after that rescue, and she is currently off the reservation in Moscow and using non-sanctioned assets to set up a rescue mission of her own. I'm calling to see if you might have some people we could borrow, if she needs them. Specifically, I need to know if you have any Russian nationals among your teams."

"I've got eight Russians," McDermott said, "and five of them are former Spetsnaz, Russian special forces. Well, I say they're Russians, but I think they're each actually from one of the former Soviet countries. I doubt any of them have any real love for Mother Russia, so they probably would be exactly what you need. You thinking of making this a military operation?"

"Possibly, as long as we can keep it non-political. Any of these people likely to be on Russian watchlists?"

"Not under the identities they're using at the moment. Like I said, they're not exactly children of the motherland. The main reason I've gotten them is because they got fed up with the way things are done back home. How soon do you need them?"

"Well, I may not need them at all, but I would prefer to have them available if I do. How soon can you get them to Moscow, and what about weapons and equipment?"

"If I call them tonight, they can be in Moscow before morning. I've got contacts there that can provide them with weapons and anything else they need, including a place to sit tight until you need them. Say the word, and I'll make it happen."

"Word," Jefferson said. "Get them over there and send me the bills. I'll let you know if I need to put them to work."

"You got it." McDermott disconnected the call and immediately started dialing other numbers. A half-hour later, he had a squad of ten men, including all but one of the Russians, packing and getting ready to head for Moscow.

"I THINK THIS IS READY," Neil said. "What I did was take everything I know about our team members and dug up some orphaned young Russians who died from various accidents and illnesses at least five years ago. I managed to get into every conceivable database and make some minor changes in the reports about their deaths, then created files on them that make it appear they were actually trained to pose as Americans. In those files, I even have records of how they were smuggled into the United States and placed into communities. Each of them would have been at least eighteen at the time, so I didn't have to worry about getting them families or anything like that."

Monica nodded. It was almost midnight and she was extremely tired, but there was an excitement about being so deeply involved in a mission like this. She had missed the freedom of working without someone looking over her shoulder, and was thoroughly enjoying working with Sarah and Neil.

"That's excellent," she said. "Now, if you can tie it into the scenario we were talking about..."

"Already did. I took the actual flights we all came in on and made sure that the identities we used for the mission were tied back to these paper people I created. I set them up into teams, which fits with what the police saw when they arrested them, with Noah and Jenny as their leaders of course, and then I've created logs of certain communications between the Committee for Restoration of The Soviet Union—which actually does exist, by the way—and Noah and Jenny. Those communications can be deciphered fairly easily, and they're orders to activate something called Mission Zeta. Well, then, I created a file that I hid deep in the bowels of the SVR labeled 'Mission Zeta,' which details how the assassination of a deputy minister by American agents could be manipulated into a restoration of Cold War politics. Cold War politics, according to this mission plan, will result in the glorious resurrection of the Soviet Union and its policies. Since every major Russian politician in the last fifteen years has talked about how the dissolution of the Soviet Union was a terrible disaster and how they wished they could bring it back, just about every news agency in the world is going to find this extremely believable."

"And incredibly damning," Monica added. "Neil, this is brilliant. Is it ready to go out to my news contacts?"

"It's ready," Neil said. "I'm also planning to send it to the CIA and Homeland Security. Both of them are likely to start raising hell over it, and the State Department should be able to use it to stall the executions, just on the basis that we want to prosecute them as spies on our end. If you can get the UN talking about it as well, we have the potential of a global viral story."

Monica cocked her head to the side and looked at him. "Viral," she said. "What about that? Is there any way you can sort of force it to appear on social media posts?"

Neil blinked and then grinned. "Actually, that wouldn't be a bit difficult. I've hacked into most of the major social sites already, so give me twenty minutes to write a bot and I'll be ready to install it."

He turned back to his computer and started typing while Monica leaned back in her chair and looked at Sarah. "We're going to pull this off," she said. "This is going to be one of the slickest things I've ever been involved in, and I want to thank you for letting me help."

Sarah shrugged. "I'm the one who should be thanking you. There's no way in the world I could've done this without your help, and you know it. I just wish you were as big a bitch as I always thought you were, so it would be easier to hate you."

Monica laughed. "Oh, come on, it shouldn't be that hard. After all, I was the one who sold you to the Chinese, remember?"

Sarah glared at her, but it was tempered with humor. "I remember," she said. "The funny thing is, that whole experience ended up making my life a lot better. I managed to work my way through a lot of old fears after that, and it was the fact that I had been captured and tortured that convinced Noah he really wanted us to be married. In a way, I guess I have you to thank for how happy I've been since then, and if we get Noah back, I'll be in your debt once more."

Monica waved a hand at her in dismissal. "You don't owe me anything," she said. "Just the fact that you trusted me enough to take the watchdogs off for a little while is payment enough. I'm sure my supervisory committee is going to go through the roof when I get back, but as long as I can tell them we were doing something important together, I think I'll be all right."

"I'll speak up for you," Sarah said. "Now, once this story Neil created spreads all over the world, what do we do next?"

"That depends on how the Russian government reacts. Personally, I expect them to cancel or at least postpone the executions. They are going to want to investigate this story for themselves, and they'll be dealing with God knows how many other countries that will be screaming for information. I wouldn't want to be in any of the high-ranking offices in Russia right now, because the one thing Russians have always done is try to blame each other. The president will blame the prime minister, the prime minister will blame the president, both of them will blame their other politicians and the politicians will be blaming each other in every possible direction. It's going to be a nightmare for any of the Russian officials, but it might just end up resulting in a house cleaning this country really needs."

"But what do we do about getting Noah and the others out of that prison? That's what I'm trying to ask."

"Well," Monica said, shifting her position to get a little more comfortable. "They are probably going to want to move all of them out of Lefortovo pretty quickly. They might try to sequester them in another prison, or they might actually take them to the Lubyanka. It's not actually used as a prison anymore, but it still has cells and facilities that work. Considering how high-profile these particular prisoners are going to be, that might be the best place for them to put them."

"And will that help us in any way, as far as getting them out?"

"It wouldn't hurt. The Lubyanka is currently the headquarters of the FSB, the federal police. Those guys are fairly tough, but they're not nearly as tough as the SVR. They're also not really the type of people to manage a prison. It might actually be possible to break them out, if they go there. Otherwise, we have to see where they end up and then plan accordingly." She looked at Sarah for a moment, then went on. "No matter where they go, Sarah, we're probably going to end up needing weapons and people who can use them. Unfortunately, I don't have those kind of contacts in Russia."

Sarah nodded. "If we get to that point, I can go to our man in the embassy. He might not help us directly, but I'm pretty sure he would know where we can hire mercenaries."

"Good, because we're probably going to need them. Then all we have to do is figure out how to get us all out of the country. They don't seem to know anything about me, so I shouldn't have any problems chartering a flight. If we can figure out a way to get all of your people to the airport, we can all fly out together."

"That might work, if it's possible. The original plan involved Noah flying us out under radar, going to Warsaw. From there, we would have gone home on a diplomatic flight."

"Well, my charter flights are not diplomatic, but I'm worth enough money in all of my identities that I rarely get any interference. If we can get your people onto the plane, there shouldn't be any problem at all."

Monica closed her eyes and drifted off to sleep, and Sarah sat quietly as she did so. Neil continued tapping on his keyboard for an hour, then finally looked up at Sarah.

"I sent it off to every news source Monica gave me, to the CIA, DHS, NSA and DoD, and I've got bots posting it on Facebook, Twitter, Pinterest and Instagram like mad. An awful lot of people are going to suddenly be surprised to realize that they have so many friends interested in what kind of crap the Russians are trying to pull."

"What you mean?" Sarah asked.

Neil grinned. "Let's just say that almost everyone on those websites is now connected to several movie stars, and those stars are currently spreading the word about the terrible Russian plot to bring back the Cold War and the threat of nuclear weapons. You know what people do when they see a Facebook post or a tweet from somebody they think is famous?"

Sarah chuckled. "They repost it or retweet it. I know what you mean, I've even done that myself. But what happens tomorrow, when all those celebrities claim they never said any such thing?"

"Nobody will care. By then, this story will have taken on a life of its own." He leaned close to his computer for a moment and tapped on it for a couple of seconds. "Here's one I attributed to that guy who plays the superspy. I posted it under his name thirty minutes ago, and it's already gotten over six thousand likes and been reposted nine thousand times. Oh, yeah, this is definitely going viral."

SLIGHTLY OVER AN HOUR later, at just after three p.m. Denver time, Allison's phone was ringing on her desk. She ignored it, because she was already on her cell phone.

"I know, it's already all over the Internet," she said. "No, I have no idea where it's coming from. Yes, Mr. President, I'm certain none of our people who were arrested are actually Russian double agents. I'll be happy to let you know as soon as I find out anything more. Yes sir, goodbye."

She dropped the cell phone and reached for the one on the desk, but it stopped ringing. She leaned back in her chair and started shaking her head. Somehow, the word was spreading through the Internet that Jenny and her team, and Noah and Marco, were all Russian agents who had been planted in the United States for the express purpose of committing some crime against Russia that would allow the Communist Party to reinstate many of the policies of the old Soviet Union.

Donald Jefferson came through her office door without knocking, something he almost never did. "You've heard?"

"I just got off the phone with the president, what do you think?"

"Any idea what's going on?" Jefferson asked. "This has to be related to what Sarah and Monica are doing, it has to be."

"Of course it is," Allison said. "This is exactly the kind of devious crap Monica would pull, but it's going to take the heat off of the U.S. for right now, so that's a good thing. The Kremlin will be doing nothing but denying, denying, denying all day, but this thing has already gotten so big that they won't be able to keep it quiet. There are a dozen news services that are already running it as if it's a confirmed story."

Jefferson nodded. "Okay, let's get Molly in here. We need to start thinking about how we can use this."

Allison picked up the phone and punched a couple of buttons, then told Molly to come to her office as soon as possible. The girl arrived only a minute later, carrying a tablet that she was staring at.

"A Kremlin spokesman has just issued a statement of denial, but he also said the president has ordered an investigation into where the story is coming from, and has postponed the execution of the alleged spies indefinitely." She looked up at Allison. "What in the world is going on?"

"It's Monica," Allison said. "We know she is over there trying to help the kids, and this is just the kind of thing she does. This will have almost every little country that used to be part of the Soviet Union ready to declare war on Russia by the end of the week if they aren't careful. Most of them don't want anything to do with bringing the

USSR back. They may be small, but if enough of them decide to fight, then Mother Russia is going to be in some serious trouble."

"Molly," Jefferson said, "what we wanted to talk to you about right now is how we can best use this in the current situation. Any suggestions?"

Molly sat down in the chair beside the one Jefferson had taken and thought for a moment. "If it were to turn out that this story is true, which we know it won't, Russia would be looking at an awful lot of angry nations pointing fingers at her. This would be considered one of the greatest deceptions any nation has ever pulled, and its obvious purpose would be to create political tensions between Russia and the United States. As far as bringing back the Soviet Union, they certainly could have used the argument that American assassins and spies meant that the U.S. was declaring itself to be a credible threat, and that only reinstating the Soviet Union could protect all those smaller countries. Now, though, since it looks like Russia staged the whole thing, all that's going to happen is that each of those countries is going to be backing further away from any diplomatic ties with Moscow. If this story isn't quashed today, you'll see massive arms buildups on every border between Russia and one of its former member countries. They'll all be preparing for war, because they will be expecting Russia to try to force them into subjugation again."

"Holy crap," Allison said. "I've been worried about trying to avoid starting a war, and Monica is over there setting up a big one."

"Oh, not really," Molly said. "All of those little countries, Kazakhstan, Belarus, the rest of them, they will all be far too frightened to actually initiate hostilities. It's just saber rattling, but it will keep the Russian military worried about what could happen. If the Russians were stupid enough to actually try to invade one of those other countries, then all of them would probably attack, but I don't believe the Kremlin is that dumb. I can assure you the prime minister is not, although the president might... No, he wouldn't be that stupid either. The point is that most of those little countries have other allies, now, so Russia wouldn't just be fighting its own little border wars. We would be talking about a major conflict, and even the United States would be involved. We might not be directly at war with Russia, but we do have some mutual defense treaties in that area. Japan and China would almost certainly get involved, and possibly even North Korea, but God only knows which side they would be on." She suddenly smiled. "On the other hand, there's going to be a lot of things hashed out inside Russia herself. A story like this is going to mean that every political faction is going to be blaming every other one. The Democratic supporters will be swearing that the Communist Party has to be behind the stunt, and the Communists will be blaming the Democrats. If it were really true, either one of them could be correct. The Communists might do something like this in order to try to bring back the USSR, but the Democrats might do it just so they can blame it on the Communists. All in all, this is one of the most brilliant moves I can even imagine. No matter what people believe at the end of the day, it's going to take Russia months, maybe even years to regain any trust in the world political stage."

"I can see that point," Allison said, "but is there any way this actually helps us get our people back?"

"Oh, of course. If we can find any way in the world to arrange a rescue now, the sheer power of this conspiracy theory is going to protect the United States completely. If the Russians say we broke them out and spirited them away, the rest of the world is going to point a finger at them and say they're lying. If they deny that they escaped or were rescued, then they won't be able to produce them when the world court or the UN or whoever decides to conduct its investigation. That will make it look like they were executed quietly, so no matter which way it goes, Russia looks bad. They can't point the finger at us, even if they know with absolute certainty that we did it, because it would only blow up in their faces. This is really, incredibly brilliant."

"Yeah," Allison said. "I just wish I had been the one to think of it. For that matter, why didn't you think of it? You're supposed to be our resident genius, right?"

Molly's eyes went wide and she stared at Allison. "Me? I–I..."

"Relax, Molly," Jefferson said with a grin. "Allison is just being the Dragon Lady. Nobody would really have expected you to come up with a plot like this, it's too Machiavellian even for us. I'm beginning to understand how Monica managed to get away with manipulating the world so long. Dear God, the woman is some kind of political puppet mistress."

"And she's off her damn leash!" Allison growled. "Remind me to make sure Neil's access to that server is terminated as soon as he gets back."

Molly made a face. "Do you really think that would be a good idea? It's very likely that being able to disconnect her from that surveillance is what is making this possible. Not only are we now much more likely to get our people back, but by the time this is over, Russia will be too busy trying to make up with the rest of the world to give Uncle Sam any problems at all."

"So much for the Gog and Magog theories," Jefferson said. "I don't know how many TV preachers are trying to say that Russia and China are the two powerful countries that will oppose God in the battle of Armageddon. Russia might have a hard time getting China to cooperate on anything for a long time to come. As I recall, the Cold War had a lot to do with the poverty conditions in China. I sincerely doubt they want to go back to it, and China is certainly big enough and powerful enough to put Russia in its place if they had to."

Allison leaned back in her chair and put her hands over her eyes. "God, this is giving me a headache." She moved her hands and looked at Jefferson. "Did you find out about the mercenaries?"

"I spoke to Peter McDermott a few hours ago, and he will have a squad of his best in Moscow by the time the sun comes up there. Most of them will be Spetsnaz, and of general Russian or neighboring descent. If you decide they need them, all we have to do is call McDermott."

Allison looked at him for a long moment, then nodded her head. "I think it's time we let the kids know we're rooting for them. Molly, I need you to get a message to Neil. Tell him that we arranged for a paramilitary group to help them out, and that we will send him the necessary contact information in the morning. Wait a minute, what time will that be for us?"

"Seven A.M. tomorrow in Moscow would be nine P.M. tonight, here," Molly said.

"Okay, good. Donald, go ahead and call McDermott and tell him we need a way for Neil and Sarah to reach his people as soon as they get there. That should be only a few hours from now, so Molly can forward that information as soon as you get it."

CHAPTER ELEVEN

President Ivan Feodor was furious. "I want someone to tell me," he said, "how in the world this has happened. How did an American assassination of a Russian minister suddenly become a crime committed by my government?"

Leonid Ivanov, director of the SVR, stood in front of the president's desk. The fury in Feodor's eyes had him rooted to the spot, for the president was known to have a volatile temper and a number of loyal friends who would not hesitate to eliminate the problem for him. Ivanov himself had replaced Yuri Leskov after the latter had been found shot to death in his own apartment. No one talked about it, but it was well known that Leskov had refused a "request" from the president only the day before.

"I do not know," he said. "Mr. President, all of this has only come to my attention this morning. I have not had any chance to investigate..."

"Then why are you not investigating right now? If you had no answer to give me, you could have sent one of your assistants to tell me that. Russia is about to become a laughing stock of the entire world, and I've already been forced to postpone the executions. My advisors are telling me this morning that I must not allow anything to happen to these prisoners, that even should one of them have an accident, it will appear that we're trying to silence them before any investigations can be conducted. Now, I want to know before this day is over whether these are American spies and assassins, or whether there's any truth to these rumors. Do you understand me, Leonid?"

"Yes, Mr. President," Ivanov said. He bowed and turned quickly, getting out of the office as soon as he possibly could. By the time he got to his car, he was already on his cell phone and demanding answers of his own.

NOAH LOOKED UP AS THE cell door opened. Captain Fedorov stood there, his face grim. "Come," he said.

Noah got to his feet and two men came in. He was handcuffed and then marched quickly through the halls with Fedorov following. They got to the interrogation room, but this time they didn't bother to hang him from the chains. He was placed in a chair with his cuffs still on. The two men left the room and Fedorov faced him alone.

"The news services, the Internet, they're all saying that you're not an American at all, but a Russian. They say that you're all special agents who were trained to pose as Americans and wait for the order to return to Russia and commit a crime. They say that this was a political ploy intended to allow the re-creation of the USSR. Is any of this true?"

Noah looked at him silently, but grinned.

"Let me explain myself better," Fedorov said. "I'm no friend of those who want to bring back the USSR. I'm no friend of those who want to bring back the KGB. If you were indeed raised in Russia and forced into such things, then I can be your friend. All I ask is that you tell me the truth."

Noah shrugged, but kept grinning. "What do you want me to say? If I say I'm an American, then you're going to hang me as a spy. If I say I'm Russian, I'll probably disappear into Siberia. You don't want to hear the truth, that I'm pretty much a nobody. What do you want me to say?"

Fedorov scowled at him. "I'll tell you this. You'll suffer less if you tell me the truth than you will if the SVR is brought in. Some of them, they'd love to see the days of the KGB return."

Noah looked him in the eye. "If these stories are actually in the news, your government is going to be very careful what they do with me and the others. There will undoubtedly be investigations that involve other nations, am I right? I don't think the Kremlin is going to want anything bad to happen to us. Or are they still planning to hang us tomorrow?"

Fedorov only looked at him for more than a minute, then slowly seemed to relax. "Your execution has been postponed," he said. "It's my understanding that the SVR is taking over all investigation where you're concerned. I was quite serious when I told you that some of them miss the old days. You may come to wish you had cooperated with me."

He stepped out of the room for a moment and then returned with the other two men. Noah was walked back to his cell and put inside, the cuffs removed and the door closed and locked.

One by one, he heard the other doors open. After almost half an hour, all of them had been questioned and brought back. Noah sat down at the table and began messaging Marco.

GET READY

I AM

NO HANG

YES GOOD

NEIL HAD SLEPT IN A bit, after being up most of the night pushing the story around the Internet. He woke at just before ten and wandered to the kitchen for a cup of coffee. His computer was on the table and he turned it on.

There was a notification that he had a message in an email account that he hardly ever used, so he looked to see what it was. His eyes bugged out when he saw that it was from Molly, with a subject that read, "Help is on the way."

He clicked on the link and the message opened up.

Neil,

I'm sending this under Allison's orders. She is aware that you're setting up a rescue mission, and that Monica is helping you. She appreciates the fact that you've done this on your own, because it keeps our country out of the potential war. However, she feels that you're going to need military specialists at some point, so she has arranged for some. She said you might remember the people who helped you in Hong Kong, because some of them are due to arrive in Moscow early this morning. You can reach them by calling +7-4011-777-5825. Tell them what you need and they will follow your orders.

Molly

"Sarah? Monica? You guys want to see this."

Both women came into the kitchen from the living room and both of them stared at the message. Sarah looked at Monica, who was reading the message for the fourth time.

"Well? What do you think?" Sarah asked. "Do you think it's a trap?"

Monica shook her head. "No," she said. "I read people pretty well, and Allison is a straight arrow. If she were trying to set a trap for us, she wouldn't offer this kind of help. She'd offer something that would require us to expose ourselves. In this case, she's offering mercenaries who will follow orders, and you don't even have to meet with them. If it was a trap, we'd have to let them know where we are."

"Neil? What's your opinion?"

"I agree with Monica," Neil said. "If this was a trap, we'd have to stick our necks out. The way she's got this set up, we could literally just send these guys off to get them while we sit tight here. I think we can trust it."

Sarah sighed. "Okay, then let's give them a call. Just be ready to hang up in a hurry if you need to."

Neil nodded, then took out his phone and dialed the number. It rang twice, and then an accented voice came on the line. "Orders?"

"Maybe in a minute," Neil said. "Can you tell me how many of you there are, and what you're doing here?"

"Tell me first your name."

"It's Neil."

"Yes, Neil. I am Yury. We are ten in number. All of us like Spetsnaz, what you call special force. We are here to assist in recover your friends."

"Good," Neil said, "that's very good. I don't have any orders for you just yet, so just stay where you are. I'll call you when I know more, okay?"

"Yes, we wait."

The line went dead and Neil looked up, wide-eyed, at Sarah and Monica. "Special forces," he said. "Ten of them. They're waiting for us to call and tell them what we need them to do."

Sarah broke into a smile. "Oh my God," she said, "we're actually going to get them out. Should we send the men now?"

Monica shook her head. "No, not yet. The president has already postponed the execution, but I'm sure he's going to move them pretty quickly. Neil, you need to get into whatever computers are necessary to find out where they go when that happens. Just keep watching, because we may be lucky enough that they'll post the orders in the computer before it even happens. It's possible we can send these guys to get them while they're being moved, which could be better. The thing is, if they get moved, we need to know where they're going."

"The news is all over the story, now," Neil said. "CNN and BBC are both jumping up and down on it, and so is every major newspaper in the world. There's probably a hundred video bloggers who've already posted videos about this, isn't that wild?"

"It's exciting, yes," Monica said. "Just don't let it distract you from the real mission. Realistically, this whole thing is going to probably set Russia back a few years in their credibility with the rest of the world, and that isn't necessarily a bad thing. Hell, I wish I'd thought of trying something like this a couple of years ago. Russia is one of the most oppressive governments on Earth, even though it's a lot better than it used to be."

"I don't care about Russia and how they stand with the rest of the world," Sarah said, "I just want my husband back. Neil wants Jenny back. Those are the important issues at the moment, can we all stay focused on that?"

"We are, Sarah," Monica said. "It's going to be okay, I promise you. I get a feel for these things sometimes, and right now I feel very strongly that your people are coming home safely. We just have to be careful not to jump the gun, because there's as much danger in trying to move too quickly as there is in waiting too long."

"I understand that," Sarah said. "Believe me, I really do, but it's all starting to get to me. I've been holding it together pretty well, but I can tell you now that I'm going to be breaking down if something doesn't happen soon."

THE DARK-HAIRED WOMAN had been waiting for almost half an hour, but she wasn't complaining. It wasn't often that someone like her was called to an audience with the Queen, and she wondered quietly what it was going to be about. The grand lady had come to see her in the hospital, once, shortly after that awful time when they had almost lost the Prince. She had been incredibly gracious, and had actually leaned down to give her a hug as she lay in her hospital bed.

A door opened suddenly and a man came quickly across the marble floor. He bowed when he was standing just in front of her. "Miss Potts?" he asked. "Would you come this way, please?"

Catherine got to her feet and followed him, and a moment later she was standing in the presence of Queen Elizabeth. The Queen rose from the chair she had been sitting on and held out her hands, and Catherine felt them touch her on the shoulders as she knelt.

"Oh, get up, get up," Elizabeth said. "All that kneeling and bobbing, there's a time and a place, you know. Now, let me look at you. How long has it been? Almost two years, now?"

"Yes, Your Majesty," Catherine said. "I'm incredibly honored to see you again."

Elizabeth smiled. "Don't be in such a rush," she said. "I'm afraid I've called you here on business, rather than pleasure. I should like very much to ask a great favor of you, if I may."

"Of course, Your Majesty. I'm ever at your service."

"I'm certain you've heard about the events in Russia," the Queen said. "How it appears that some factions over there have attempted to create an international crisis between Russia and the United States, in order to resume certain attitudes from the past."

"Yes, Your..."

"Dear girl, please stop saying Majesty. A simple 'yes, ma'am' will suffice."

"Yes, your—yes, ma'am."

"In the course of the long life such as I've had, one makes many friends. Some of those friends are in powerful positions in the United States today, and I've been informed rather quietly that one of the men currently imprisoned in Russia is actually an old friend of ours. I'm not sure what name you knew him under, but he was credited with saving your life, as I recall, and he certainly saved that of my son. Do you know to whom I refer?"

Catherine's heart began racing and she felt a flush come to her face. "Yes, ma'am, I do."

The Queen smiled again. "He was certainly memorable, wasn't he? In any event, it seems to me that if he is involved in this, then it probably is not quite what it appears to be. I feel that I would be much more comfortable about all of this if I had someone in Moscow whom I believe I can truly trust. This is why I sent for you, Miss Potts. I wonder if you would consent to be my eyes and ears on this matter."

"You want me to—to go to Moscow?"

"As my personal representative, yes," Elizabeth said. "You would report directly to me, to keep me advised of the situation as you see it."

"Your Majesty," Catherine said, momentarily forgetting herself, "it would be an honor."

The Queen smiled and Catherine found herself basking in it. "Oh, I'm so pleased," Elizabeth said. "Can you leave immediately?"

"ACCORDING TO CNN," Allison said, "twenty-seven countries have demanded explanations of Russia's ambassadors about this situation. The good old U.S. of A. is one of them, incidentally."

"Are you surprised?" Jefferson asked. "After they've been screaming for the last several days about how we assassinated one of their ministers? Our president is no fool, Allison, he's going to jump on this bandwagon with both feet. The longer Russia can be kept off balance, the stronger we become in the eyes of the world once again. With half the world believing that the assassination was carried out as an inside job by Russian agents, I would imagine he's feeling pretty good right now."

Allison chuckled. "It's almost like this is their 9/11. We had an awful lot of people thinking that was an inside job, too, remember?"

"Remember? I still think so. If you ever watch the videos of the south tower coming down, it's kind of amazing that some of the lower floors blew out many seconds before any of the debris from above could have gotten there."

"Donald, there are a dozen videos on YouTube debunking that theory. Go watch them, why don't you, so you can stop talking about that."

"I've seen them," Jefferson said. "I even got Wally to sit down and look at them, and he agrees with me. There's no way that tower fell just from the impact of the airplane and the burning fuel. No way."

"Change of subject. I got a phone call from Nick Weber a little bit ago."

"Weber, Weber," Jefferson muttered to himself. "Oh, one of your old partners at the CIA, right?"

"Yes, he's Deputy Director of Analysis over there, now. He wanted to thank me for overseeing the Kalashnikov situation. I guess the family is getting settled into their new home in Seattle."

"Well, good, I'm glad to hear it. Did you happen to thank him for giving us a mission so screwed up that it may cost us our best people?"

"Oh, I don't think I put it quite that way. Anyway, he told me something I found interesting. Some of his people had picked up chatter suggesting that there are actual Russian deep cover agents here in our country who are on the verge of panicking over all of this. According to Nick, they have recordings of more than half a dozen such sleepers who are discussing the possibility of turning themselves in and asking for asylum."

Jefferson burst out laughing. "Now, that's amazing. Monica Lord goes to Russia, spreads a bunch of big lies, and ends up possibly saving our country from God only knows what these people might have done at some point in the future. Sometimes I think Noah may have given us a fantastic gift when he brought her into the fold. Incidental-ly, how is her committee doing, with her being off the reservation?"

"I covered her ass," Allison said. "I told them that I needed her help with a top-secret mission and that she'll be back in a week or two. I did not tell them that even we can't watch her at the moment, though. Not sure how they would've taken that news."

CAPTAIN FEDOROV WAS sitting in his office in the Lubyanka. He had been removed from the case of the American spies, replaced by Colonel Leschinsky of the SVR. Leschinsky's job was to inves-tigate the claims that the Americans were actually Russian sleeper agents who had been placed in America to await orders. Those orders, according to the stories flying around the world, would cause them to come into Russia as Americans and perpetrate an assassination.

The plans behind them, the stories said, included relaunching the old Cold War and prompting the rebirth of the USSR. Fedorov knew that there were many people in the government who would love to see such things happen, but he personally scoffed at the idea. The old Soviet states had enjoyed independence since the early nineties, and he knew enough to doubt that any of them would ever welcome the chance to return to Soviet Socialism.

There was no doubt in his own mind that these were genuine American agents, but Leschinskyhad refused to listen to him. Grant-ed, Fedorov thought, it was quite possible that the old KGB might have come up with this kind of ridiculous plan, but the KGB was gone. The type of thinking that could engender such a plan was no longer common among Russian officials, and there was no one who might actually conceive of it who could possibly make it happen.

Sitting at his desk, Fedorov used a pen to doodle on his desk pad. The words and numbers he had scribbled there told him that such an operation would cost billions of rubles, and even the SVR did not have enough black ops budget to finance it. In his opinion, it was a red herring, a smokescreen, and it was quite possible that Russia could collapse under its weight.

It had been only fifteen hours since the stories began appearing online, but already there were demands from governments around the world for answers. Eleven countries, including the United Kingdom, were already demanding a special session of the United Nations, and proposing to levy sanctions against Russia until the matter was resolved. Should the UN decide that the stories were true, those sanctions might become very grave and potentially permanent.

There was a tap on his office door, and he looked up to see Anya Kerensky looking at him through the glass. He motioned with his fingers for her to enter and pointed at the chair beside his own. Anya was one of his best officers and often showed initiative that far surpassed that of any of her colleagues.

"Anya," he said. "At least I have the pleasure of your company during my exile."

"Exile?" Anya asked. "Sir?"

Fedorov smiled. "Have you not heard? I've been banished from Lefortovo for the duration of this event. Leschinsky feels that I've failed to accomplish anything in my questioning of the suspects, and so I have been sent back here to twiddle my thumbs. What can I do for you, lovely Anya?"

Anya blushed. Short and chubby, she had never heard the word lovely used to describe her before, but the little part of her that lived deep inside encouraged her to take it while she could.

She was a good investigator, however, and had been in his unit for a little over a year. Officially, she was listed in his Table of Organization as an intelligence analyst, because of her encyclopedic knowledge of the cultures of other countries. Fedorov had quickly learned that she was capable of using that knowledge on the fly, and often called her in when investigations took an international turn.

She was also his choice when it was necessary for someone in his unit to deal with foreign police. Anya had become invaluable in that regard, and he had changed the T/O to reflect her job title as his "Intercultural Coordinator," and she was adept enough that many international callers now asked for her by name. Some of them seemed to think that she was working for them, rather than for the FSB.

"It's a fancy title," he had told her at the time, "but all it means is that you can deal with the calls from police in other countries. They give me a headache, so I'm dumping them on you."

He gave her his attention, now. She had a tendency to come up with things that were important, and he had learned to trust her judgment.

"I came across something I thought might help," she said. "I was looking at the photographs of the arrested spies and one of them looked familiar to me. I ran him through our facial recognition system, but nothing came up. Still, I couldn't shake the feeling I had seen him before, so I've been thinking about it all day." She smiled suddenly. "About twenty minutes ago, it struck me that I had seen the man when I was a patrol officer stationed at Sheremetyevo. That was just before I came here, about a year ago, so I went back through some of the old files of cases I had worked on out there, and stumbled across this." She leaned forward and laid a freshly printed eight by ten photo on his desk.

Fedorov picked it up and looked at it, and then he suddenly sat forward in his chair and began to stare at it in earnest. "Where did this come from?"

"Do you remember the situation with Nicolaich Andropov? He was a powerful man in the SVR until it was learned that he was running a rogue operation."

"Yes, yes, of course," Fedorov said. "He was stripped of his authority and rank and fled the country. He was brokering information at one point, but then he became obsessed with the man who killed his son. If I remember correctly, that man killed him, as well."

Anya nodded. "That's correct, sir," she said. She pointed at the photograph in his hand. "That's a photo of the man we suspected of being an American assassin at that time. It appears that it was he who killed Vasily Andropov, son of Nicolaich. This photo was taken as he arrived in Moscow. We only noticed him because he was greeted by a man from the American Embassy, but he was the only American to fit the description given by the survivors."

Fedorov stared at the photo for several seconds. "I wonder, Anya," he said, "if you realize just how great a discovery you've made. This does appear to be Mr. Winston, it's quite obvious. However, that would mean that he has acted as an American agent before, which could help us to prove that these are not Russian agents after all." He got quickly to his feet and pulled on his jacket. "Come, Anya," he said. "We must go and see Leschinsky immediately."

Anya's face lit up. She hurried back to her own office to get her jacket and met Fedorov at the front door, then followed him to his car. She smiled when he opened her door for her.

The late afternoon traffic slowed them down a little bit, but Fedorov got there in good time. When he went inside the front offices of the Lefortovo prison, he was met at first with resistance, but he had always known how to command obedience and respect. The staff member who tried to dissuade him from seeing Colonel Leschinsky quickly ran out of arguments and let them pass.

CHAPTER TWELVE

Leschinsky was in a foul mood. His boss, Ivanov, was crawling all over him to get to the bottom of whatever was going on with the suspects, and yet he was not allowed to use any of the normal tactics for extracting information.

"I've been ordered to move them," he said after he stopped being angry about the interruption. "The president seems to be concerned that someone may wish to kill them while they're in custody."

"More than you?" Fedorov asked. He ignored the glare it got him. "I want to show you something," he said. "Anya has found something very interesting." He passed over the photograph and Leschinsky grudgingly turned his eyes to it.

He looked at it for a moment, then looked back up at Fedorov. "What am I supposed to be seeing?"

Fedorov's eyes grew wide. "Isn't it obvious? That photograph was taken more than a year ago, of the man suspected of killing the son of Nicolaich Andropov. I find it interesting that it's the same man you currently hold under the name of Samuel Winston."

Leschinsky looked back at the photo. He tilted it to get better light, with his head thrown back so that he could look through the bottom of his bifocal glasses. After almost a minute, he looked back at Fedorov.

"I see a resemblance," he said. "Our Mr. Winston, however, is taller than this man. Look at the poster in the background, it should appear lower. There's no way this is the same man."

Fedorov grinned. "Leschinsky, you old bear. Do you hope to claim the credit for this discovery to yourself? I've spent enough hours with Winston to know that this is him. Since he is already known as an American agent, it's simply beyond the realm of possibility that the story of his being a Russian sleeper could be true. This is the evidence you need to break the story, but I'll not have Anya cheated of the recognition she deserves for finding it."

Leschinsky scowled at him and handed the photo back. "It's not the same man," he said. "You may try to convince someone else, if you wish. Until you do, and someone gives me orders other than those I've already received, I shall proceed to move them somewhere safe." He turned and walked away.

The grin had vanished and Fedorov was stunned. He looked at the photo again, just to reassure himself that he had not imagined what he'd seen, but there was still no doubt in his mind that he was looking at a picture of Samuel Winston. He started to speak, to call out to Leschinsky, but Anya put a hand on his arm.

"Please, let's go," she said. "If he refuses to see the truth, then it means it's a truth that someone does not want exposed. Let's go, let's just forget this."

"But..." Fedorov said, but Anya put a hand to his mouth to silence him.

"Please? Please, this frightens me," she said.

Fedorov looked down the hall where Leschinsky had gone and saw him speaking with another man. That man turned his face to look at Fedorov and Anya, then looked back at Leschinsky.

"I think you're correct," Fedorov said. "Let's go."

They left the building quickly and went to his car, and were back on the street only a minute later. Fedorov was quietly ranting, letting out the anger that was building up inside himself at the knowledge that the truth was going to be covered up again. Anya was quiet, looking around from time to time to see if they were being followed.

A car had appeared behind them and Anya was watching it closely. It was staying at a steady distance away, even when Fedorov slowed or sped up, and this was making her nervous. She turned to look at Fedorov, to tell him that they seemed to have someone following them, but she never got the words out. Her eyes grew wide, but then the freight truck ran into the driver's side of Fedorov's car.

The big truck was moving a lot faster than the speed limit. When the sedan flipped over, the truck bounced upward and continued right over the top of it and somehow managed to keep right on going.

The sedan rolled three times and finally landed on its roof, which had been smashed flat. People who had been standing on the street ran over to see if they could help whoever was in the car, but they stopped and stared instead.

There was a bloody mass hanging out the driver side window. It took a moment for the onlookers to realize that it was probably what was left of someone's head.

NOAH LOOKED UP WHEN the keys rattled in his door. A man he had not seen before stood there looking at him, as if he were trying to make up his mind about something. Noah sat where he was on the bunk and looked directly into his eyes for a moment, and then the man stepped inside.

"Mr. Winston," he said. "I'm Colonel Vladimir Leschinsky, with the SVR. I've been placed in charge of your safety while you're in our custody."

Noah nodded and grinned. "Sam Winston," he said. "You'll forgive me, I hope, if I harbor a wish that your hospitality won't last much longer, won't you?"

Leschinsky smiled. "I believe you may well get your wish, but I'm not certain how soon. I'm told that you've been made aware of the stories about you and your friends?"

Shrugging, Noah looked at him and shook his head. "I've been told something about some crazy idea that we're supposed to be Russian spies who were hiding in America. First off, that doesn't make a lot of sense to me, and second, all of you people keep talking about 'my friends.' The only person I know here, assuming he's here somewhere, is my old buddy Harold."

"As it happens, I cannot as yet prove differently. However, I've only moments ago been shown evidence that you've been to Russia before. There was a photograph taken of you sometime in the past, at Sheremetyevo Airport. Your hair was considerably shorter than it is now, so I know the photograph is not a recent one. I'm told that you were identified at that time as the man who killed Vasily Andropov. Would you care to refute that accusation?"

Noah squinted at him. "Vaseline drop off? What kind of a name is that?"

The Colonel burst out laughing. "Oh, yes, the American sense of humor. I cannot tell you how it pleases me to hear it once again. It has been a long time." He turned and looked at the guards that were standing in the hall behind him. "Close and lock the door. Mr. Winston and I have matters to discuss."

The door was closed and Noah heard the lock click into place. He strained his ears to be sure that the guards had walked away, then looked up at Leschinsky. "I'm sorry, what was it you wanted to talk about?"

Leschinsky pulled the chair away from the table and sat down. "Mr. Winston, I've been in this field for a number of years. This is not the first time I've heard of the *Sovetskiye Spets*, the Soviet Specials. Do you know what I'm referring to?"

Noah curled his upper lip. "Is that a menu item at a Russian restaurant?"

The Colonel shook his head. "No. The Soviet Specials were the graduates of a special training course in which they were trained to speak, act, and live as everyday Americans. Once they had graduated from their training, they were carefully inserted into communities around the United States, using brilliantly crafted identities. Most of them were couples, men and women who were assigned together. Their identities and documentation showed that they were married, although a few of them got married after arriving there. Many of them had children, and some of those children were eventually told the truth. I know that a number of them were willing to embrace the loyalties of their parents and were brought under the control of loyal Russian handlers."

"Hey," Noah said, "that's a popular theme in books and movies. I think there was even a TV show about it, not that long ago. Are you trying to tell me there was actually some truth to those stories?"

"Oh, yes. The GUSP, our General Directorate for Special Programs, was very active in this regard from the early 1970s until 1991. When the USSR was ended, there were quite a number of these agents in the United States. Many of them were left in place, and their identities are, of course, some of our greatest secrets."

Noah put on an expression that he hoped would convey the idea that he was mulling this over. "And you're saying that people think that's who I am? Who we are, me and these other people you keep talking about, right?"

"Indeed, this is true. As of this moment, most of the world believes that's who you are. To be perfectly honest, I first thought that those news stories were only some sort of disinformation that was put forth by the CIA, but seeing that photograph of you has made me wonder. If you're the man who killed Vasily Andropov, then it strikes me as quite possible that you're exactly who these stories claim you to be."

Noah shook his head and squinted. "Wait a minute, wait," he said. "You're telling me that somebody who looks like me killed this Vaseline whatever a year ago, and that makes you think I really am a Russian agent? Do me a favor, let me have some of whatever you're smoking, would you? It's got to be a whole lot better than anything I've ever had before."

The smiles and laughter suddenly vanished, and Leschinsky leapt up off the chair and grabbed Noah by his throat. "Do not laugh at me," he said. "Vasily Andropov and his father, Nicolaich, were two of the most hated men in Russia. Nico was the type of man who would set people to following you, to find ways to blackmail you into doing his bidding. Vasily, his son, was one of the most evil and perverted creatures that has ever walked upon the Earth. The two of them had many enemies, and some of the most powerful of those enemies were Grigori Pacheco and Pavel Boskovich. To you, those names probably mean nothing. They were, however, the two most powerful men in the GUSP, and Vasily had toyed with and raped both of their daughters."

Noah's eyes went wide. "I think I'm catching on," he said. "So, now you're thinking they may have activated some of these sleeper agents to come over here and kill him. Am I right?"

"It would make sense. Pacheco and Boskovich could have arranged his death locally, but it might have left trails that Nico could follow. He would have killed them both in retaliation, and killed their families at the same time. Their children, their parents, brothers, sisters, aunts, uncles, grandchildren... All would have died in terrible ways."

Noah nodded. "But if it was some American who did it, then it doesn't come back on them, right?"

"That's correct. I know that after Vasily was killed, Nico was driven out of the Russian intelligence community and became a rogue. He sold information to the highest bidders, he arranged assassinations, he used the influence he gained from blackmailing so many people to enrich himself in many ways, and all because he had an obsession. He wanted to find the American who killed his son. He was absolutely convinced, as were his superiors at the time, that this assassin was an agent of the American government. Rumor has it that Nico also died at the hands of that assassin, but the whole thing is shrouded in mystery and intrigue to the point that we may never know the truth."

Noah shrugged again. "Okay. And you're telling me all this because..."

Leschinsky smiled again. "I've two daughters, Mr. Winston. The eldest of them is now sixteen years old, and the younger is only fourteen. Three years ago, Nicolaich Andropov wanted me to cooperate with him on a certain matter. I refused, and the next day I received an email containing photographs of my daughters. Both of them were naked, Mr. Winston, and there were tears in their eyes. Vasily Andropov was holding each of them by her throat."

Noah said nothing, but continued to look into Leschinsky's eyes.

"Moments later, the email and the photographs vanished from my phone and from my computers. Immediately after that I received a telephone call from Nico, who told me that my cooperation was no longer optional. To protect my daughters, I did the thing he wished me to do, and I'm not proud of that. From that day on, I looked for any possible way I could to strike out at the Andropovs, but I never found an opportunity. It should not be hard for you to understand that I'm grateful to whoever ended the life of that monster."

Noah cocked his head and nodded. "I can completely understand," he said. "And I'll even be honest enough to tell you that, right at this moment, I really, really wish I was that man. The kind of gratitude you're talking about might actually do me some good, but unfortunately, I'm not him."

"You asked me to forgive your wish to leave our hospitality. I'll now ask you to forgive my belief that you're a very convincing liar." Leschinsky released him and broke out in another smile. "Now, to business. I've been ordered to move all of you to a safe and secret location. The president is concerned for your safety, and it's absolutely necessary for us to keep you very safe. Many countries are demanding answers, and it may be necessary for you to be available for questioning at any time. It's likely that all of the major world powers will send investigators, as well as the United Nations. We must do everything we can to ensure that you're available to speak with them." He walked toward the door for a moment, then stopped and turned back to face Noah. "It will not matter what you say when you're questioned," he said. "The investigators will form their own opinions based on how they perceive you, rather than on your replies. I can tell you that you'll be moved sometime in the next few hours, all of you together, to a rather lovely and luxurious estate about an hour from here. There, you'll no longer be confined to a cell, but you'll be given a bedroom and the freedom to enjoy the house and the grounds. There will be guards, of course, to prevent your escape, but we will be doing everything possible to ensure that you're comfortable."

Noah chuckled. "And all because of some crazy news stories," he said. "You know, this could be a pretty good premise for a book, itself. Maybe I could write one, someday, if I get out of this alive."

"Perhaps," said Leschinsky. "At the moment, all I can tell you is that you're going to live longer than you might have expected this morning." He turned and tapped on the door, and a moment later the guards opened it again. He stepped out, turned again to look back at Noah, and smiled before walking away.

Noah waited for a few moments to be sure he was gone, then quickly got up and grabbed a pencil. He sat in the same chair Leschinsky had just occupied and began messaging Marco.

WE ARE BEING MOVED

WHERE

COUNTRY HOUSE SOON

SHIT

YES

THE PLANE TOUCHED DOWN at Sheremetyevo at just after five P.M., and Catherine Potts breathed a sigh of relief. She hated flying, she always had, but sometimes it was just necessary. Besides, while a lot of her compatriots and colleagues supported the idea of letting the monarchy come to an end after Elizabeth, Catherine had always had a fondness for the grand old lady. When the Queen of England asked a favor, Catherine was not going to be someone who would turn it down.

She stayed in her seat for a few moments while other people gathered their carry-ons and made their way off the plane. When the center aisle traffic was a little slower, she got up and retrieved her own bag, then held it in front of her so that she could squeeze between the seats. The stewardess helped her get past the last few, and then she was walking through the movable ramp and into the terminal. She smiled when she spotted a Burger King and a Taco Bell, but she didn't have time to worry about dinner at the moment. She had to get her baggage and find the embassy shuttle driver that was supposed to be waiting for her.

The airport was surprisingly busy, but she got to baggage claim without any problem. Her bags came through after only a ten-minute wait, the green diplomatic labels still in place over the locks. She'd been a bit surprised when her supervisor, Mrs. Carriker, had informed her that she was suddenly appointed to the position of Queen's Royal Ambassador, a rarely used posting that would entitle her to diplomatic immunity while in Russia.

Bags in tow, she made her way through Migration Control, where her diplomatic passport was stamped and handed back to her. She then proceeded to the main entrance of the terminal and spotted a young man holding a hastily made cardboard sign with her name on it. She walked up to him quickly.

"I'm Catherine Potts," she said.

The young man broke out in a big smile. "Cor," he said. "Oh, forgive me, but the last QRA I had to pick up was a gentleman older than my granddad, so I was expecting someone, er, a bit more advanced in years."

Catherine chuckled. "Well, I've been told I look a bit younger than my true age," she said. "I'm probably near old enough to be your mum."

"Pull the other one, it's got bells on. Sorry, ma'am, I'm Jared Ogilvie, special attaché to the Embassy of the United Kingdom in Moscow." He winked conspiratorially and leaned close as he took her bags. "Special attaché, you know, that's the title you get when you're the bugger gets sent out on errands."

"Well, you seem well suited to it," she said, following him out of the building. He led her to a rather ancient-looking Bentley limousine, where he stored her bags in the boot. A chauffeur opened the back door of the car for Catherine and she slid inside. A moment later, Jared walked around the car and got in on the other side. "Look, you've got a chauffeur of your own and everything. Pretty posh job, I must say."

Jared grinned. "Yes, well, it's a bit of a necessity, what? Bloody Russians don't want our sort roaming around unsupervised, so they require us to hire locals as drivers. That's Alexei. He pretends not to understand any English, and we pretend that he can't hear anything we're saying, anyway. Still, we only have to be a little careful what we talk about in the car, so it's not so much of a nuisance."

"I see," Catherine said. "Well, my visit has no secrets attached to it. Her Majesty simply asked me to come over here and report back my opinions on this current case. Can you tell me anything new about that?"

"That's a real cock-up," Jared replied. "Of course, the Kremlin denies it, but the problem is that there are so many factions in the government here that nobody is absolutely sure there isn't some truth to it. We know for sure that the KGB had such sleeper agents in place prior to 1991, and many of them are still there. Some have brought their children into it and are still awaiting orders, but there's considerable evidence that new sleeper agents are being recruited and trained even today. The big issue in this case is that nobody knows who was behind these particular people. MI6 has determined that there are at least eight former KGB programs that employed sleepers in the West, and some of them are still functioning. Most likely, the original handlers from the KGB are getting some sort of funding that allows them to keep their operations going without any direct connection to the current Russian Federation government. All of that means that the people who were arrested could be descendants of one of the old groups or they might be part of an entirely new cadre of sleepers. If the latter, then nobody is quite sure who would be running them."

Catherine thought over what he had said for a moment. "What about the theory that this is a Russian plot to allow them to reinstate Soviet policies and government? What do your people think about that?"

"The Russian Federation has already annexed, or tried to annex, some parts of the old Soviet Union," Jared said, "particularly Crimea and parts of the Ukraine. It's well known that most of the government feels the downfall of the USSR was a disaster, despite the fact that Russia has been much more popular on the world stage and much more prosperous domestically since it happened. The problem in this instance is that it's beginning to look like Russia deliberately staged the assassination of one of its own people in order to create an environment of suspicion and distrust that would undermine relations between the U.S. and all of the other former Soviet states. It's very possible that most of those former states would have willingly accepted a return to Soviet domination after that assassination, on the theory that they would be safer as part of a new USSR than they would be on their own. With this story out and prevalent, however, those same potentially cooperative states are now gearing up for war. Russia could soon be facing a dozen different wars on its borders, and this would be a geopolitical and economic disaster for the country."

"For Russia, yes," Catherine said. "What about for the rest of the world, though? Wouldn't the rest of us be better off if Russia were to suffer some loss of credibility and prestige?"

"If only it were that simple. Our local analysts are of the opinion that, if these border wars begin, Russia is going to adopt a scorched-earth policy. Rather than try to fight these countries into submission, President Feodor would commit enough troops and equipment to quickly subdue two or three of them, then conscript their soldiers in-to the Army and move out to crush all of the others. The only thing that might stop him from doing such a thing would be intervention by the United States or China, but there's a high probability that Russia would employ tactical nuclear weapons against either or both of them."

Catherine looked out the car window at the people walking by on the streets. "And we would be dragged into World War III." She looked back to Jared. "Am I right?"

"Quite likely, yes. What it all boils down to is that, if these people are American agents who committed an assassination on sovereign Russian soil, then the normal protocols may still prevent any of these disastrous scenarios from coming to pass. The Yanks deny any knowl-edge of these agents, the Russians scream and yell that the Yanks were lying, the agents are executed and the whole matter tends to fade out of the world's consciousness within a few days. On the other hand, if they turn out to be Russian sleepers who carried out the assassination in order to create an atmosphere that would allow the reformation of the USSR, then it's one of the biggest acts of fraud in history. The backlash would be incredible, both inside and outside of Russia."

"Like the conspiracy theories surrounding the attacks on the World Trade Center in 2001," Catherine said. "It's been claimed ever since that the attack was orchestrated from within the American government, and that it was done to force the average American to overlook some of the things their government would do in the name of keeping them all safe."

"Quite right. This would be an absolute Russian nightmare." He leaned toward her. "I just learned that there already seems to be some interagency fighting going on. An FSB Captain who had been involved in the case until this morning was killed about half an hour ago. Car was run completely over by a lorry, and the bloody thing disappeared right after. Might not be suspicious except he and a woman from his office had just gone to visit the SVR Colonel who replaced him, trying to show him evidence that one of these people they've got locked up might have been here before and done another assassination."

Catherine stared at him. "You think he was killed because of that evidence?"

"Not so much what I think," Jared said, "it's our intelligence people who are in an uproar about it. Apparently they found a photograph of one of the men that was taken at the airport more than a year ago, and the bugger was suspected then of killing several people. One of them was the son of an SVR bleeder who turned out to be working several different sides of the fence. You might remember, his name was Andropov."

"Andropov? Really? Jared, can you get me a copy of that photograph? One of the reasons I was sent here is because the Queen has heard a rumor that one of these men is the one who prevented the murder of Prince Charles some time ago. As it happens, that man once had an interest in Andropov. I'm fairly certain this is going to confirm what she was told."

Jared took a phone out of his pocket and quickly sent a text message. "I'm not certain whether we can get it or not," he said, "but I'll try."

CHAPTER THIRTEEN

The door swung open. Noah looked up to see who was coming in and his eyes widened in surprise. Just outside the door, each of them handcuffed and wearing shackles on their legs, stood Jenny, Marco, Randy, Dave, Jim, and another man that Noah didn't recognize. Five guards holding automatic weapons stood around them, and Colonel Leschinsky motioned for him to stand.

"As I told you earlier," Leschinsky said, "it's time for us to move you. Unfortunately, it is necessary for us to transport you as prisoners, so please do not resist."

Noah stood and turned his back, and a moment later he felt one of the guards putting handcuffs on him. He stood where he was as the shackles were applied, then turned carefully around.

"Resistance is futile," he said. "I learned that from Star Trek."

The guard took hold of his arm and walked him out the door, and then Leschinsky motioned for all of them to follow him. They were taken down a long hallway and told to enter a small room with benches around its walls. Once they had gone in and taken seats, Leschinsky leaned in.

"You all need to wait here for a short time," he said. "I assure you, it will be only a few minutes."

Noah watched him close the door, then looked around at all of the others. His eyes came to rest on Jenny, and he smiled. "Hey, there, cute stuff," he said. "What are they accusing you of?"

Jenny glared at him hatefully. "Do I look like I'm in any mood to be hit on?"

Noah chuckled and turned to Marco. "Watch that one, Harry," he said. "Just a little bit on the bitchy side."

Marco shook his head. "Did anyone ever tell you you're crazy, Sam? This is not exactly the time or the place to be trying to pick up a girl."

"Nonsense," Noah said, "I can never pass up the chance to talk to a pretty girl like that. Life is too short, man, you gotta try."

"Lighten up, asshole," Randy said. "That's my wife you're talking about."

Noah looked at him. "Geez, really? Look, man, I'm sorry. This is just how I deal with stress, okay? I have to make jokes, and if there's a pretty girl around, then I..."

"Just shut up," Randy said. "Do you not understand that we're probably on our way to die?"

"Die? I sure hope you don't know something that I don't know. That Colonel Lifshitz, he said they're taking us out to some luxury resort place, just to keep us safe."

Jim scoffed. "Yeah, I heard that line, too. Never trust a Russian, that's what I always say."

Marco cleared his throat. "Sam, did they tell you what this is all about? First, they said we were American secret agents, then the next thing I know, they're saying we're some kind of Russian spies. Did any of that make sense to you?"

"Not a bit," Noah said. "I told that other guy, the captain, we were just trying to steal the commissary money. He didn't believe me. Saying we were trying to steal something about an execution plan."

"Yeah, that's what they told me. Crap, you actually told them about the money? You have any idea what stealing that much money, hell, even trying to steal that much money, you got any idea how much prison time we're going to get?"

"Hey, the way I look at it, this is Russia. You get arrested in Russia, you might as well figure on going to prison no matter what it's about. I thought, maybe if I was just honest with them, they might cut us a break, you know what I mean?"

"You guys are so stupid," Randy said. "They keep trying to tell me that I'm some kind of assassin, and that my wife murdered a couple of men. Hell, we just brought some friends and came here on vacation. Went out to watch the whales and saw some boat blow up. These assholes are crazy."

"I just want to go home," Jenny said. "That's all I want, just to go home and forget this ever happened."

The door to the room opened suddenly and Colonel Leschinsky stepped inside. He stood in the middle of the room and looked around, then began clapping his hands.

"Bravo," he said. "Bravo. An excellent performance. If this were a movie, you would probably win an Oscar, each of you. Of course, this is not a movie, and you've just wasted an opportunity to discuss your situation more honestly."

"Discuss what?" Jenny asked angrily. "You want us to discuss this dickhead you threw in here with us? We've told you over and over, we don't know anybody else. We didn't assassinate anybody, and we don't know anything about who did." She sat back in a huff.

Leschinsky laughed. "As I said, a wonderful performance. Gentlemen, and dear lady, we will shortly be taking you to the place that will be your home while we try to determine the truth of who you are. This would all be so much easier if you would simply tell us. I might add, it would all come to an end that much sooner, as well. If, in fact, you are the Russian sleeper agents that so many sources allege you to be, then it is quite possible that you will actually regain your freedom. Would anyone like to talk about this?"

Noah looked up at him. "Hey, you know what? Here's the problem the way I see it. If any of us was to jump up and say, 'yes, I'm a Russian spy who was living in the U.S. and waiting to come back here and kill somebody,' then you guys are suddenly going to start asking us all kinds of questions about Russia. We don't know about Russia, or at least I don't and Harry doesn't. We wouldn't be able to answer those questions either, so we'd end up right back in the same boat we're in now."

Leschinsky looked at him. "You may be right, Mr. Winston," he said. "But the fact of the matter is that you are either American espionage agents and assassins, or you are Russian sleeper agents. I can assure you that we will find out the truth, and then we will take whatever action is appropriate." He gave them a big smile. "All that this means for you at this time, however, is that you are going from a prison cell to a mansion. This is so that we can prevent anyone who might want to silence you from finding out where you are. That could be a terrible thing."

A soldier stuck his head in the room and said something in Russian, and Leschinsky nodded to him as he replied. He turned back to face them again. "Your ride is ready," he said. "If you will all please get to your feet and follow me, we can depart on our journey as soon as one more traveler arrives."

"THERE'S ONLY ONE WAY I can think of to get you a look at that photograph," said Ronald Barrons, intelligence analyst for the British Embassy in Moscow. "It's in the possession of the woman who was in the car with Federov when he was killed, and she's probably lucky to even be alive. When they pulled her out of the car, she said she'd seen the lorry coming and ducked down, so when it hit, she was thrown into the floor of the car. That's the only reason she wasn't crushed by the roof."

Catherine nodded. "So where is she? I want to see her as soon as possible."

"She's in hospital, of course," Peterson replied, "and they would not normally allow a foreign national to visit her at all, but you've got special status. As a QRA, you can be admitted to see her to express the Queen's good wishes, and you can ask her about the circumstances of the accident. With any luck, she'll tell you about the photo and show it to you."

"Then make it happen. The sooner I know whether this is the same man the Queen asked me to verify, the better I'll like all of this."

Peterson ducked his head in a nod, then turned to walk away. Catherine sat behind the desk in the tiny office she'd been given to use during her visit and thought about how she would feel if it did indeed turn out to be Alex Colson.

She had met Colson only a few times, starting with a case where he was trying to find an information broker named Jeremy Pendergrast. She had helped him locate and abduct the man, which had then taken him to Russia, where he rescued the daughter of the president of Mauritania from some Russian agents who were holding her in order to pressure her father into a political alliance he did not want.

The second time was when he was sent into London to impersonate an international assassin known only as Adrian. Adrian was scheduled to take a job for a quasi-terrorist organization, and Colson was supposed to identify and eliminate them. He succeeded in that mission, but then he learned that Adrian was planning to assassinate Prince Charles, and turned his efforts to stopping that from happening.

The very last time she had spoken to Colson had been on the telephone, just after Adrian had killed her entire team and left her bleeding in the street. She had begged him to find Adrian and kill him, and then passed out. When she awoke a day later, she learned that a passing drug addict had picked up her phone and that Colson had convinced the man to call 999. If he had not, she probably would have bled out on the spot.

She owed him her life, and her country owed him even more.

Peterson returned a few minutes later, a smile on his face. "Miss Kerensky is awake," he said, "and would be pleased to receive you. The hospital is only a few minutes away. Shall we go now?"

"God, yes," Catherine said. She grabbed her bag and was up out of the chair like a shot, then followed Peterson out of the embassy.

Peterson snapped his fingers at Alexei and the chauffeur jumped to attention. He opened the back door of the limousine and waited as the two of them entered, then closed the door and got behind the wheel.

"European Medical Centre," he said to the chauffeur, and the man put the car in gear. He turned to Catherine. "Don't let the name fool you," he said. "The European Medical Centre is a typical Russian hospital. Actually, I should not say that, it's truly a bit better than most. Miss Kerensky was probably fortunate to be taken there."

As Peterson had predicted, the ride seemed to take only a few minutes. Alexei pulled up in front of the main entrance and let them out, then went to park the car while they hurried inside. Peterson spoke to the information desk in Russian, and a moment later a young woman approached to lead them to Anya's room.

As the Queen's Royal Ambassador, diplomacy required that Catherine could go where other foreign diplomats could not. Peterson was told he had to wait outside while Catherine went in to speak with Anya, but he didn't seem terribly surprised. Of course, despite the fact that he was listed as an assistant agricultural attaché, it was almost certain that the Russian intelligence services would be aware that he was actually in the intelligence business, himself. It stood to reason they wouldn't want him in a position to question someone who might have damning information.

Catherine smiled at him. "Don't worry," she said. "I can manage." She entered the room and immediately froze.

The woman in the hospital bed looked like some sort of industrial plumbing experiment. There were pipes and hoses all around her, many of them going directly into parts of her body. A nurse standing beside the bed looked up at Catherine and smiled. "You are from the Queen?"

Catherine tore her eyes away from Anya and looked at the nurse, relieved that the woman seemed to speak English. "I am," she said. "Goodness, she looks to be in very serious condition."

"I'm Irina," said the nurse. "Miss Kerensky was very fortunate. Most of her injuries are not terribly serious, though she'll be in some pain for a time. This equipment is mostly just to help her be more comfortable."

"I see," Catherine said. "I was told she was awake."

"I'm awake," Anya said. Catherine looked at her and saw that one eye was open and watching her face. "They told me you are from the Queen of England?"

Catherine smiled brightly. "I am," she said. "Her Majesty heard about your accident and asked me to come and extend her wishes for your speedy recovery."

"Really?" Anya asked. She turned to the nurse. "Irina, could you leave us for a few minutes?"

The nurse glanced at Catherine for a second, almost looking nervous, but then smiled at Anya and nodded. She walked out of the room and closed the door behind her, and Anya turned back to her visitor.

"Either you are lying," she said, "or you are seeking information. Which could it be?"

Catherine smiled and stepped up close to the bed. "You are quite perceptive," she said. "In fact, I've been told that you and the gentleman who did not survive were in possession of a photograph of one of the alleged Russian sleepers, a photograph that was taken some time ago. I'm hoping you'll tell me more about this photograph, and that you still have it."

Anya stared at her for a moment. "What is your interest?"

"Her Majesty sent me here because she has reason to believe that one of the men is someone to whom our country owes a great debt. Based on certain knowledge of my own, I suspect it may be the very man in your photo."

"Which would mean that he is almost certainly not a sleeper agent," Anya said, "but in fact an American spy. Would that not be the case?"

Catherine only looked at her for a moment, then pulled a chair closer to the bed and sat down. It put her almost eye to eye with the young woman. "The man I'm speaking of was, as far as I know, an American. He came to Great Britain with the intent of putting a stop to a certain terrorist group, and he did do so. In the course of that effort, however, he learned that there was an assassin who was planning to kill one of the royal family. On his own initiative, because we were unable to find or stop this assassin, he did so, at great personal sacrifice. If it is the same man, I do not know why he is in your country. The only thing I can tell you is that he does nothing without being certain that it needs to be done. He operates not on the code of any government, but on a code of his own."

Anya looked deeply into her eyes for several seconds. "I do not have the photograph," she said. "According to the police who were present when I was taken from the wreckage, there was no photograph to be found. This tells me that one of them secured the photograph, and that I'm not supposed to have it. It tells me also that the photograph is what cost the life of my superior, Captain Fedorov."

"Why you believe that to be the case?" Catherine asked her.

"Captain Fedorov had been in charge of the interrogation of these prisoners until this morning. Shortly after the news began running the story that they were Russian deep cloak agents, he was removed and replaced by an SVR officer, Colonel Leschinsky. I had been helping him with some of the research, and one of the men in the photographs looked familiar to me. Some time ago, I was assigned to Sheremetyevo Airport on a security detail, and I was on duty when an alleged American agent passed through the airport. When it was learned that several men had been killed in Kubinka, one of them the son of a ranking SVR officer, and that the description of the killer fit this particular man, his photograph was widely circulated. He had already escaped the country by then, but we did not know that at the time." She carefully reached to pick up a glass of water with a straw and took a sip, then put it back. "I have a very good memory for faces. When I saw the photos of the prisoners, one of them looked like that man, so I went back and found the file from that time. I put the photos side-by-side on a computer and compared them. There's no doubt in my mind that it was the same man."

"And you showed this to your superior?"

"Yes. He agreed with me, and said that we had to show it to Colonel Leschinsky. We drove out to Lefortovo prison and met with the Colonel, but he insisted that it was not the same man. He told us to go back to our offices and forget it, but then he sent someone to follow us. Both the captain and I were concerned, because Leschinsky refused to look at the evidence, but then we were struck by a freight truck. Captain Fedorov is dead, and I've no doubt that my life depends on forgetting that photograph completely."

Catherine sat there and looked at her for almost a minute, nibbling gently on her own bottom lip as she did so. "Miss Kerensky, have you any idea why the SVR would want to keep this information from coming to light?"

Anya hesitated, but only for a couple of seconds. "Colonel Leschinsky said that he had been ordered to move the prisoners because the Kremlin is concerned for their safety. As of now, no photographs of any of the prisoners have been released to the public. If it were possible to prove that one of those prisoners truly was an American agent who had been to Russia before to commit an assassination, the people would demand that they be publicly executed, as was originally intended. If the press ever gets to photograph them, then the photos that were taken at Sheremetyevo more than a year ago would make that clearly evident. My concern is that the SVR does not want those photos to come to light until they're ready."

Catherine's eyebrows lowered. "Until they're ready?"

Anya nodded slowly. "Until they can be certain that the photographs will not show that one of those agents had previously been to Russia. I've been thinking about this since I was brought to the hospital. The only reason I can imagine that they would not want that truth to come out is because they plan to replace the prisoners with agents of their own. The prisoners are being moved somewhere, may have already been moved. I would imagine that the SVR plans to interrogate them unobserved for a few days, and then replace them with Russian agents. The prisoners themselves will be put to death quietly, their remains destroyed or disposed of. A new narrative will begin, in which the president will almost certainly claim that the sleeper agents were activated by his opponents, his enemies in our government. Their purpose, he will claim, was to force his hand in a return to open hostilities between Russia and the United States."

"And what purpose would that serve?" Catherine asked. "There's already talk of the UN imposing sanctions against Russia; wouldn't that only guarantee them?"

"Not if the president and the prime minister were unaware of the plan," Anya said. "In that case, the State Duma would have no choice but to rule that they would have clear justification to remove opposition members from the government, including from both the upper and lower house. This would effectively make Russia a dictatorship, with the prime minister in absolute control of the government until such time as new councilors and ministers could be elected. That would take at least a year, and would mean that the prime minister would have plenty of time to affect massive changes in our constitutional law. If this is done slowly enough and cleverly enough, the people of Russia will welcome the changes, they will not realize soon enough that they're simply being returned to the shackles and chains of communism."

Catherine stared at her. "And it wouldn't be long," she said softly, "before there would be a new Russian Empire, starting with the former members of the USSR but probably spreading even further. Am I correct?"

"Without any doubt," Anya said. "It will all happen if they manage to replace those prisoners with their own agents. I would even dare to guess that the new agents will testify before the State Duma and identify those opposition members whom they claim gave them their orders. If they do this, they will be hailed as heroes of the Russian Federation."

"Is there any way to prevent this from succeeding?"

Anya closed her eyes for a moment, then snapped them open and looked into Catherine's own. "The only way I could imagine is if photographs of the current prisoners can be found and exposed. That would warp the plan, since it would then be impossible to substitute other agents. The only problem with that is that it may already be too late."

Catherine nodded. "Why are you telling me all this? If anyone in your government learns that you've figured this out, you run the risk of being killed."

Anya gave her a sad smile. "Because you might be one of the few people who will believe me. Please understand, messenger of the Queen, that I do not wish to live in the Russia that we would become. If this plan is allowed to succeed, I would prefer to die."

"And I would prefer to see you live," Catherine said. "I will do what I can to prevent this from happening, but it will mean sharing this information not only with our own intelligence service, but with our allies. The only thing I can promise you is that I will not use your name. Let us hope that no one connects the information to me, or to my visit with you." She got to her feet and gently patted Anya on the shoulder. "I do wish you well, and I can assure you that I speak for the Queen, as well as for myself. Perhaps one day we can talk again. I think I would like that very much."

Anya smiled up at her. "As would I," she said.

CHAPTER FOURTEEN

Prime Minister Viktor Petrov pressed the intercom button on his phone. "Boris," he said. "Come to my office, please."

Boris Petroski felt his hands go clammy and sweat broke out on his upper lip. Petrov rarely called him over the intercom; he usually stepped out of his office and simply called out to him. Boris pressed his own intercom button and said he would be right there, then got slowly to his feet and walked down the hallway. It occurred to him that anyone watching might think he was walking like a condemned man on the way to the gallows.

He reached the prime minister's office and stopped just outside the door to compose himself. He quickly ran his hands over his face, wiping off the obvious traces of sweat, then opened the door and stepped inside.

"You wanted to see me, Prime Minister?" Boris said.

"Yes," Petrov replied. "Boris, we have intelligence agents from all over the world coming into Moscow. It's necessary for us to sequester those individuals who seem to have been involved in the assassination of Minister Kalashnikov, but I'm concerned that our plans have already been leaked. I was going to put them in a safe house near Novinki, but Colonel Leschinsky has expressed some concern about it. It has been used quite often of late, he says, and suggested that we find a more remote location, somewhere that has not been used for housing prisoners like this before. I recalled that your family has an estate near Stolbovaya. Would it be available? There would be compensation, of course, but I need to know that no one besides you would be aware of our purpose in using it."

Boris felt a flood of relief so great that he had to clamp his sphincter shut to avoid pissing himself. He drew himself up proudly and smiled. "Prime Minister, it would be an honor to provide the estate. Only the staff are there at this time, to keep the house fresh. My family will not even know that it is being used."

"And your staff? Can they be trusted?"

"They are only three, Prime Minister. The butler and housekeeper are man and wife, and the gardener is their son. I can inform them that they must be discreet, or I can send them away for a time, whichever you desire."

"They can stay," Petrov said. "I'm going to send you along with the prisoners and their guards. You can explain to the staff that they will not be allowed any contact with the outside during this time. There should be no telephone or Internet that they can reach, and none of them will be allowed to leave the grounds for as long as the prisoners must be housed there. It shouldn't be more than a week or two, but it is possible that resolving these issues will take longer."

"Yes, Prime Minister," Boris said. "When will we be going?"

Petrov leaned back in his chair and crossed his legs. "I've just ordered Leschinsky to prepare the prisoners for transport immediately. I want you to go directly to Lefortovo and ride with them. You do have your travel bag in your office, do you not?"

There were occasional times when Boris was needed to travel on short notice with the prime minister, so he had developed the habit of keeping a packed bag in his office at all times. "I do," he said. "May I have permission to let my wife know that I will not be coming home tonight?"

The prime minister smiled. "Of course. Give her my best, but do not tell her where you are going or the reason for the journey."

Boris was dismissed and went back to his office. He quickly called his wife and told her that he was being called away on diplomatic business and did not know when he would be home. She expressed concern, but he assured her that he was in no danger and would be home as soon as he could.

When he got off the phone, he picked up his bag and stepped out of his inner office. His secretary, Vasily, looked up at him, saw him carrying the bag, and raised his eyebrows. "Are you going somewhere, sir?"

"It's these prisoners," Boris said. "The president wants them taken out of Lefortovo to somewhere safe, so he has conscripted my family's country estate. I've been ordered to go along to make sure the staff does not give them any problems."

Vasily nodded. "Yes, sir. Will you be returning in the morning?"

"Probably not. I'm not sure when I will be back, so cancel my appointments until further notice. With any luck, I won't be gone more than a few days. The president is simply concerned that, with all this attention, someone may try to do harm to the prisoners. We can't afford to let anything happen to them until these allegations are all sorted out."

"Yes, sir, I understand. Please let me know if I can do anything to assist."

Boris smiled and thanked him, then walked directly out to his car. He was still relieved that the prime minister had not asked about his earlier visit to Lefortovo, but it was highly unlikely that he knew anything about it. Petrov was very transparent and had a tendency to speak exactly what he was thinking. If he had any question about why Boris might have gone to the prison, he would have simply asked.

The late afternoon traffic was worse than it had been earlier, so it was just after six when he arrived at Lefortovo prison. He was greeted inside the front entrance by an SVR officer who escorted him directly to the rear exit, where two large vans stood waiting at the gate. Colonel Leschinsky was standing beside one of them and broke into a smile when he saw Boris.

"Boris, my old friend," Leschinsky said. "It is kind of you to allow us the use of your family's property. My orders are to ensure that no one has access to these prisoners until the president and the prime minister feel it necessary, but I do not know who to trust at this time. Seeking a property that's not connected directly to any government agency seemed most prudent to me."

"Colonel Leschinsky, it is my pleasure. Besides, you're getting me out of my office for a few days. For that, I will be forever in your debt."

Leschinsky laughed. "Then let us go," he said. "You and I will be riding with the prisoners. Come, give your bag to the sergeant and we can go."

The man who had brought Boris to Leschinsky took his bag and carried it to the back of one of the vans while Leschinsky opened a door on the side of the other and climbed in. Boris followed him and found that they were sitting in a pair of seats that faced to the rear, and that the prisoners were already inside. Each of them was chained to a seat and there were two armed guards sitting in folding seats on each side.

Each of the prisoners glanced at him and Boris suddenly began to sweat again. If any of them said anything about recognizing him, Leschinsky was bound to become curious.

The blond-haired man turned his attention to Leschinsky, and the others did likewise. Boris forced himself to relax, but he saw no sign that the prisoners gave any indication of his earlier visit. Hopefully, the messages he had delivered to them were of enough importance that they would continue to protect him.

"Oh," Leschinsky said, "I almost forgot. Your telephone, you must turn it off and remove its batteries. We can take no chance that anyone might be able to trace its location."

Boris took out his phone and fumbled with it for a moment before he figured out how to take off the back. When he pulled the battery out, Leschinsky reached out and took it from him, dropping it into his own pocket. Boris grinned at him, then put the phone away again. For a brief second, he wondered if he should mention that he always carried a spare battery, but then he thought better of it. Considering that he had been ordered to take messages to these prisoners, it was highly likely that the tiny woman and her employer would want to know where they were taken.

While Boris was loyal to his country, he was even more loyal to his life. He would look for an opportunity to send a message telling the puppeteer about this change in the SVR's plans. If he failed to do so and the puppeteer ever found out, he knew, it would not be himself that would suffer. He had a wife and he had children; their safety was more important to him than anything else in the world, and the puppeteer had shown him clearly that it was impossible to protect them in any other way but by absolute obedience and cooperation.

LARRY CARSON WAS JUST about to leave the embassy for the day when John Wilkerson caught his attention. The janitor was pushing a broom through the ground floor main hall and turned to go into a small conference room that was used for visiting tourists. Larry followed him in and shut the door behind him.

"What's up, John?" Larry asked.

"I got a message a few minutes ago that I thought you'd be interested in," John said. "I have a double who just told me that your people are being moved. I guess they left Lefortovo about twenty minutes ago, headed for Boris Petroski's country house at Stolbovaya."

Larry's eyebrows squeezed together. "Seems like an odd place to take them," he said. "Petroski, Petroski—who is he again?"

"He works in the president's office, a lawyer who used to be with the SVR. They call him a crisis advisor, he sort of tells the president what he can and can't get away with when he's under a lot of pressure."

"Maybe that explains it. I'm pretty sure they consider this a crisis, all right. Probably don't want to take them to any of the regular safehouses, so the best bet might have been to commandeer somebody's party pad."

"Maybe," John said. "I just figured you'd want to know. Any word on the girl that disappeared on you?"

Larry smiled. "The Dragon Lady called a while ago to tell me that she and the computer geek are working on a rescue mission. I guess the outfit is behind them on it, but she told me to stay clear. Plausible deniability, right? Make sure we can swear up and down we didn't know anything."

"That's the name of the game. Let me know if I can be of any help."

"Sure will," Larry said. He left the room and started toward the front door, but then thought better of it. It was almost seven P.M., so it would be almost nine A.M. back at Neverland. He turned around and went back to his office, picked up the phone and told the operator to give him a secure line. He heard a couple of beeps and then the dial tone returned. He quickly punched in the number and sat back.

"Brigadoon Investments," said the receptionist. "How may I direct your call?"

"Allison Peterson, please," Larry said. "Larry Carson calling, from Moscow."

"One moment, please."

Music began to play, and it took Larry a moment to realize that he was listening to Barry Manilow. For just a moment, he was lost in the Copacabana, and then Allison came on the line.

"Moscow? Report."

"Yes, ma'am," Larry said. "Our CIA field man just told me that our pigeons have been moved to another coop. Apparently, they're being taken down to Stolbovaya to the country estate of one of President Feodor's advisors, a guy named Boris Petroski. I thought you would want to know about it."

"You're damned right, I do," Allison said. "Let me know if you hear anything else."

"Yes, ma'am," Larry said. The line had already gone dead, so he hung up his phone and headed out the door to his car. For once, he might actually surprise his wife by getting home in time for dinner.

ALLISON HADN'T EVEN bothered to hang up the phone. She had gotten the call by holding down the switch hook, then let it up again and immediately dialed Molly's office. "Get down here," she said, "and bring your computer. We've got to get a message off to Neil, ASAP."

She hit the switch hook again and then dialed Jefferson. "My office, right away."

This time she hung up the phone, but Molly was already rushing through her door by then. Allison held up a finger to tell her to wait, but it was only a few seconds later that Donald Jefferson rushed in.

Allison told both of them what Carson had said, and Molly instantly turned to her computer.

"Boris Petroski is the crisis advisor to President Feodor," she said after a few seconds. "I'm cross-checking for property records at Stobolnaya. There's nothing under his name exactly, but there's something under Nikita Petroski. Checking, checking—looks like an extremely impressive estate. Over a thousand acres, and the house was built during the time of Czar Nicholas. Neoclassical, more than a dozen bedrooms, an honest-to-goodness ballroom—quite a place. Let me check one more thing—yes, Boris Petroski is the son of Nikita Petroski. Nikita, incidentally, is a man, Boris' father."

Jefferson shrugged. "Nikita wasn't always a woman's name. Ever heard of Nikita Khrushchev?"

"Okay, okay," Allison said. "I'm not that concerned about the history of Russian names. Molly, get a message off to Neil right away, let him know about them being moved and about the estate. Tell him I suggest they send the soldiers to start watching the place." She looked at Jefferson. "Donald, I don't know what it is, but something about this makes me nervous."

Jefferson frowned. "I don't know," he said. "To me, it seems like a bit of a logical move. With all the international uproar over who they're supposed to be, I can imagine that the Kremlin wants them kept safe, somewhere."

"Yes, but why? Why are they safer in some country mansion than they would be in one of the most impregnable prisons in the world?"

SARAH, MONICA AND NEIL were sitting at the little kitchen table. They had just finished eating dinner, which consisted of Ramen noodle soups and tea. They had spent most of the afternoon trying to work out a plan, but the best they could come up with was to have the mercenaries continue to stand by. Sooner or later, Neil was certain, there would be an announcement on the news that would give them an idea of when the rescue mission had its best chance of success.

Neil's computer chimed and he glanced at the screen. "Um, guys? I just got an email from Molly. Take a look." He turned the computer so that they could see the screen.

Neil,

Noah and the rest have been moved. They are on the way to the Petroski Estate near Stolbovaya, about forty miles south of Moscow on the M2. The estate is about four miles west, halfway between Stolbovaya

and Chernetskoye. Latitude 55.2565 longitude 37.3429. AP suggests
sending troops to observe.

Molly

"Damn," Monica said. "There's something fishy about this. Petroski is my man in the president's office. Why in the world is he involved in this?"

"I don't know," Sarah said. "Is this something bad?"

Monica stared at the screen for a moment, then shook her head. "Probably not. Most likely, they were just looking for somewhere to hold these guys and wanted something off the grid. Something that isn't connected directly to the government, you know what I mean? Boris has this estate, it belongs to his family. I'm sure the president is fully aware of it, and probably asked him if they could use it. Let's face it, it's definitely out of the way."

"It is that," Neil said. "I'm calling the soldiers." He picked up his phone and dialed the number Molly had given him before, and Yury's voice answered.

"Orders?"

Neil gave him the coordinates of the estate and told him to take his men and carefully put the place under observation. They were not to take any action until they heard from Neil. The soldier replied that they would leave immediately and report once they had a chance to reconnoiter the place, and the line went dead.

Neal looked to Sarah. "I'm beginning to understand why the Dragon Lady gets the big bucks. I don't want to sit here and plan this out and give orders, I want to be out there. When this goes down, I want to be in the middle of it."

Sarah shook her head. "I know what you mean," she said, "but you and I aren't soldiers, Neil. We are not the combat type. It comes down to having to raid the place, I think it's best that we let the trained professionals handle it."

"She's right," Monica said. "Neil, they've probably got Russian commandos guarding them down there. If it comes down to a gun battle, you want the most experienced professionals possible handling it. It's going to be bad enough already, trying to get them out in the middle of a firefight, but if it has to go down that way..."

Neil shoved his computer away. "I know, I know," he said. "You just got to understand one thing. Noah always came back for one of us. Always. That's kind of our thing, we never leave anyone behind."

"And we won't. But this time, Noah isn't here to lead the rescue. I think it's definitely better to have these people on board and ready to move."

CATHERINE HAD FILLED Peterson in while they were on the way back to the embassy. He had listened without interrupting, only nodding now and then. When she finished, she simply looked at him for a moment. "Well? Is she right?"

"She's not only almost certainly right," Peterson said, "she's absolutely brilliant. She managed to figure all this out on her own, while laying in a hospital room with broken ribs and a collapsed lung. That's pretty damned impressive."

"You agree, then? They probably are planning to kill the Americans?"

"Oh, that was pretty much a certainty already. Either way it goes, those particular individuals are a liability. If it's determined that they genuinely are American spies and assassins, then the government absolutely has to make an example of them. They will be publicly executed, and the Russian state media will continue blasting that they were American agents, no matter how much the Yanks deny it. On the other hand, should it turn out that they were some kind of Russian deep cover agents who pulled off this assassination just to try to bring back the Soviet Union, that could be a disaster. The way this girl worked it out is just about the only possible option the Kremlin would have. The president and the prime minister would have to stand solidly together on it, and they would have to have someone loyal enough to ensure that every person who has seen these people is eliminated. Every guard, every clerk, anyone who ever saw them clearly becomes a potential liability. When they finally parade their well-rehearsed captured agents before the media, they must be absolutely certain that no one who has ever seen them is alive." He turned to Catherine. "Unfortunately, that means that the young lady you just spoke to will probably not live out the night."

Catherine shook her head. "That poor girl. And what sodding kills me is that there's absolutely nothing we can do about it."

"Fear not," Peterson said. "Back home, we might get away with going to the press, but here it wouldn't matter. Either the press would ignore the story completely, or they would check with the Kremlin to see how it should be handled. Either way, nobody learns anything about her or the risks she has taken."

They pulled into the embassy parking lot and Catherine got out of the car. As soon as she got inside and to her office, she picked up the telephone and asked for a secure line. Once she got it, she dialed a special London telephone number and waited. She heard a lot of strange noises as the call was switched from one router to another, but finally it began to ring and was answered.

"Brigadoon investments. How may I direct your call?"

"Allison Peterson, please. London calling via Moscow."

"One moment, please."

Music began to play, but it was cut off almost instantly. Allison's voice came on the line. "London, report."

"Her Majesty was told by somebody that a certain hero of the Royal Family was involved in the Moscow fiasco," Catherine said. "She sent me over here as Queen's Royal Ambassador, to be her eyes and ears. As soon as I arrived, I stumbled across a bit of information that I considered important and decided to check it out. I just spent a fascinating twenty minutes with a brilliant young woman, and I felt it necessary to report to you what I've learned."

Catherine spent the next thirty minutes repeating everything Anya had told her, adding in the things that Ronald Peterson—who was no relation to Allison, incidentally—had contributed.

"Well, this isn't good," Allison said. "London, are you restricted there in any way? Can you move about the city freely, on your own?"

"Of course," Catherine said. "Her Majesty is fully aware of my affiliation with your organization, and understands that there are times when my duty to you must come first. What would you have me do?"

"Hang on a moment." Allison put her on hold and the music began again. Catherine listened to Ray Stevens singing about a squirrel getting loose in a church for a moment, and then Allison returned. "We've got a couple of people on site, there, working on extraction. I'm going to ask you to go and meet with them, tell them everything you just told me. Get a pen, so I can give you the address."

"Got it, I'm ready." She jotted down the address Allison gave her, then listened as Allison told her about the prisoners being moved to the country estate. They talked for another minute about how that move might fit right into the information she had just reported, and then said goodbye. As she stepped out of her office, she spotted Jared Ogilvie, the special attaché who had met her at the airport.

"Jared? Could I see you for a moment?"

Jared smiled and followed her into her office again. "What can I do for the pretty lady from back home?"

"Well, first, stop trying to chat me up, I already said I'm too old for you. Now, I need a way to get around the city without using Alexei. Any notions?"

The smile had disappeared with her admonishment, but it suddenly returned. "Bloody hell," he said in a stage whisper, "are you a bloody secret agent? Need to give our snoop driver a bit of the slip?"

Catherine rolled her eyes. "Jared, grow up. How did you manage to get assigned here, anyway?"

The young man looked like he was at least slightly crushed. "My dad's in parliament," he said. "He thought this would be good for me, look good on my CV, right? Any road, you want a car. We got a few of them, and it just happens that one of the duties of a special attaché is to see that they're taken care of. Now, do you want something fast, or something that won't be noticed?"

"I think something discreet," she said. "I'm not much of one to draw attention to myself."

"Right, then," Jared said. "Got just the thing for you. BMW X6 hybrid. Nearly 500 horsepower, all-wheel-drive, it'll go anywhere you want to go and get you there in a hurry. Lots of them around the city, so nobody will pay much attention. It's right out back, come along and I'll fetch you the key."

Catherine smiled, then reached out and grabbed the young man by clamping his face between both of her hands. Before he knew what was happening, she pulled him close and kissed him on the lips, then let him go quickly. "Okay, show me," she said. "Oh, and one more thing. Can you get me a gun?"

He stared at her for a moment, then broke out into a huge smile. "I knew it, I bloody knew it. You're a bloody secret agent! I've a Glock 17, will that do?" He reached up under the back of his jacket and pulled it out.

Catherine took it from him, pulled the slide back enough to verify that there was a round in the chamber, then dropped it into her purse. "Absolutely perfect," she said. "Now where's the bloody car?"

CHAPTER FIFTEEN

The van had turned off the highway sometime earlier and the road underneath it had become rather rough. The seven prisoners bounced around in the hard plastic seats, but they didn't complain. No one had told them how long the ride would be, but it wasn't like they had any choice in the matter.

Then the van turned again, this time on to what sounded like gravel. They rolled along slowly for about five minutes, weaving around as if it was dodging obstacles, and then it came to a stop. They heard the front doors open, and a moment later, the side door slid back.

Leschinsky and Boris climbed out, but the guards made no move to indicate that the prisoners should get up. They sat where they were for several minutes more, but then Leschinsky came back to the van. He said something in Russian to the guards, then looked at the prisoners.

"All right," he said. "You can come out now. We're going to take you inside the house and show you to your rooms, and then we'll take those chains off. We've brought along some clothing for each of you, so that you can shower and change when you wish. You might want to do so quickly, though, because the cook is preparing to make your dinner."

The guards climbed out of the van and watched as the prisoners followed, and then they started toward the house. They got only a few feet when Leschinsky stopped them, then spoke quickly to one of the guards. The man passed his automatic rifle to one of his comrades, then took out a key and began removing the handcuffs and shackles.

When he was finished, he tossed them inside the van with a clat-ter, then took his weapon back. Leschinsky motioned again and the prisoners, now walking freely, followed him into the house.

They went up to the second floor, where a number of bedrooms were fully furnished. Randy and Jenny, because they were supposed be married, were given one room to themselves. Noah, Marco, Dave, Jim and the other man were each given a room of their own. There was a pair of large paper bags on each bed, and Leschinsky explained that those contained new clothing in each of their sizes and a pair of soft shoes each.

"As I said," Leschinsky said, "you may take the time now to show-er and change clothing. When you are finished, come down and join me in the dining room. Dinner will be served in about an hour, so you should have enough time." He glanced at Jenny and Randy. "De-pending, of course, on how you use it."

He turned and went down the stairs and the guards followed him. Noah watched and saw that they apparently took up stations on the ground floor. He went quickly into his room and checked the windows, and wasn't surprised to see that they were covered with steel bars.

He went back out to the hall, where the rest of them were still milling around. He caught the eye of the extra man and walked up to him. "Sam Winston," he said, holding out a hand.

"Tony VanHorn," the man replied. "I work at the Consulate Gen-eral's office in Vladivostok. Somehow, these idiots have the idea that I was mixed up with this other bunch who blew up some big shot."

"Yeah, well, don't feel too bad. Harold and I were just trying to pick up some spare change, and somebody told us there was lots of money stashed in the office of that prison we just left. Probably not the brightest thing we've ever done."

Jenny carefully maneuvered herself to stand close to Noah, and Randy and Marco got into position around them. With VanHorn still close by and talking, it was unlikely anyone could hear them speak softly to each other.

"How did you end up in the middle of this?" Jenny asked.

Noah kept looking at VanHorn, but spoke at the side of his mouth. "Did you honestly think Neil was going to let us sit back and watch you die? He was freaking out, so I talked the boss into letting us come after you."

"And you got yourself caught," Jenny hissed. "How did that happen?"

"I know you won't believe me, but it was actually part of the plan. The idea was that Harold and I would get inside and try to make contact with you. Obviously, things didn't go according to plan."

"No shit, Sherlock. So, what are we supposed to do now?"

"Sarah and Neil knew what to do. They recruited someone to help, someone with the power it took to get the messages to us in the prison. I don't know what they've got planned out, but just be ready. They'll be coming for us."

"I don't see how," Jenny said. "We don't even know where we are, so it's doubtful they do."

"They'll find out. By now, the boss has figured out who we recruited and will be backing their play. There are probably at least a dozen intelligence agencies watching this situation, so it won't be long before they know where we're at. Just stay ready, because we're going to be leaving. See what you can come up with for improvised weapons, because we're going to need to do our part from the inside when it goes down."

"Will do," she replied. "Just really hope you're right. If they can't find us, we're probably all going to die."

"Can't argue with that," Noah said. "As far as I can tell, everyone from the Moscow area who has seen our faces is here with us. Looks to me like they might be planning to eliminate us and put in some

puppets. They want to eliminate anyone who would know the difference, too."

"Oh, geez, are you always this cheerful? I didn't want you to agree
with me, I wanted you to tell me everything was going to be okay."

"It probably will," Noah said. "Neil seemed pretty determined to
get you back. Sort of reminded me of me, when Sarah was taken."

Jenny didn't say anything else, but took Randy's hand and walked
into their room. Noah pretended to talk to VanHorn for another
moment, then turned and went into his own bedroom. Two minutes
later, he was in the shower and letting the water run as hot as it could
go.

CATHERINE'S GPS DIRECTED her to the address she'd been
given, and she parked the BMW next to the big SUV. A moment later, as she was climbing out of the car, a tall, thin young man stepped
out and looked at her.

"Hello, Neil," she said. "I'm supposed to tell you that Molly sends
her regards."

Neil stared at her for a moment. "And you are?"

"Catherine Potts," she replied. "I'm MI6, but I'm also the E & E
London station chief. I worked with Camelot a couple of times in the
past. The last time was on the Adrian affairs."

"How did you find us?" Neil asked. "We never told Molly where
we were."

Catherine shrugged. "I haven't the foggiest how she knew, but Allison gave me the address. Perhaps you let it slip inadvertently?"

Neil motioned for her to come inside, then held the door open
as she did so. "I'm pretty sure I didn't," he said. "The only thing I can
figure is that she somehow pinpointed my computer. It's got a direct

satellite connection, so I suppose that's possible. I imagine I could figure out how to do it, if I took enough time."

He pointed at Sarah and Monica and introduced them. Catherine shook hands with both of them and then joined them at the table.

"I'll get right to the point," she said. "Have they notified you yet that our people have been moved?"

Sarah nodded. "Yes," she said. "Molly sent us an email about it just a little bit ago."

"Good. Allison filled me in on all of that just a short time ago, just before I left our embassy to come to see you. Now, what's the plan and what can I do to help?"

Neil filled her in on the mercenaries McDermott had sent down, and that they were already on the way to the estate to begin observation. "As soon as we hear back from them on what the situation looks like down there, we'll probably just tell them to go for it. That's what I've got in mind, anyway. Don't get me wrong, I'd rather be down there myself, my girlfriend is in the middle of all this..."

Catherine did a double take. "Wait, what? Your girlfriend?"

"Yeah. My girlfriend is Cinderella."

Catherine's eyes were just about to bug out of her head. "I know I can't possibly have heard you correctly," she said. "I've never met Cinderella, but I've been privy to a couple of her after-action reports. Are you sodding stupid? I mean, I know she's very good at what she does for the organization, but she's a bloody psychopath! I've read where she's literally skinned men alive, starting with their most important bits and cauterizing as she goes along!"

Neil looked like he was about to snap, so Sarah jumped in the middle of the conversation. "Catherine, relax. Yes, she can be pretty violent when she's out in the field, but when she's with Neil—well, she's just about the sweetest little thing you've ever seen. From what I understand, she's just naturally submissive on the inside, but she never gets to let that side of herself out except when she's with Neil." She held out her left hand so that her rings could be seen. "And it's not just them," she said. "Camelot and I got married a few months ago."

Catherine's mouth opened three times, but no sound came out. Finally, she just grinned at them. "Well, I suppose everyone needs some love in their lives." She looked at Neil. "I apologize, Neil. I should never have gone off like that when I don't even know the girl. It was wrong of me, and I hope you'll forgive me."

Neil sniffed, then shrugged. "I'm over it," he said. "When you meet her, you'll understand."

Sarah nodded. "Seriously, she's a very nice girl. Well, when she isn't killing people."

Catherine started to say something, but thought better of it. Instead, she began telling them about Anya and the things she had learned from her. It took almost twenty minutes, and the longer she talked, the more frantic Neil was becoming.

Neil was ready to take off toward Stolbovaya immediately, but his phone rang at that moment. He glanced at it and saw that the call was coming from Yury, then answered quickly. "Yes?"

"We have found the location and have scouted it carefully. There are fifteen soldiers on guard and about a dozen civilians. Some of the civilians seem to be under guard and are not permitted to wander far from the house. I am thinking these are the prisoners."

"I'm thinking you're right," Neil said. "Have you come up with a plan to get them out?"

"There will be resistance," Yury said. "The soldiers appear to be well trained, and they do not expose themselves. We would do best to go in as quietly as we can and take them down one by one. In this way, we can reduce the resistance before we must engage fully."

Monica's phone rang at that moment and she looked at it in surprise. Her eyes went wide, and she looked up at Neil. "It's Boris," she said. She motioned for the others to be quiet and put the phone on speaker. "Go ahead," she said.

"This is Petroski," Boris said. "Because you sent me to see those prisoners, I felt you would want to know that they have been relocated. They are at my family's estate south of Moscow, to keep them safe while we're learning what we can of the stories that surround them."

"Boris, are you alone?" Monica asked.

"Yes. I must speak quickly, though, because it is forbidden to have a phone here. I must go..."

"No, hold on. Boris, I think that you are in danger. I've come across information that makes me believe there's a plan to kill all of these prisoners and replace them with agents who will pretend to be the sleepers. If they do that, anyone who knows the truth will become a liability."

There was silence on the phone for a moment, and then Boris came back. "If you are correct, then I am already dead."

"Not necessarily," Monica said, smiling at Neil. "Go to the prisoners and find the big, blond man. Tell him that his tiny new friend says rescue is coming within the hour. Tell him to make sure his people are prepared, and then I want you to try to get to somewhere safe. It could be a closet, it could be a bathroom, just lock yourself in somewhere. Will you do that for me?"

"I will," Boris said. "I will go and tell them now. I must get off this phone."

The call disconnected and Monica put the phone down. Neil began speaking again.

"Yury, we have someone inside that house who is going to alert the prisoners that rescue is coming. They will do whatever they can from inside to help in the fight. Give them one hour from now before any shooting starts, and then go and get them out."

"One hour," Jacob said. "Yes, sir."

Neil's line also went dead and he put the phone on the table. He looked at the three women and smiled nervously. "Am I the only one here who just plain hates waiting?"

"Oh, no, luv," Catherine said. "I detest it. Look, what happens after?"

"After?" Sarah asked.

"She means after extraction," Monica said. "We are counting on the mercenaries. Supposedly, they have all the transportation and equipment necessary. When they call, we'll set up for them to meet us at my airplane. It's big enough to get us all out of the country, quickly."

"That's assuming there's not an alarm out for them already," Catherine said. "What have you got in mind in that case?"

"Well, the original plan was for Noah to fly us out," Neil said. "There's a small twin-engine plane waiting on a private airstrip, and we can go under radar and get into Poland. The embassy there can get us out on a diplomatic flight, so nobody will actually know what happened to us."

Catherine pursed her lips and looked at him. "Well, I think that would best be an option of last resort. Only I wish there were a way to ensure no alarm goes out, once they've escaped."

ONE OF THE THINGS THE big mansion had over the prison was a library, and Noah had wandered into it. He browsed through the titles, most of which were written in Cyrillic, but he was surprised to find an entire section of books written in English. There were Westerns, classical literature, a few science fiction novels, and even some discount romance novels. Noah chose one of the latter and sat down in an overstuffed chair to read.

Noah had begun reading romance novels when he was in high school. Back then, his best friend Molly was his girlfriend, not so much because of any romantic feelings between them, but because neither of them wanted to actually invest in the effort into a relationship, nor did they want to be ridiculed for not having one. The solution, Molly had explained to Noah, was for them to simply pretend to be dating.

Noah, having no emotions, wasn't really sure how to act with a girlfriend. Molly had explained a few things to him, but she had also given him a stack of tawdry romance novels to read. They helped him understand how to act when other people were around, and he even learned a few things about how to please a girl. He had tried some of them on Molly, who knew exactly what was going on, but still did her best to be surprised each time.

In the last couple of years, since he had met Sarah, he had often thought about the romance books he had read back then, and on more than one occasion he had reminded himself that buying a few might be a good idea. Somehow, though, he just never got around to it. Since there was nothing to do at the moment but wait, he logically felt that it was a perfect opportunity to try to learn some new romantic ideas and techniques.

He heard Boris come into the library, but continued reading. One part of his mind could read while another part kept track of what was going on around him. After a moment, he knew that Boris was simply standing not far from his chair and watching him, so he tucked a finger inside the book and looked up at the Russian.

Boris was carefully standing with his back to the door, so that anyone coming in would not be able to see his face at all. When he didn't speak at first, Noah gave him a quizzical look and cocked his head to one side.

Boris licked his lips nervously and began to whisper. "I have a message for you, from your tiny new friend. In one hour, you and your people must be ready. Rescue is coming, but you must help those who come by doing what you can from inside."

Noah nodded slowly, to show that he understood. Then he winked. "Personally," he said, "I just like reading about all the hot sex scenes in these books. Have you ever tried one?"

Boris' eyes widened for a moment, but then he realized that Noah was only offering camouflage. Neither of them wanted the Colonel or any of the guards to realize what they were talking about, so Boris chuckled and shook his head. "I think I prefer something more adventurous, such as a war story." He turned and walked out of the room, and Noah resumed reading.

He counted off ten minutes in the back of his head and then put the book back on the shelf. He walked out of the library and up the stairs, noting that all of the guards were still staying on the ground floor. Knowing that Colonel Leschinsky was still convinced they were some type of spies, though, he expected the house to be bugged in several different ways. Keeping the guards downstairs, he was sure, was simply an attempt to get them to talk to one another.

Marco was laying on his bed, so Noah walked into his room. "Hey, Harold," he said. "You ready for some fun and excitement?"

Marco looked up at him. "I think chasing ants around the room would be more fun and excitement than anything happening at the moment. What have you got in mind?"

"Oh, I don't know. I was thinking, maybe in about forty-five minutes or an hour, we might try to get some kind of a game going. Maybe something a little challenging, something to rescue us from this boredom. You interested?"

Marco shrugged. "Sure. Anything beats this crap. You want to see if we can get the others involved?"

"Yeah, let's give it a try. I'll tell you what, though, you talk to the little hellcat and her husband. Okay? I'll get the other guys."

Marco laughed, but headed toward the room Randy and Jenny were sharing. Noah glanced through the doorway as he passed it and saw that they were laying on the bed, each of them facing outward with their backs to one another. They both looked around when Marco entered the room and began talking to them, but Noah went on in search of the other men.

He found Jim doing sit-ups in his room. "Hey, man, you got a minute?" Noah asked.

Jim stopped his workout for a moment and looked up. "What do you want?"

"Me and Harold, we thought maybe we'd get a game going. In about forty-five minutes or so, get something exciting happening. Compared to all this boredom, I'd be willing to just darn near go to war."

Jim looked up at him for a moment and Noah saw the recognition in his eyes. He understood what Noah was saying and was ready to do his part.

"Sure, count me in."

"Cool. I'm going to go talk to the others."

YURY LOOKED AT HIS watch. The hour was up and it was time to make his move. He quickly signaled the men in sight and watched as they relayed the signal to the others. He waited until he was sure the message had gotten all the way around the house, then began moving slowly toward it through the trees.

Each of the men was equipped with a silencer, some of the best quality he'd ever seen. He heard a soft *phtt* sound, and then another, and then one of the soldiers guarding the place was just in front of him. He squeezed the trigger once, the cough of the silencer seeming far louder when he was this close, but the man dropped without making a sound into the leafy ground under the trees.

Seven of the soldiers were outside, and each of them died without even having a chance to raise an alarm. It had taken almost six minutes, but now his men were crouched against the outer walls of the house. Slowly, they began moving toward the doors, weapons held carefully in front of them, ready to fire at the slightest sign of a hostile guard.

NOAH DECIDED IT WAS time. According to the only clock he saw in the house, it was approaching nine o'clock in the evening, and the house was relatively quiet. He stepped out of his room and bounced down the stairs.

One of the guards was standing beside the front door, just past the entrance to the library. The man looked past Noah up the stairs, and he glanced behind himself to see Marco, Jenny and Randy following him down. He looked back at the guard and smiled, then stepped into the library.

The other three joined him a moment later, and then he heard more footsteps on the stairs. He raised his voice so that the guard would be able to hear him. "Okay, I looked everywhere for a deck of cards and couldn't find any. I figured what we could do, since we don't have any other games, we can build houses out of books. Whoever builds the biggest house wins, right?"

Jim, Dave, and Tony stepped into the room and Noah went over the idea again. Each of them was enthusiastic in their agreement and they all started pulling books down off the shelves. For a couple of minutes, they looked like a bunch of kids playing in the sand at the beach, but they were just a bit more intense in their efforts.

"Hey, can I use these?" Randy asked. He was holding up a pair of heavy metal bookends, L-shaped sections of iron with the famous Russian hammer and sickle embossed into them. "They could be great for support."

Noah grinned at him. "Hey, yeah," he said. "Are there any more? We could all use them."

"I don't know, you just got to look around." Everybody went back to the bookshelves and four more of the bookends were found. They were exactly like the others, and Noah figured they weighed a good three pounds each. Wielded with force, their corners could become extremely deadly weapons.

Colonel Leschinsky stepped into the library. "What is this?" he asked with a grin. "Some form of American entertainment?"

Noah smiled. "Yeah, you want to play? We are each going to build the biggest house we can out of books. Don't worry, we'll put them all back when we're done."

"Intriguing," Leschinsky said. "I can't help but note that you are using the largest and heaviest books. You are not by any chance thinking of trying to overpower the guards, are you?"

"Oh, I can't honestly say the thought hasn't crossed my mind," Noah said, "but then I remembered that they have guns and I don't. Doesn't exactly seem like an even match."

"No, I can see how it would not. Please, gentlemen and lady, do not be foolish. This incarceration, I believe, is only temporary." He looked around the room at each of them. "May I speak frankly?"

Noah shrugged. "Go for it."

Leschinsky tilted his head back and drew in a deep breath, then looked directly at Noah. "There are those in Russia who believe that a return to the old ways is in our best interest. I am one of those, but I am one of very many. Should it happen that you are in fact agents of Russia who are working toward that goal, I can assure you that you will find in me an ally."

Noah raised an eyebrow. "Your president is behind this?"

Leschinsky shrugged, his grin only slightly subdued. "He is not," he said. "We feel that it is time for a new regime, and this will help us to achieve that goal. All I need to do is ensure that you are loyal Russian agents and the prime minister is ready to act."

Noah snorted. "Geez, and I thought American politics were screwy. Your prime minister wants to bring back the Soviet Union?"

"Many of us feel that this is necessary. The prime minister sees the president as a fool, as do many of our people. A return to Soviet socialism may cause Russia to suffer the ire of the rest of the world for a short time, but it will eventually mean that Russia will be the greatest world power of them all." He looked around at all of them once more. "And you have the opportunity to become heroes, to become part of the greatest nation that ever existed."

Jenny sneered at him. "Look, jackass, how many times do we have to tell you, we're not Russians, and we're not agents of anybody?"

Leschinsky grinned at her and tilted his head to the right as he looked her in the eye. "But, you could be. From this place, I've been ordered to produce proof that the people we arrested and brought here are in fact heroes of Mother Russia. At some point in the next few weeks, it will be necessary for me to introduce those heroes to the world. They will be met with honor and admiration, and will be rewarded with wealth and power. You can become those heroes, no matter who you might have been before."

It took a moment before anyone could speak, and then Noah, Jenny and Marco all tried to talk at once. The men glanced at one another and decided to let Jenny go first.

"Wait a minute," she said. "You're saying that if we, I don't know, confess to being these Russian sleepers, then we can become heroes in this country?"

"Absolutely. You will have luxurious homes, freedom to come and go throughout Russia, you will be heroes of the new Soviet Union that will rise. Now, I ask you, would this not be preferable to being quietly executed and buried in an unmarked grave?"

It was at that moment that there was a knock on the front door of the house, but it was soft. Leschinsky seemed not to notice, but Noah's ears picked it up. He was in the act of placing two large books side-by-side and listened as the guard on the door turned and opened it.

The guard had undoubtedly expected to see one of his compatriots standing there, and so he was not prepared when the slim bayonet suddenly went up under his chin and pierced its way into his brain. He made not a sound as Yury and one of his men caught him, lifted him and carried him off the front porch, but Noah caught the sudden silence. He jerked his head up and looked toward the door, a move that was guaranteed to catch Leschinsky's attention, and it succeeded.

Leschinsky instinctively turned his eyes toward the door, and Noah took two steps in that brief second and brought a pair of the iron bookends together as hard as he could on the sides of the Colonel's head. Leschinsky dropped straight to the floor, dead even before his knees gave out, and Noah tossed one of the bookends to Marco as he knelt beside the fallen colonel.

A quick search of the man's body turned up a Grach MP-443 pistol, and Noah snatched it up and tossed the other bookend to Tony VanHorn as Yury and his men came streaming through the front door. The whole thing was over in a matter of seconds, as the silenced SR-3M submachine guns spat out their quiet death.

The mercenaries searched the house quickly, and there was one last commotion when one of them opened the closet and found Boris Petroski sitting cross-legged on the floor. "No, no," he called out, "I am not one of them. I was told to tell these prisoners to be ready for you, and I did so."

Dragged out of the closet, Boris was hustled down to the library where Noah and the rest were still gathered. Yury pointed at him and looked at Noah. "This one?"

"He was the one who let us know you were coming," Noah said. "I think he's on our side."

"Oh, yes," Boris said. "I work with—with someone who seeks your safety. May I call him?"

"Let me guess," Noah said. "This person talks to you through something that makes the voice sound mechanical?"

Boris looked at him for a moment, then nodded. "Yes."

"Go ahead, then," Noah said, "but put it on speakerphone. I want to be able to hear it."

Boris looked at the pistol in Noah's hand, then nodded vigorously as he took out his phone. It took him a moment to put the battery back inside, and then he powered it on and dialed a number. As Noah had said, he put it on speaker.

"Boris," came the familiar distorted voice. Noah reached out and took the phone.

"He's here, but this is the man who visited at your home. Our location has just been cleared, and I wanted to check in to see if there are any new developments."

Noah heard other voices in the background, but the distortion made it difficult to tell who they were for sure.

"We are discussing the matter of immigration," Monica said. "How many will be in your party?"

"There are seven of us here, plus two with you, for a total of nine. We picked up another guest during our little vacation."

"Have your transportation take you directly to the rental desk at the usual location. I will have accommodations ready when you arrive, and the rest of your party will be with me."

"I need to delay that," Noah said. "We've come across some information that needs to be reported back to our headquarters. I think it's quite possible we may not be finished with our visit, yet."

Monica hesitated for a couple of seconds. "So be it. Your technical man will send coordinates to the head of your transportation team. They will bring you to us, and we'll discuss these matters privately. Let me speak with Boris, please."

Noah handed the phone to Boris, who stared at it nervously. "This is Boris."

"Under the circumstances, I wonder whether it is safe for you to return to your employment. Would you like me to extract you?"

Boris looked at the armed men surrounding him and swallowed nervously. "It appears to me that the person who brought us here was acting against the interests of my employers. I believe that I will be in a unique position to bring that fact to light, and that this may strengthen my future."

"Very well," Monica said. "You will remain there. Give my friends one hour and then call for help. Be certain to make it clear that you were a victim and managed to survive only by hiding. The prisoners were extracted from your location by Russian soldiers from a rival faction and you believe they hope to use them in propaganda against your employer. Do you understand?"

"I understand perfectly," Boris said. "As always, I shall do as you say."

The line went dead. Boris turned off the phone and put it into his pocket, then looked at Noah. "I will do as he has said," he said. "I will raise no alarm for one hour. Will that be sufficient time?"

Noah looked at Yury, who nodded. "It'll be fine," he said.

CHAPTER SIXTEEN

A large truck drove up to the house and Noah and the rest were led into it. The back of the truck was fitted with seats similar to a bus, and there was plenty of room for all of them as well as the mercenaries. Yury smiled as he closed the doors; the operation had come off without a hitch and he had not lost a single man.

The truck began moving and Noah leaned back in his seat to relax. Everything that had happened was running through his mind, and he was mentally preparing for the report he would make to Allison.

In Noah's opinion, Jenny's mission should have come off without a problem. The plan was perfect and well executed, but somehow the FSB had gotten onto them. While it was possible that they genuinely stumbled across them because of finding the two security men, Noah had the distinct feeling that there was more to the story.

Those security men would not have been on the boat with the Kalashnikovs, so it was unlikely they would be considered missing so soon. Since their charges would have been out on the ocean for the day, they would have almost certainly been free to do whatever they wanted. Even after the explosion took place, their absence shouldn't have been noticed until late in the day, even the following day. Somehow, the FSB had been notified that they were eliminated.

Logically, the only explanation was that the watchers were being watched. Someone realized that they had not left their rooms and made a phone call, but who would have been paying attention to them? The only answer Noah could come up with was that they were somehow involved in the faction that was behind the move to bring back the Cold War, but that would mean that Jenny and the men were only targeted because they were Americans.

Jenny had told Noah about the witness who claimed to have seen her leaving Khrushchev's room, but she was adamant that no one had seen her. "No other door on that floor was opened," she said. "Not even a crack, seriously. Nobody could have seen me leaving that room, and yet somehow they knew I left there in a man's shirt with my dress rolled up under my arm."

Noah believed her. They were trained to notice even tiny details that could compromise them, and he was certain she would have known if any door within view had been open at all.

Looking at the problem from a different angle, Noah considered the possibility that she was seen elsewhere in the shirt, with the dress under her arm, and that the investigators had simply concluded that she had left Khrushchev's room that way. Had Dimitrovitch actually said she was seen leaving the room? Or had he only said that someone saw her wearing the shirt? Noah had not been present for that interview, but he would be willing to bet on the latter.

Now, he could add in the information that the Prime Minister of Russia was actively working against the president in order to eliminate the freedoms and democracy they had achieved since the fall of the Soviet Union. A return to the old Soviet policies and empirical practices would undoubtedly mean problems for Russia with the rest of the world, but Leschinsky might have been right. It was quite possible that when the dust settled, the new Soviet State would be far more powerful than Russia alone had ever been.

Colonel Leschinsky had been a high-ranking member of the SVR, and that would mean that there were probably others in the organization who also supported this radical faction. If the SVR was involved, then there were undoubtedly many members of the military who would support the idea, as well.

Noah considered the implications for the rest of the world if the USSR were to be reborn. There were so many current moves toward globalization, but the friction that such a move would cause would most likely set those plans back by decades. The new union would be too great a threat, simply on the basis of the fact that any of the former member states who returned or were subjugated would simply mean a massive influx of new soldiers for the Russian military. It wouldn't be long before Russia would be capable of mounting an army that could counter any attempt by the UN or other nations to keep them from attempting world domination.

The Cold War would almost certainly be resumed just about where it left off. The new union would be hard at work rebuilding its own nuclear arsenal, just to make sure that other world powers like the United States and the U.K. were not stronger. China, Japan and almost every other country would be cautious, because they would not want to risk the possibility of war with such a massive military machine.

No matter how he looked at it, this was an extreme danger to the peace and security of the United States and probably the rest of the world. For that reason, Noah felt that he should get this information back to Allison so that she could pass it on to the CIA, Homeland Security, the NSA, and whoever else might need to weigh in on it.

The next question was what could be done about the problem. Political organizations were like the fabled hydra, and cutting off the head usually only resulted in several more springing up. Countering this threat would take more than simply eliminating its figureheads. Noah needed to turn this over to the think tanks and geniuses whose job it was to make such decisions.

Which meant he could stop thinking about it. He let himself relax and was asleep a couple of minutes later, comfortably enjoying the rocking of the truck as it rolled up and down the road.

He woke instantly when the truck came to a stop and followed the rest out the back door quietly. He guessed that it was probably approaching ten thirty, which was late enough for it to be quite dark on a nearly moonless night like this one. He saw that they were in the yard of a house, and he saw Sarah and Neil coming out the door as he approached it.

Sarah saw Noah and ran into his arms, throwing her arms around his neck and covering his cheek with kisses. Neil and Jenny were in a similar position a few feet to the right.

"Oh, Noah," Sarah said. "Oh, God, I was so scared. I don't know what I would've done if..."

"I'm back," he said. "Everything worked out, and that's all that's important. Come on, let's get inside. I've got to get a report off as quickly as possible."

She let go of his neck and put an arm around his back as they walked together to the house. "Okay, what's going on? Monica wants to get us all out of the country as quickly as possible, and I can't say I think that's a bad idea."

"I'm afraid that's going to be up to someone above our pay grade. I stumbled across some information that I'm not sure anyone else has, and it could be about the most important bit of intel yet. I need to go over it with all of you and then we'll make our report together."

The truck started up and drove away and the newly released prisoners piled into the house. Jim Marino was at the tail of the line and closed the door as he entered. Noah saw Monica standing in the kitchen doorway and nodded to her, then spotted Catherine Potts. He gave her a nod as well, then turned to the assembled crowd in the living room.

"Okay," he said. "Neil, I need you and Jenny to join us in the kitchen. The rest of you, find somewhere to sit and take a load off. We've got to make a report back home, and then we may have to wait a while before we're ready to leave. Tony, come here. Tony, this is my wife, Sarah. Sarah, this is Tony VanHorn. He's CIA, he got caught up in this because he was picked to carry weapons to Jenny and her team. The FSB in Vladivostok was able to identify him, so he's coming in from the cold."

Noah didn't bother to introduce him to Monica and Catherine, but told him to make himself comfortable. He took Sarah, Neil and Jenny into the kitchen and joined Monica and Catherine at the table.

"Monica, I appreciate you coming to help. I figured, under the circumstances, you were the only person outside any government agency who might be able to help figure this out and accomplish what we needed."

"My pleasure," Monica said. "Believe it or not, it sort of felt nice to be a good guy for once."

"One day," Catherine said, "somebody is going to tell me the story behind this. You've got this little bitty woman sitting here, and she seems to know more about what's going on in the world than any of my superiors, in either country."

"Sorry," Noah said. "I'm not sure how MI6 rates a security clearance, but I don't think yours is going to be high enough to know the story behind Monica. Just be glad you've met her, and be even more glad you lived through it."

He looked around the table at all of them. "Here's the situation as I see it," he said. "The reason Jenny and her team got captured is because they probably interrupted another attempt on Kalashnikov's life, a genuine one. Somebody was watching the security men who were watching him, because they shouldn't have been listed as missing so quickly. With Kalashnikov out on the water, they would have been able to stand down and take it easy for the day. Nobody should have realized they were off the job until late that night, maybe even the next day. For them to be under surveillance, someone was probably planning to eliminate them, anyway. When the boat blew up and they were already dead, whoever was behind that must have simply chosen Jenny and the guys to blame because they were Americans. I suspect it was pure chance that they actually picked the right people."

"You'll forgive me if that's not a lot of consolation, right?" Jenny said. "I'm still trying to figure out how they knew I was the one who killed those guys."

"Well, it could be that whoever was watching them actually saw you do it. It occurs to me as I think about it now, there might have been surveillance devices inside those rooms. We're talking about a very powerful group of people, involving high-ranking officers of the FSB, the SRV, probably the military—and I've learned that it's all coming together under the direction of the Russian prime minister. The plan was to stage an assassination and use it to embarrass Russia badly enough that she could justify rebuilding the USSR. The people organizing it are aware that this would cause some temporary problems for Russia, but they've come to the conclusion that it would be worth it because the new Soviet Union would be far more powerful than it ever was before. Their plan is to build a whole new union based on Soviet principles, but to make it the world's premier superpower."

"Holy mother of God," Monica said. "Noah, the implications are staggering. If the PM is involved, this thing's got to be huge."

"I agree, especially since a major part of the plan is to embarrass and get rid of the president. Done properly, this whole fiasco about sleeper agents and such could destroy his party. The only political party with any power left would be whichever one is behind this plot, the people holding the carrot and the stick. By using a little bit of carrot and a lot of stick, it wouldn't take them more than a year or so to have a new union put together. The Kremlin would command one of the largest standing armies the world has ever known, and if they decide to exercise any kind of force, things could get pretty dicey for the rest of the major powers in the world. The U.S., the U.K., China, you name it, the Kremlin would be capable of handling just about any-body."

"I'm making notes," Neil said. He had opened his computer and was typing like crazy the whole time Noah was talking.

"Good." Noah turned to Catherine. "Catherine, first tell me why you're here."

She snorted. "I'm here because Her Majesty found out from someone that you were in a pickle. She appointed me QRA, Queen's Royal Ambassador, and sent me over to find out just what in the bloody hell you Yanks were doing. When I got here, one of our blokes told me enough to make me worry, so I called Allison and she filled me in. Since I was already here, she thought I might as well come join the girls and Neil to see if I could be of any help."

"When you see her again, please give her my thanks. Now, you've just heard everything I said. Can you tell me what you believe the U.K.'s take would be on a new Soviet Union?"

"We'll be sodding buggered, that's what," she said. "The USSR was one of our greatest enemies, and most of the world would be shocked if they knew how often we came close to war with them. I mean, it would be like David and bloody Goliath, wot? Even today, it's seemed prudent to keep a couple of Trident submarines close enough to launch a strike if we had to. If this new union is anything like the old one, we'll be expanding our nuclear arsenal just as bloody hard and fast as we can."

Noah looked at Monica. "What's your opinion?"

"A new Soviet Union would undoubtedly adopt an expansionist policy. It wouldn't stop at just reclaiming their own member states, they would want more. They would almost certainly sweep down through Asia into the Middle East and Africa. Afghanistan, Iraq, Iran, all of them would fall. I'm not sure what they would try to do with Israel, but Saudi Arabia would almost certainly end up one of their members. If they get down into Africa, the Kremlin could end up controlling ninety percent of the hemisphere. What we do end up with is a world that was divided into two major philosophies, socialism in the East and democracy in the West. The two are mutually exclusive, so I wouldn't give it five years before we were looking at World War III."

"And in all your travels, you've never run across this plot before?"

"Not even a whisper. Believe me, if even one major intelligence agency had heard of this, I'd know it. This is the kind of thing that would have rattled around every intelligence HQ that came across it, there's no way I could've missed it."

"That's what I was thinking. Now, if you had run across it before, what would you have done?"

"Well, this would certainly have fallen under the heading of oppressing the people. I'd have been looking for a way to kill it, obviously. That's what's going to have to happen, now. We've got to find a way to kill this thing before it can get any bigger."

"I don't suppose you can speculate on how that might be done."

"Well," Monica said, "you said the prime minister is actively involved. I don't know if it would actually kill it, but we could definitely put a crimp in its operation if we can convince the president and his party that this is a genuine threat. Some quiet threats of a potential preemptive attack, especially if we could claim support from a few other countries, would cripple it for a long time, at the very least."

Noah looked at Neil. "Are you getting all this?"

"You better believe it. I'm summarizing a bit, but I'm making sure that all the major points are in here."

"Okay. Do whatever you gotta do to get that to Allison, and send a copy to Molly. Sarah, where's my phone?"

Sarah jumped up and ran to the bedroom, coming back a moment later with Noah's iPhone. He took it and powered it on, then touched the icon that would dial headquarters. Both his phone and the ones at headquarters had built-in encryption that would prevent anyone from listening in on the conversation.

"Brigadoon Investments, how may I direct your call?"

"Camelot calling for Allison Peterson."

"Cam—one moment, please."

The hold music started, but vanished almost instantly. "Camelot, report," Allison said.

"I am pleased to report that the rescue mission has been implemented, with all team members present and accounted for. We also picked up a stray, a CIA operative named Anthony VanHorn. He was burned in the investigation into Cinderella. We are still in country at the moment, but we've come across some other information that I feel is critical. Neil has just sent that information to you and Molly."

"I'm looking at it now," Allison said. "Good God, Camelot, how do you fall into these things?"

"It's a very long story, so we need to save that for when I get back. I felt this was important enough that we needed to get the report off to you now, so that we are still in country if you want us to take any kind of action while we're here."

"All right. I'm going to call Molly and now and we'll go over all this, then see who else we need to share with. I'll be back in touch within a few hours. What time is it there?"

"Almost eleven P.M."

"Then get some sleep. From what I'm seeing in this report, we're going to have to make something happen pretty quickly."

"We'll be ready." He ended the call and laid the phone on the table, then looked at the others. "We all need to get some rest. I've got a feeling our mission has only really just begun."

MOLLY CAME INTO THE office and took a seat. She wasn't surprised to find Donald Jefferson already there.

"Have you read it?" Allison asked.

"Twice, already," Molly said. "This is a potential disaster in the making, you know that, right?"

"Of course I do. Donald, opinion?"

"I have to agree with the things that Monica said," Jefferson replied. "I think she might be a little optimistic on her projection of World War III. I'd be surprised if it took more than three years to get there."

"I've emailed this off to Nick Weber at the CIA, John Hardy at NSA, Paul Karcher at Homeland Security, the joint Chiefs and the president, with all references to Monica redacted, of course. I expect the calls to start coming in in the next few minutes, and I'd like to have something to say by the time they do. Talk to me, people. What do you recommend in this situation?"

"If we could identify," Molly said, "which of the primary Russian politicians are involved, I'd suggest a surgical removal. The problem is that the only one we know for sure about is the prime minister himself, and assassinating him could fall right into the hands of the people behind it all. He'd become a martyr, most likely, and we don't need to give them something that powerful."

"Agreed," Jefferson said. "As noted, the point of this thing is to embarrass President Feodor, make him resign or get him ousted. I think we need to try to turn the tables. If we could turn this into some kind of embarrassment for the prime minister, it should strengthen Feodor's party considerably."

"That's a wonderful idea, but how do we go about it?" Allison asked. "And would it really have any effect on the rest of the action behind this?"

"No, it probably wouldn't," Molly said. "I'm sure they've got someone else ready to take over as the primary figurehead, in any case.

I think the best move might be to approach the president himself, let him know everything we know about this and see what he can do about it internally."

"Yes, Monica mentioned that. She also suggested some kind of preemptive strikes. Any idea what she might be talking about?"

"I took it to mean a potential invasion," Molly said. "She mentioned getting other countries to back it up; if these plans can be exposed without damaging the president in the process, it's possible we could insert a peacekeeping force, maybe even from the UN. Barring that, I would say we need to find intelligence on the leadership and start going after them directly."

"Yes, but where? I wouldn't have a clue how to start looking for that kind of intelligence, would you?"

"Actually, I think I would. I think the key is sitting right there with Noah at the moment. Monica, when she was doing all her nefarious little things, had an awful lot of people under her control. If anyone could find a lead on who is running this thing, I think it would be her."

Allison chewed her bottom lip for a moment. "I think you're right," she said, "but we have to handle that pretty quietly. Most of the government isn't ready to trust her very far, and I can't really blame them. We'd basically be turning her loose again, and that might be dangerous both politically and personally."

"Ask the president," Jefferson said. "He's never been one to back down from a fight, and he's always willing to use whatever tools are available. I think this might be a good time to defer to his authority."

Allison started to speak, but the phone on her desk buzzed at that moment. She reached over and hit the speaker button. "Yes?"

"It's the president on line one," came the receptionist's voice.

Allison reached over and hit the appropriate button. "Mr. President," she said. "I take it you got my message?"

"I got it. You want to tell me just what on Earth it is?"

"There's a faction inside Russia that is trying to bring back a lot of the Cold War policies, reinstate the Soviet Union or form a new one. The goal seems to be to implement a major expansionist, possibly even an empire-building policy. This whole recent debacle about our people being arrested seems to have been engineered with the goal of planting the seeds of that possibility in the minds of the people. It's also very embarrassing for the current president of Russia, and since we now know the prime minister is one of the top people in this faction, we're looking at quite a potential threat."

"What does the CIA have to say about this?"

"I haven't heard back from them yet," Allison said. "I sent it to Nick Weber, he is the Deputy Director of Analysis over there now. He and I go way back, and I know I can trust him not to let it get into the wrong hands."

The phone buzzed again. "Hold one, Mr. President," Allison said. She hit the hold button, then tapped the button for the receptionist. "Go ahead."

"John Hardy on line three and Nick Weber on line four."

"Tell Hardy I'm on the phone with the president and I'll call him back." She reached out and punched the button for line four. "Nick? What you think of that?"

"I think I'm beginning to believe the end of the world is coming," Weber said. "Where on Earth did you get all this?"

"Camelot," she said. "Hang on, I've got the president on another line and I'm going to patch you in."

She pushed a couple of buttons, then scowled at the phone. "Mr. President?"

"Yes, I'm here."

"Good, I managed to do it. I've brought Nick Weber in with us."

"Afternoon, Mr. President," Weber said.

"Hello, Nick. What's your take on all of this?"

"Sir, I think that this is something we should have known about months ago, and I can't come up with a reason why we didn't. I'm trying to figure out just what might be a good plan of action, but short of identifying the key players and eliminating them, I'm not sure what to suggest."

"Nick," Allison said, "did you see the suggestion about going directly to the president over there? If we could get him to publicly oppose this faction, and turned as much of the intelligence community as possible onto identifying those key players, we might have a good chance of at least stopping them from any immediate action."

"The only problem I see with that," Weber said, "is that President Feodor is a bit of a wet noodle. He talks a good game when he's trying to rally voters, but he doesn't really have much of a backbone. As much as I hate to say it, it looks to me like he was deliberately supported for election so that he could be used in this way. Once he got into office, he appointed Viktor Petrov as prime minister, so he had to have believed at the time that Petrov was going to back his policies. Now, looking at things from the angle of this information, I'd say there's a pretty good chance that the Russian rumor mill is already running crazy with the idea that the Kremlin is going to start attacking the former member states of the USSR. If Petrov can actually convince Feodor to start talking about it—you know, he has made the comment in the past that the USSR was actually a good thing—it will completely destroy any support he had. He wouldn't actually have to invade a single country, but even the thought of it would be enough to make most of them gear up for border wars."

Allison scowled. "Then how in the hell are these people trying to use this to bring the Soviet Union back? If the countries that used to be part of it are going to see this as a threat, they'll never get any of them to agree."

"I disagree," Weber said. "If Russia tries to force them back into membership, then no, it's doomed to failure. On the other hand, if the president and his party are discredited, then it leaves the prime minister a perfect opportunity to suggest that a voluntary reorganization of the Soviet Union would only make all of the countries stronger. He has to at least say that he's going to preserve their individual democracies and sovereignties, but once they sign on, there aren't many of them that would have enough independence to be able to stand up to whatever he wanted. He accomplishes the same thing he wants people to believe the president is trying to do with threats, and he can do it without even an angry word."

"This is giving me a headache," said the president. "It sounds like a schoolteacher I knew once. She would stand in front of the class and threaten all of us with failing grades if we didn't do something she wanted, then promise us all some kind of treat if we did it. You never knew from one minute to the next what it was she really wanted, because you were too busy trying to figure out if you were going to get a swat or a cookie."

"Sir, I don't think that analogy applies," Weber said. "It's more like—the people in those countries are going to be angry that the government of Russia, whom they see personified in the president, is going to try to force them to come under its dominion once again. They'll be so angry that, once he is kicked out of office, the prime minister will be able to say, 'hey, look, the bad guy is gone. Come join up with us and help make sure no more bad guys get into office.' It's not so much a matter of rewarding them as telling them they can have the power to prevent such a thing from ever happening again. It's a lie, of course, because once they have joined, then they've pledged their military forces and resources to support whatever Mother Russia wants. If Mother Russia decides it wants to build military bases in Kazakhstan, then its president won't be able to prevent it. Same thing applies to every other country involved, but a smooth operator like Petrov could probably pull it off."

"Nick," Allison said, "what about quiet threats of military action? If we go directly to the president, and let him know that we are prepared—and by we, I'm saying the U.S. and its allies—that we are prepared to initiate military action to prevent the reunification of the USSR, would he be able to control enough resources to make sure we don't have to go that route?"

"I'd say no, and here's why. Petrov is going to have a lot of the ministers in his pocket. If Feodor does anything at all to try to limit Petrov's power or curtail his activities, those ministers are going to pull all of their support. Without them, the president is pretty much helpless. It wouldn't take much for the ministers to orchestrate his downfall, I'm afraid."

"Then the only real option we have is to find a way to identify the people who actually have power in this faction. You got any clues on that?"

"Well, not yet," Weber replied. "But bear in mind, I have only just put some of my top people on looking at recent Russian events and traffic from this perspective. They should be able to figure out who's involved, but it's going to take a little time."

"Nick," the president interjected, "how much time are we talking about? And while we're at it, how much time do you think we have before this blows up in our faces?"

"Mr. President, a best-guess estimate on how long it will take my people to figure out who's involved would probably come in around 6 to 9 months. As for how long we got before this faction might try to implement their plans, I'm going to say no more than a year, and probably less than six months. Just the fact that they were ready to launch an operation of this magnitude on such short notice, that tells me there is a lot more going on than we know about."

"So we could be talking about seeing this happen even before we know who's involved?"

"I'm afraid that is a possibility, Mr. President."

Allison cleared her throat. "Gentlemen, I'm going to make a suggestion. Mr. President, Nick Weber is actually on the advisory board
that is overseeing the activities of Monica Lord. It's now necessary for
me to reveal to you that Monica Lord is currently sitting in Moscow
with two of my teams. When Team Cinderella was arrested, I authorized Team Camelot to conduct an off-books rescue mission. In the
course of that mission, Camelot felt it necessary to allow himself to
be captured and arrested, and then made arrangements on his own
to temporarily sever our monitoring capability on Monica so that his
team could recruit her assistance. From what I understand, she has
been quite invaluable to them, but I think she may be even more
invaluable to us right now. While her methods may be deplorable,
she nevertheless has the most extensive network of double agents the
world has ever known. Many of them are in Russia, and some are in
positions of great power, I'm sure. I propose that we ask her to use
those agents of hers to try to identify these oft-mentioned key players."

"Toward what end, Allison?" asked the president.

"Well, Mr. President, I just explained that I currently have two
full teams sitting in Moscow. While assassinating Petrov would probably turn him into a martyr, chipping away at his power base would
cripple him. There are only seventeen ministers, but each of them has
several deputies, and then there are the heads of about thirty government agencies. Altogether, we are probably talking about less than a
hundred individuals who hold true power in Russia. If ten percent of
them could be quickly eliminated through assassination, most of the
rest would quickly and quietly desert the prime minister, rather than
risk getting killed. Present company excluded, most politicians aren't
real keen on giving their lives for what they believe in."

"Don't worry about hurting my feelings, Allison," the president
said. "Nick? What do you think about what she just said?"

Nick Weber was quiet for several seconds, then cleared his throat. "Mr. President, I'd have to say I believe that's the best suggestion I could imagine at this time. I'm not even going to imply that I'm a fan of the idea, because I'm not. I don't trust Monica Lord, especially when we can't look over her shoulder. However, Allison is correct in saying that she has the biggest network of double agents in the world. Had she been working for me all this time, I would've found a lot better ways to use them, but I don't even have access to a list of them, yet."

"Well, do you think it would be better to bring her back and demand that list? Let someone on our end be the one giving the orders?"

"Mr. President, at this point, I feel that the best person to be pulling Monica's strings is Allison Peterson. We are actually talking about strategic assassinations of functioning governmental officials. I don't think there's anyone else I would trust to make the right calls."

"Allison, that's good enough for me. I've known Nick for about six years and I trust his judgment. I'm going to leave this in your hands, but I'll be waiting to hear from you on how it turns out."

The president dropped off the call without another word, and Weber said goodbye a moment later. Allison turned off the phone and looked at Molly and Jefferson.

"Well, that shit didn't go anywhere near the way I wanted it to go."

CHAPTER SEVENTEEN

"Camelot," Noah said as he answered the phone. It had wakened him instantly when it rang, and the time display said it was almost 7 A.M.

"It's Allison. Camelot, I'm afraid I'm about to dump a lot of responsibility on to you. I've been going over this all evening and I've spoken with the president, with CIA, Homeland Security, National Security Agency, everybody I can think of."

"Yes, ma'am," Noah said.

"You've got Monica over there. It's time you put her to work. Out of all the people she has managed to blackmail, there's bound to be quite a few in Russia. We need to know as much as we possibly can about who the key players are in this faction that wants to bring back the Soviet Union. Specifically, we need the names of any of the ministers or agency heads who are involved, any of the wealthy elite, anybody whose name would be recognized in the news over there. Have her gather that information as quickly as possible and then select some of them for termination. Notify me of who you choose, but I'm giving you blanket authorization to use your judgment. The idea is to undermine the prime minister as thoroughly as we can. If being part of this faction is going to cost them their lives, most of these people will abandon it in a heartbeat. What I want you to do is give them every reason to believe that the price truly is that high."

"Yes, ma'am," Noah said. "I'll get her on it right away."

"Very good. Report when you have opportunity." The line went dead.

"Allison?" Sarah asked beside him. The little house had only two bedrooms, and she had commandeered one for herself and Noah.

Neil and Jenny got the other one, so everyone else was camped wherever they could, except for Monica and Catherine. Monica was curled up in a comfortable chair, while Catherine was sleeping on the small sofa.

"Yes. She wants me to have Monica use all of her resources in Russia to find out the names of any high-ranking or important people involved in this plot. Once we have a list, I'm to start choosing some of them for assassination. The idea is simply to make them all afraid that being part of that will get them killed, so that the prime minister doesn't have the support he thinks he's got."

"Okay," Sarah said tiredly. "I will start the coffee."

Noah pulled his pants and shirt on and padded out to the living room in his bare feet. He gently tapped Monica on the shoulder until she woke, then motioned for her to follow him into the kitchen. It took him only a minute or two to explain what Allison wanted, and she nodded sleepily.

"You've already met one of my people," she said. "Boris Petroski; he actually works for the prime minister, so he should be a good source. And she's right, I've got several others."

"I'm just curious," Sarah said as she sat down at the table, "but how do you keep track of them all? You must have hundreds, right?"

Monica grinned. "Over a thousand. And no, before you ask, I haven't personally been involved in getting what I need to have control over them. In a lot of cases, I simply found out about their particular proclivities from someone else. It's amazing what people will tell you when they think you can destroy their lives by sending an email."

"Good grief. Do you keep a little black book with all their names and phone numbers or something?"

Monica shook her head. She tapped her temple and said, "Nope. It's all up here. That way, nobody can get it without my consent. It really isn't that hard to remember things, if you try. I read a book on how to memorize long lists many years ago and I never forgot it. No pun intended."

Sarah just shook her head.

When the coffee was ready, they each got a cup and sat down at the table again. By then it was well after seven, and Monica took out her phone. She looked at it for a moment, tapped a particular icon, then dialed a number and set it to speaker.

"Good morning, Boris," she said. "I trust you made it home safely?"

"Yes, about an hour ago. It has been an interesting night. I handled everything the way you wanted, so there does not seem to be any problem."

"That's very good. I have something new, however. I understand you overheard some of what was said before everything got exciting last night. I was speaking of the reference to your employer and his plans."

"I heard it," Boris said. "Is this of interest to you?"

"Yes. I need you to find me the names of those who are high in its ranks. Ministers, other politicians, heads of different agencies, businessmen and -women, anyone involved in those plans."

There was silence on the line for a moment, and then Boris asked nervously, "Is it going to be bad for me if I am on that list?"

Monica slapped a hand over her mouth to keep from laughing out loud. She got herself under control in just a couple of seconds and turned back to the phone. "You are safe, as long as I can trust you. That's how it has always been. Do you have such a list already?"

"There is one. It is not here at home, but at my office. I was planning to stay at home today, but..."

"Boris, get me that list. You know how to send it to me. How soon can you get there and send it off?"

Boris sighed. "You will have it within the hour. May I say that I was forced into this thing. It is not something that I would have wanted."

"Good for you. Give me the list." She cut off the call and looked at Noah. "Damn, that was easy."

"Assuming he has a reasonably complete list, it was very easy. On the other hand, you said he works for the prime minister? I can imagine that it would have been hard to keep this whole thing secret from him in any case. It was probably safer to recruit him than to risk him finding out on his own."

"I'm just curious," Sarah said, "but do you think this guy might be in danger? I mean, wasn't he sent out there to die, as well?"

"That's possible," Monica said. "The way I'm reading it right now, he probably wasn't actually in any danger. If he's privy to the prime minister's involvement in this thing, he was probably there to act as Petrov's eyes and ears."

"I hope so. It'd be a shame if he got to his office only to find out he was going to be arrested and executed."

Monica scowled at her. "I think you've been around Noah too long, you're such a pessimist."

"I'm not a pessimist," Sarah said. "I just naturally expect things to go wrong."

An hour later, Monica asked Noah to wake Neil. She had a special web server set up that allowed for people to send her documents untraceably, but she would need Neil's computer to get to it. Noah went down the hall and tapped on the bedroom door, and Jenny called out for him to come in.

He opened the door and found the two of them cuddled up together on the bed. Neil was awake and looked up at him.

"Need you and your computer in the kitchen," Noah said. "Monica needs to retrieve a document from online, somewhere."

"Okay," Neil said. "I'll be there in a minute."

Noah stepped out and pulled the door shut behind him and immediately heard giggling. He went back to the kitchen and sat down and noted that it was almost ten minutes later before Neil finally showed up. Jenny was with him, and both of them were smiling.

Neil set his computer up on the table and opened it, then slid it over to Monica. "I've entered all the right passwords, so it's ready for you."

Monica stared at it for a minute, then looked at Neil. "Where's the browser?"

Neil groaned, then reached across and pulled the computer back over to himself. He touched an icon on the screen and something that looked a little like a web browser opened up. He pushed it back over toward her again.

"Sorry," he said. "I forgot you wouldn't know that. I don't trust any of the commercially available browsers, so I wrote my own."

Monica grinned. "Not a problem. Maybe one of these days when you're not too busy, you can help me with some of my own Internet security issues."

Neil shook his head. "Call geek squad," he said. "You can't afford me."

Monica typed in a URL and then entered information into several fields of the form that appeared. It took only a couple of minutes, and then she clicked on a link and a scanned page opened up. It was a list of names, and as she looked down it, her eyes went wide and her mouth came open.

"Holy cow," she said. "Look at this. All but two of the ministers are involved, almost all of the department heads—Noah, he's got half the government behind him. No, more like three-quarters of it."

Noah slid his chair over and looked at the list, which was headed "Committee for Restoration of the Communist Party." There were fifteen senior ministers on the list, more than three dozen deputy ministers, twenty-six agency heads and about a hundred other names. Noah didn't recognize any of them.

"Do you know who any of those people are?" he asked.

"Oh, yeah," Monica said. "Serge Chernov is Minister of Defense, Ivan Grichkin is minister of transport, Alexander Trepov is the finance minister, Boris Stolpin is minister of agriculture... A lot of important names on here."

"Let Neil copy that list," Noah said. "I need him to start locating some of these people. Jenny, you and I are going to have to start taking them out. We need to start with the ministers, I think. They'll have the most impact on the prime minister, and then we can move on to some of the others if it's necessary."

Jenny grinned. "I'm ready when you are," she said.

Neil took the computer and copied the list into another file, then started hunting the individuals on it. An hour later, he sent something to the printer and turned to Noah.

"I've located six of the ministers," he said, "and I've been able to find their itineraries for the day. They each have some light security, but nothing you can't handle."

"Good. Send the list of their names to Allison, then find me photographs so that she and I can study them."

"I'm ahead of you, boss," Neil said. "I'm printing out a quick dossier on each, with itineraries and photos attached."

By that time, everybody else was awake. Noah sat down with Sarah and Marco and began planning for the three ministers he would take out, while Jenny took her own team into the living room and began working on hers.

"I wish we had your computer, Jim," Jenny said.

"I have one in my car," Catherine said. "Is there wi-fi here?"

"Not the usual kind," Neil said. "My computer goes direct to satellite, but I can turn on a wi-fi sharing program, so another computer can log on through mine. Go ahead and get it and I'll set it up."

The only real problem was transportation. The only vehicles they had were the Nissan Armada that Sarah had rented and the BMW Catherine had acquired from the British Embassy. Noah didn't want to risk either of them being spotted, so he picked up his phone again and called Larry Carson at the U.S. Embassy.

"Carson," Larry said as he answered the phone.

"This is Camelot," Noah said.

"Holy shit," Larry said. "I heard you guys all escaped last night, but I sure didn't expect you to call me. You got any idea what's going on around the city right now?"

"Not really. Care to fill me in?"

"Well, the FSB and SVR are both in uproars. At the moment, they're each blaming the other for letting you get away, but there was one guy down there who claimed he was hiding in a closet and said it was a bunch of Russian soldiers who came and got you. Is that true?"

"Let's just say it's true enough and leave it at that. Have you been advised of the current situation regarding the plot to return to the USSR?"

"Um, I'd have to say no. Can you tell me?"

"Probably not. I'd imagine it's coming through the proper channels for you, but for now I need some wheels, gear, and some weapons. You still got that Russian supercar I drove before?"

"Oh, yeah, the Marussia B2. It actually belongs to the CIA, but I can get it if you need it."

"I do. I also need a second vehicle, something with power. Any suggestions?"

"Well, the only other thing we've got with any power is a year-old Nissan sedan. This one was actually custom-built for the embassy, and it's got a V-6 cranking over three hundred horsepower. Ought to get you where you want to go in a hurry. Will those work?"

"As long as you can rig it so they don't trace it back to the embassy. I can't guarantee I can bring them back in one piece, and my mission isn't one you want to be connected to."

"Well, that changes things, doesn't it. Let me think for a minute." He was quiet for nearly 30 seconds, then came back on the line. "Well, I can't give you either of those. What I can do, on the other hand, is call on a guy we use when we need a disposable car in a hurry. Can I text you on this number?"

"Yes. Tell me about this guy."

"His name is Ivan, and he restores older cars for some of the rich people. On the side, though, he's always building extremely fast cars that most people would never even notice. We've got kind of an arrangement with him when we need a car in a hurry. I'll send you his phone number and location, and all you have to do is tell him I sent you. You do have a source of funding, right? He'll happily hide the transaction, but he wants to get paid when a car leaves the lot."

"Not a problem," Noah said. "Send it on."

"Now, as for weapons, can you tell me what you need?"

"A couple of sniper rifles, at least two submachine guns, nine pistols, and plenty of ammunition. You could toss in some good knives while you're at it. I also need identification and passports, nine sets. I'll have a list and photos emailed to you shortly."

"You and your Christmas lists," Larry said with a chuckle. "I can have all of this ready within the hour. Got somebody who can come by and pick them up?"

"Yes, I can arrange that. Talk to you later."

Noah ended the call and his phone chirped a moment later to tell him he had received a text message. He passed it off to Neil, who immediately started researching Ivan and his clandestine sports cars.

Moments later, Neil whistled in admiration. "Larry wasn't kidding," he said. "This guy Ivan builds some awesome machines. He's known for restoring old cars, but he also likes to take simple, transportation-type cars, the kind nobody pays any attention to, and turn them into street sleepers. We're talking about typical Japanese sedans with more than four hundred horsepower."

"That should work for what we need," Noah said. "Get us two of them, okay?"

"You got it," Neil replied. He clicked a link on the company's website and was shortly talking with a salesperson who seemed to speak perfect English. It took only fifteen minutes to arrange the purchase of a couple of Toyotas from the late nineties, each of which was powered by an aftermarket, turbocharged V-6 engine.

"Okay, I used the same corporation that bought the airplane. Buying the two cars cost slightly over four million rubles, but they're ready to pick up. I'm printing out the documents now."

Noah turned to Catherine Potts. "You're the only one here that has diplomatic tags, so you can move around the city more easily than anyone else. Would you take Sarah and Dave out to pick up the cars?"

"My pleasure, sir," Catherine said. "Would you like me to stop by your own Embassy and pick up the other toys? As you pointed out, I have diplomatic license. No one's going to be stopping my car and searching it."

"That would help a great deal, if you don't think it will get you in any kind of trouble."

"Her Majesty probably expects me to get into a bit of trouble, going 'round with your lot," Catherine said with a giggle. "I don't think it will cause much of a stir, though. Our people visit yours fairly often, I'm sure."

"Then it sounds like a plan. Everybody ready?"

Catherine, Sarah, and Dave left only a few moments later, and Catherine was the first of the three to return to the house. Noah and Randy went out to her car to bring the boxes of weapons inside, and Sarah drove in as they were opening the trunk. She pulled the Toyota up close to the front porch and jumped out with a smile on her face.

"This baby is sweet," she said. "Plenty of power and it can turn a corner at close to fifty miles an hour."

"Good," Noah said, "we may need that. Where's Dave?"

Sarah smiled. "We decided to come back by different routes. If one of us got noticed, we didn't want it automatically leading to the other one."

"Good thinking," Noah replied. "Jenny and I have our first strikes planned. We've got to move pretty quickly, so let's get inside and start getting ready."

DIMITRI NOVAK, MINISTER of Justice for the Russian Federation, stepped out of the back of his official state limousine at the junction of Tverskaya Street and Kamergerskly Mall. The Mall was a wide, pedestrian-only street that was lined with hotels, theaters and shopping. One of its most famous locations was the Moscow Art Theater School, and Novak was visiting to attend a performance featuring his grandson, Alexei, in a starring role.

Because it was a private event, rather than one that was sponsored by the government, Novak was accompanied by a single member of his usual security team. Alex Jovanovich was a former FSB agent who had accepted Novak's offer to head his personal security. Since ministers did not normally come under the protection of the FSB, Jovanovich found the offer to be quite generous and had happily accepted. He had stepped into the position of commanding eight other security personnel, but on days like this one, he preferred to accept the duty himself.

"Alexei is very proud," Novak said as they made their way toward the theater. "He has worked hard to become the best actor he could be, and I feel that it will do him good to see that I support his choice of career. Besides, how often do I get to simply sit and enjoy entertainment?"

"I agree," Jovanovich said. "You should schedule such things more often, Dimitri. A little relaxation, they say, is good for the heart."

Novak laughed and looked at his bodyguard, who had also become his friend. "And this old heart needs all the good it can get. Perhaps we..."

A shot rang out and Jovanovich suddenly looked strange. It took Novak a second to realize that the look on his bodyguard's face was that of a man who had just had most of his brain blown out the side of his skull, but the spraying blood and gore that splattered across two women passing by was obvious. The women were screaming and people were starting to run, but Novak turned to see who had fired the shot that killed his friend.

A tall, blond man stood near the entrance to the Megapolis Hotel, his arm outstretched. Novak saw the pistol, but barely had time to register what he was seeing before a brief flash became the last sight he ever saw.

Ten feet from Novak, near the entrance to the theater, Marco suddenly began screaming and running. Between the gunshots and the screaming of the women and Marco, the milling crowd suddenly went into a mass panic. There were people running in every direction as Marco ran directly toward Noah.

The pistol quickly shoved into his pocket, Noah turned and ran with everyone else. With Marco shouting in Russian for everyone to run—*Beg! Beg!*—no one was paying any attention to the man who had fired the shots.

Novak's limousine had driven away as soon as he had exited it, and Sarah stopped in precisely the same place only two minutes later. Marco ran around the car to get into the back seat behind Sarah while Noah opened the passenger door and slid into the front beside her. As soon as the doors were closed, she had the car in gear and was moving forward.

"He's in," Sarah said.

The cell phone in her hand came to life. "Okay, things are going well," Neil said. "I've kept the police busy with alarms going off all over the city, keeping them away from your actual locations. Someone just called in a report of the shooting, though, and the dispatchers are trying to get officers available to respond."

"Good job," Noah said. "How's Jenny doing?"

AGRICULTURE MINISTER Boris Stolpin came down the hall with a smile on his face. The pretty, petite brunette sitting in the lobby of the building was the cause, because Boris greatly enjoyed looking at pretty girls.

This one was a reporter for a magazine out of New York and wanted to speak with him about the plans for Russia to increase its annual agricultural output. Those plans had been the subject of a speech he had given only a month earlier and he was delighted to have gotten such attention so quickly.

"Miss Stephanie Perkins?" Boris asked. "I am Boris Stolpin."

The girl got to her feet quickly, a bright and very attractive smile on her face. "Oh, thank you so much for seeing me," she said. "I know it was sudden, but my editors said while I was here, they wanted me to try to get a short interview."

"Is my pleasure," he said with a smile of his own. "Won't you come up to my office?"

"Oh, sure. I'd love to see where you work, where you come up with all of your great ideas."

Boris laughed. "Well, in that case," he said, "I would have to show you my lavatory. Some of my best ideas come while I am, shall we say, sequestered away."

"Oh, my goodness," Stephanie said, giggling. "That's actually kind of—interesting. To be honest, I have some of my own best ideas in the bathtub. There's just something about laying back naked in a tub full of water that sort of, I don't know, maybe it frees my mind. Lets it wander wherever it wants to go and sometimes it comes up with something really good."

"Now, I shall have to try that," Boris said. "Although I doubt I could become as comfortable in the bathtub as you might. Nor as beautiful, I might add."

That beautiful smile returned. "Okay, I heard you were a charmer. I should tell you that I usually get in trouble for trying to mix business with pleasure."

"Then perhaps we could take care of business with the interview and then look into pleasure? Perhaps I could take you to dinner?"

She looked him up and down appraisingly. "I can't say I would object to that idea," she said, licking her lips. "I just need to get the interview first, so that I can tell my editors I did my job. Is that okay?"

"Of course." They entered an elevator that rattled and clanked as it rose. "We can take as much time as you need."

"I really, really appreciate this," Stephanie said. "I've only been with the magazine for a few months and this is the first real official interview I've gotten to do. They had me over here to do a story on the ballet and then someone decided they needed an interview from you. Since I was already here, they decided to give me a chance at it. If I do good, it'll probably mean a promotion. Oh, gosh, I'm running off at the mouth. I'm so sorry."

"Not at all," Boris said. "Your excitement is quite delightful." The elevator clanked to a stop and the door opened. Boris led the way down the hall to the right, then opened the door to his office.

His secretary looked up as they entered and Stephanie felt a sudden chill in the air. It was rather obvious that the secretary had a crush on Boris and wasn't pleased to see someone much prettier than herself getting his smiles.

Boris noticed. "Natasha," he said to her, "this is Ms. Perkins, who has come to interview me for her magazine. We shall be occupied for some time. Why don't you go ahead and take the rest of the day off? I can close up the office today and I will see you tomorrow morning."

Natasha, who was the epitome of frumpy, forced herself to smile. It wasn't lost on her that Boris had spoken in English, obviously in an attempt to impress the pretty young girl. Natasha understood English perfectly well, but she responded in Russian.

"*Spasibo, ser,*" she said. She kept her eyes on him as she shut down the computer on her desk, then reached down and picked up her handbag and her coat. A moment later, she walked out the door and made a point of locking it behind herself.

"Please forgive Natasha," he said. "Sometimes, I think she forgets who here is the boss and who is the employee."

Stephanie giggled. "Looks to me like she's got a thing for you," she said. "Maybe you should pay some attention to her sometime."

He feigned surprise. "Oh, do you think so? Well, perhaps I should. Please, come on into my office where we can become more comfortable."

Stephanie followed him through the inner door and made the appropriate noises at the luxurious appointments of his office. There was a desk that looked like it belonged in a museum and a pair of beautifully upholstered chairs sitting in front of it, but he gestured toward the absolutely magnificent sofa that was set to one side, against the wall.

"We can sit here," Boris said. He led the way to the sofa and took a seat close to one end, while Stephanie sat in the middle.

"Okay," she said with a giggle, "this has got to be the most beautiful leather sofa I have ever seen. Oh, my gosh, it's just incredible." She licked her lips again. "Are you in any kind of a hurry? I mean, am I taking up important time?"

"No," Boris said, his smile twinkling. "I am all yours, for as long as you want me."

She put her hands over her face for a moment, then looked at him again. "Okay, this is going to sound crazy, I know, but—have you ever, like, you know, done it on the sofa?"

Boris leaned toward her and lowered his voice. "Never with anyone as beautiful as you," he said.

The girl bent double, she was giggling so hard. When she sat up again, she looked at him with her bottom lip held in her teeth. It took her a second to speak, but then she said, "I think it would be hot. If you want to, I mean."

Boris stood and took off his jacket, then began unbuttoning his shirt. Stephanie watched him for a moment, her smile growing wider, then got to her own feet. She took off the jacket she was wearing and dropped it on the sofa, then stepped close to him and put her arms out around his neck. He lowered his hands and put them on her waist, then began lowering his face toward hers.

He felt her hands move and then her left hand was against his chest. He smiled down at her, but then he saw the long, slim blade she had palmed when she took off her jacket, and his eyes grew wide for only a second before she spun herself to get behind him. The blade flashed across his throat, cutting all the way into his larynx.

He pushed away from her, but it was too late. He tried to call out, but no sound would escape except a hiss. He tried to get to the door. The knife flashed again, severing the tendon in the back of his knee, and he went down.

Half a minute later, his eyes went dull. Stephanie picked up her jacket, turned it inside out so that it was now black instead of red and slipped it on, then lifted her purse off the sofa and walked around the spreading pool of blood to the door. She opened it and walked into the receptionist's office, then pulled it shut behind her.

In the receptionist's office, she took off the brown wig and dropped it into her purse, pulling on a short, curly black one. She checked herself in a hand mirror, dropped it back into her bag, and then walked out the door. Like Natasha had done, she locked it behind her.

"SHE FINISHED HER NUMBER one just before yours arrived," Neil said, "and she's on the way to her number two."

"Good. So are we. Can you clear the route for us?"

"I'm already on it. Every policeman in that part of the city is being suddenly diverted to the area you just left. There won't be any interference along the way for you. I've already taken care of that for Jenny, and she'll be on station at number two in about four minutes."

"Good work."

CHAPTER EIGHTEEN

Allison looked up as her office door opened and saw Donald Jefferson enter with Molly right behind him. "And I thought I was the only one up this early," she said.

"Do you have any idea what an uproar is going on in DC right now?" Jefferson asked. "Four Russian ministers are confirmed dead in the last ninety minutes. The Prime Minister of Russia is currently screaming about American assassins, but the propaganda machine over there is going crazy with the story of the sleeper agents who were snatched out of the government safe house by the Russian military. That story is spreading like wildfire, and it's quite possible that Russia will split in half over it."

"He's exaggerating," Molly said. "On the other hand, this is definitely going to destroy the Committee. We've got CIA assets over there that are spreading the word that the ministers were killed by those sleepers, as part of a hostile takeover of the organization. Petrov is trying to deny it all, but we leaked enough information to tie him to the Committee, and President Feodor is already drafting an order to remove him from office."

Allison nodded. "I heard an hour ago that he was extremely cooperative when our ambassador went to visit him earlier. I gather we assured him that he's not in any direct danger from these sleeper assassins, but that continued peaceful relations between our two countries was dependent on the destruction of the Committee."

"Whatever works," Jefferson said. "And I'm not ruling out the possibility of a Russian civil war just yet. Sometimes we get lucky, you know?"

She looked at Jefferson. "Well, there are still two more on the target list. Reach out to everyone, I want to know about every bit of feedback that comes in. If we have to take out more of the Committee members, we need to do it soon. We can't afford to give them time to regroup and do any damage control, it's too important to shut this down."

"Agreed," Jefferson said. "I'll call NSA and Homeland, Molly can take the Joint Chiefs and Strategic Analysis. Between those four, we ought to get a pretty good handle on what's going to happen."

The two of them turned and left the office, leaving Allison staring at her computer screen. She was scanning news websites in Russia and trying to get a sense of the mood of the people as the story of a failed coup began to spread through the media.

She was still watching the news stories twenty minutes later when her phone rang again. The switchboard told her that it was the president calling, and she took a deep breath before she pushed the button to accept the call.

"Mr. President," she said. "What can I do for you?"

"You can tell me you know what's going on in Russia," the president said. "I'm hearing rumors of some 'American death squad' running loose over there. I trust that's your best people?"

"Would I send anybody else? It's being handled, and from what I'm seeing in the Russian media, it's being handled quite effectively. The Committee for Restoration of the Communist Party is catching the blame for the assassinations, because our propaganda machine is the best in the world. We've got people all over Russia swearing that the committee is going through a hostile takeover by a faction that hopes to see the USSR restored exactly the way it was. That's the last thing in the world any of the old member states want, and most of the Russian people hate the idea, as well."

"As well they should," the president said. "The true Communist Party in Russia is actually pretty small, made up mostly of old folks who just don't know how to live under a democratic government. Freedom isn't something they understand, not after so many years of living under communist rule."

"I agree. As dangerous as this situation is, we don't dare sit back and let these people bring back the Cold War. Every analysis I've seen of the situation says that the new Union would end up controlling half of the freaking world. There is no way we could avoid a final nuclear conflict, and I'm just not ready to go back to the Stone Age, not yet."

"I'll tell you something, if you promise never to reveal I said it. There are times when I think that could be exactly what this country needs. Get rid of the Internet, get rid of nuclear weapons, get rid of everything technology has given us since about eighteen seventy-five, and we'd probably all be a lot happier."

"Bite your tongue," Allison said. "A lot of the advances we've made have been in medicine, things that make life better. Hundred and fifty years ago, most women died in childbirth before they ever reached the age of twenty-five. I'm not ready to go back to those days, thank you."

"Hey, I never said it was perfect," he quipped. "I just said people were happier. Do a little historical research, you'll find out I'm right."

"I'm perfectly happy with technology, thank you. I don't know what I would do without my cell phone, and if it weren't for modern medicine, I wouldn't even be here. That attack a year and a half ago would have killed me and quite a few others."

"Allison, if we didn't have all this technology, that attack never would've taken place. Your department wouldn't even exist, you know that."

"Do you have to be such a downer? I suspect all of your security advisors are probably trying to get hold of you about now. Why are you tying up the line with me?"

"Because you're the only one of them who isn't afraid of me. If I want to know just how bad things really are, I know to call you. How bad are things, Allison? Tell me straight."

Allison sighed. "If everything goes according to plan, the Committee will be on the run within the next few hours. They don't dare try to reassert themselves, not when so much is hanging in the balance. The last thing in the world they need is to let the Russian people think they are still intact. If we were to publish the list of all of their top members, it wouldn't be our people taking them out alone. An awful lot of the Russian military and even some civilians would get involved."

"Then why haven't we published it?"

"It isn't time yet," Allison said. "I want my people out of there before we get to that point."

The president was quiet for a moment. "Allison, are you going to be able to get them out?"

"Of course. I always have a backup plan, especially when my original backup plan goes south. At the moment, I have four different options for removing them from Russia. I'm just waiting to see which one is most likely to succeed."

"Woman, you give me headaches. Keep me posted, will you?"

"I sure will. Go talk to your advisors, and let me know if any of them want to do anything stupid."

She disconnected the call and leaned back in her chair. If everything went according to plan for the next few hours, they might just barely manage to avoid ending up in World War III in the not-too-distant future.

If it didn't...

BOTH NOAH AND JENNY had taken out two of their targets and each of them was closing in on the third. For Noah, that meant climbing a building on the outskirts of a residential area where Ivan Gritchkin made his home. Ivan was Minister of Transport and the youngest member of the Council of Ministers.

At forty-six years old, Ivan was one of the most powerful men in Russia. Noah was almost surprised that he would have anything to do with the Committee, since the Communist Party had always relied on what they referred to as "Elder Statesmen" to be in control. Under the Communist Party, Ivan would never have risen higher than a clerk in a minister's office.

He had only been just in his teens, however, when communism came to an end in Russia and democracy was introduced. His views on the subject might not be as much his own as those he heard from his parents or grandparents. Regardless of why, he was still far too powerful to be allowed to pursue such a goal, and the fact that he was going to be at home on this particular evening put him on Noah's target list.

The building Noah scaled was originally an office complex, but it had been purchased some years earlier by a real estate consortium. It was now divided into dozens of luxurious condos and many Russian businessmen and -women were calling it home. Noah had no issue with any of them, and the only reason he even had to come near them was because their building was the only one tall enough to allow him a line of sight into Ivan's bedroom.

Marco had gone ahead while Noah took care of Yuri Moskovich, Minister of Education and Science. Yuri had met his end while riding in his limousine on the way home, via the M7. The FSB, together with the local police officers, were trying to figure out just how the accident had happened. Since the limousine had crashed head-on into a massive concrete pillar at more than one hundred and fifty KPH, it would take their combined forensics departments a week to determine that the driver had been shot through the head before the accident occurred. Ironically, the bullet that killed him had not caused the car to slow. Somehow, it had gone faster and faster until it finally was brought to a sudden halt as it struck the pillar under the E115 overpass.

It was actually Sarah who had pushed the car to such speeds. Once Noah had taken out the driver, she had put the Toyota behind the limo and let the bumpers kiss, then she eased into the throttle and let the powerful V-6 do its job. It only took about half a minute to get it up to crash speed, and then she fanned the brakes to help her stay on the road as the limousine shot into the median and headed for the pillar. It worked out even better than they had planned, and the big limousine was completely destroyed.

Meanwhile, Marco had gone to the top of the condo building in the guise of a repairman, carrying a big toolbox. Once he was there, he set up the sniper rifle Carson had provided and waited for Noah while keeping binoculars trained on Ivan's house. The young minister was at home and Marco could see him through the living room window. He seemed to be watching television and his beautiful wife Irina was curled up beside him.

A hand touched Marco on the shoulder and he barely managed to keep from dropping the binoculars as he spun his head around. Noah was there, looking at the way the rifle was set up and nodding. "Looks good," he said. "What about the target?"

"He's watching TV," Marco said. "His wife is sitting beside him on a loveseat, and at least one of his kids is there. Looks like a boy, probably around ten or eleven."

"That would be Roman," Noah said. "You were close, he's twelve."

Noah sat down on the toolbox and hefted the stock of the rifle to his shoulder. The bipod that held the barrel was braced on a block set on the edge of the building, which kept it perfectly positioned for the shot. Noah looked through the powerful scope and saw Ivan clearly, then lowered the stock again as he began calculating the various factors required to make a shot over a distance of twelve hundred meters. This was not the longest shot he had ever made, but it was necessary to figure in the wind, the elevation, the amount the bullet would drop as it traveled through the air, and other factors in order to determine precisely where to aim if he wanted the bullet to strike Ivan perfectly.

Eight minutes later, Noah picked up the stock again and embraced it against his shoulder. He made minor adjustments to the scope, then placed its crosshairs directly on Ivan's face through the window. He started to squeeze the trigger, but then hesitated.

Irina's face was very close to her husband's as she leaned sideways to rest her head on his shoulder. Noah adjusted his aim, putting the crosshairs over the center of Ivan's chest. The big, fifty caliber round would do sufficient damage to ensure that he would die, even if Noah were to miss striking the heart directly. He checked his aim, slowly released his breath and then held it, and squeezed the trigger.

The big gun roared and bucked, but Noah kept his eye against the scope. As soon as the gun dropped back down, Noah saw that his shot had been true. Ivan was almost cut into two pieces and Irina was running away from him.

"Let's go," Noah said. He dropped the stock, peeled off the gloves he had been wearing, and the two of them hooked their carabiners onto the ropes Marco had hung down the back of the building. Less than thirty seconds later, both of them were on the ground and walking calmly away, their rapelling harnesses dropped into the bushes. They walked less than two hundred yards before a Toyota Camry pulled up beside them, then they got into the car as Sarah drove away.

"All done," Noah said.

JENNY'S SECOND TARGET had been Alexei Piotrovich, the Minister of Industry and Trade. She didn't anticipate a lot of difficulty with that one. Alexei would be having dinner at the Old Tower restaurant, not far from Red Square, a fairly common place for tourists to visit. Jenny changed into a pair of jeans and a western shirt, added a wig that was blonde with brown streaks, and then she and Randy took a taxi to the restaurant. They walked in like any other tourists and Jenny spotted Alexei sitting with a beautiful younger woman.

She pointed to a window near where he was seated. "Oh, can we sit over there? I love to look out at the city, it's so beautiful."

The maître d' smiled and escorted them to a table beside the window. They were less than ten feet from Alexei's table and they both made a show of playing the tourist. Jenny kept looking around, and when she finally caught Alexei's eye, she gave him a smile and a flirtatious wink.

While he was already with a beautiful woman, Alexei was not the kind of man to ignore any woman who seemed to think he was attractive. He knew that he was not a bad-looking man for his fifty years, but his taste had always run to women in their teens or early twenties. The girl with him at the moment looked to be around twenty-five, but that pretty blonde American was obviously younger. Alexi wasn't about to pass up the opportunity to find out who she was.

One of the perks of being a minister was that you could get away with things the average citizen could not. Alexei had discovered this early on and had cultivated friendships that would help him to achieve certain goals that might not be heartily approved by the public. More than one young American woman had been brought to him for his personal enjoyment and then been listed as simply missing. This one, married though she might be if the man with her was any indication, looked like she could be a lot of fun in such a situation.

All he needed to do was get her name and hotel. His friends would take care of the rest, including that husband.

Ironically, this was not something that the American intelligence community had stumbled across. Jenny had no idea that she was being sized up as a potential victim for rape and murder, and if she had known, she probably would've encouraged him. It would have made killing the bastard so much more fulfilling.

She waited until the woman with Alexei got up to go to the ladies' room and then gently kicked Randy under the table. He excused himself and wandered off toward the men's room, and Jenny carefully watched until he was out of sight before looking at Alexei again. He was staring directly at her, and she pretended to be shy for a second, then looked up and winked again.

Seconds later, Alexei stepped over to her table and sat down in Randy's chair. "Please forgive me for being so bold," he said, "but you remind me so much of a lady I met about a year ago. Would you happen to be named Janet?"

"Oh, no," Jenny said shyly. "I'm—my name is Krista, Krista Borden."

"Ah, that's too bad. However, I must say that Krista is a beautiful name for such a beautiful woman. You are visiting our city?"

Jenny nodded, smiling brightly. "Yes, it's my first time. My husband brought me over here because he wanted to check out the architecture, that's what he does, he's an architect." She leaned toward him and lowered her voice to a whisper. "He's a very boring architect, to be honest. If he wasn't loaded, I would've dumped him already."

Alexei smiled. "I see you have a sense of adventure," he said. "May I ask where you're staying?"

"Oh, yes, we're at the Marriott. It's just a few blocks away from here, a beautiful hotel."

"Oh, really? I have friends who stay there quite often. Perhaps I will see you there. I am coming by tomorrow, in fact. I must bring some papers to someone who is staying there at about ten o'clock tomorrow morning."

Jenny looked at him for a moment, then gave him a sultry smile. "My husband has some business to take care of tomorrow," she said. "I'll be all alone."

"Well—if you would perhaps like some company?"

Jenny looked at him for a moment, licking her lips. "Are you a good kisser?" she asked.

"I've been told that I am very good," Alexei said. "Perhaps tomorrow you can find out."

Jenny looked around quickly. "How about if I find out right now? Would you go outside with me for just a minute?"

Alexei laughed heartily. "You are truly adventurous," he said. "Certainly, let's go." He rose quickly to his feet and Jenny did likewise, hurrying past him so that he had to follow her outside. She went out the door and turned to the right, hurrying into the shadows cast by the lights of the city. There was one place that was almost invisible, right behind the outdoor dining area that was closed at the moment. It was dark and deserted, and exactly what Jenny was looking for.

Alexei had followed her with delight, and when she turned to face him, he hurried toward her. She held out her arms with a smile on her face, and he quickly stepped up and reached for her, and that's when the blade slipped through his solar plexus and found his heart. Before he realized what had happened, she gave it a twist and shook it from side to side, effectively shredding his heart muscle in less than three seconds.

Jenny stepped back quickly, out of his reach as his face registered shock, and then instantly stepped in again to punch him in the throat. He made a choking sound, then looked down at himself and saw the grip of the knife protruding from his chest. Some part of him must have known he was dying, then, because he only looked up at her and stared. He made no attempt to cry out, no effort to turn and run, but simply stood there and stared at her as blood poured down his body.

It took slightly more than a minute for him to lose consciousness, but that was enough. There was absolutely no hope he could be saved, even if he were found at that moment by best paramedics in the world. Jenny carefully stepped around the blood and walked off toward Revolution Square. Randy, who had been waiting behind the Burgermeister building next door, stepped out and joined her.

Dave pulled up as they approached Revolution Square and they got into the car. He followed the road around until he came to Ulitsa Olhotnyy Ryad, then turned left to go west into the city.

"Without a hitch," Jenny said. "How long before we get to the last one?"

"Probably about ten minutes," Dave said. "Neil and Jim have the police running wild goose chases all over the place, so we shouldn't have any problems."

"Well, time is getting short, so I'm not going to be able to play with this one. He should be arriving at his mistress' place in about twenty-five minutes, so let's get me close so I can get everything set up."

"You got it, boss lady," Dave said. He drove sedately, carefully not drawing attention to the car that was barely noticed anyway.

Just over ten minutes later, Dave stopped the car at the intersection, five houses down from the one Jenny wanted. It was the home of the young woman who happily fulfilled the desires of Serge Chernov, Minister of Defense for the Russian Federation, in return for the comfortable house and generous allowance he gave her.

Ironically, Chernov was the only one of the Ministers who was automatically entitled to protection by the FSB, and yet he insisted on leaving his security behind when he visited her. Svetlana, he explained to his security team, preferred to live in the fantasy that they were a genuine couple. If the armed security agents accompanied him, it ruined the effect for her.

Even more stupidly, he allowed his visits to her home to be listed on the itinerary that was given to his security team. Neil had managed to get a copy of it from the FSB computers, and Jenny had all but begged Noah to let her have Chernov as one of her three targets.

Dave parked the car at the curb and Jenny got out. She went around to the trunk of the car and opened it, then reached inside and picked up the submachine gun. It wasn't often she got to use one of these, and something about the vibration as it *rat-a-tat-tatted* fifty rounds of pure death out of its barrel just lit her fire. Since Svetlana lived on a quiet street, she had decided it would be fun to liven things up a bit.

There were some large bushes in the yard of the house beside hers, and Jenny hurried from one yard to the next until she got there. No one seemed to have noticed her, and she slipped into the bushes without making a sound or drawing any attention. Now it was just a matter of waiting, and Jenny had learned long ago how to wait.

In her head, she sang songs as she waited. She sang all the way through four of her favorite country hits before Chernov's antique Zil sedan pulled up in front of the house. A quick look around confirmed that no one else seemed to be within sight, so she crouched under the bush and watched as he got out of the big car.

She waited until he had walked all the way around the front of the car and stepped into Svetlana's yard before she opened fire. The gun rattled, sending a thrill through her, and Chernov did an insane-looking little dance and fell onto his back. She had seen that several of the bullets had made their way through his face, so the job was done. While Svetlana began screaming, standing at her door and staring out at the end of her tenure as a sugar baby, Jenny trotted calmly back toward the Toyota and tossed the submachine gun to Randy in the back seat as she got in.

"Okay, boys," she said cheerfully. "All done, let's go back to the house."

DONALD JEFFERSON WALKED into Allison's office and flopped into his usual chair. "I just got the word that six of the Ministers are confirmed dead. Three others seem to have gone into hiding, and the prime minister, Petrov, has resigned his position and is currently in protective custody of the SVR. The NSA says the Committee is almost certainly out of business, but they would like to see a few more of the members eliminated from time to time over the coming months. I think that's just to remind the remaining ones that there are those of us out here who are not going to put up with a return to those days."

"We've got a couple of the new teams that need some practice on real missions. Some of the members aren't going to be that hard to get to, so those would be good missions to let them get a grip on what they're doing. Tell NSA to send the proper request through the proper channels and I'll review them the way I always do."

"Already did," Jefferson said. "They always try to get me to run around obstacles for them, but I never do. You'd think they'd have learned, wouldn't you?"

"It's the fact that they are political animals," Allison said. "They're just too damned stupid."

CHAPTER NINTEEN

It was almost nine o'clock that evening by the time Jenny and her team were all back at the house, and Noah was standing on the porch waiting for them. When Jenny stepped out of the car, she snapped off a parade-ground-perfect salute and smiled up at him. "All missions accomplished, sir," she said. "It felt good to be back in action, at last."

Noah nodded. "All right," he said. "I'm calling it in."

He took out his phone as they entered the house and pressed the icon to dial headquarters.

"Brigadoon Investments, how may I direct your call?"

"Camelot calling for Allison Peterson."

"One moment, please."

The music played for roughly four and a half seconds, and then Allison came on the phone. "Camelot, report."

"All six targets were acquired and eliminated," Noah said. "No difficulties on our end. We are awaiting orders."

"You can't imagine how glad I am to hear from you," Allison said. "The word of your activities has spread all over the world, and our propaganda divisions are working ridiculous amounts of overtime, which is a euphemism for having an absolute field day spreading out pure bullshit! I understand the Russian president is being extremely cooperative with our ambassador on this matter, and the prime minister has been removed from office and is currently in what they are calling protective custody. He's probably on his way to Siberia as we speak, which would suit me just fine. Now, where do we stand on getting you out of Russia?"

"We have clean IDs and passports and Monica has offered to take us all back on her charter. At the moment, that seems the best option, but I wanted to get your input on it."

"That plane is sitting at Sheremetyevo, right?"

"Yes, ma'am."

"The problem with that is the fact that all of you were photographed when you are arrested. There's very little doubt in my mind that the FSB has people all over every airport holding those pictures like a hand of playing cards. You try getting to the charter gate, you might end up shot dead." She cursed under her breath. "Can you think of any way you can get onto that plane without being seen?"

"I don't think it would be easy. The chances we would have of getting through the terminal building and out to that aircraft are probably pretty slim. The only ones who can certainly make it are Monica, Sarah and Neil. If we decide to go that route, I want to send them ahead. Let them get into the plane and be ready to take off if things go wrong."

"Noah, I'm afraid it wouldn't matter. If you and the rest are captured or killed while trying to get to that plane, it would probably be shot out of the air. The only hope you've got of catching that charter out is if you can get onto it without the FSB spotting you."

"The issue there is the fact that the IDs we have all use our real photos, and we know that the SVR has some fairly sophisticated facial recognition software. Pretty good chance they'd spot us even with disguises. The only possible way I can think of to get us onto that plane would be in boxes, something that would prevent anyone, including computers, from seeing our faces."

"Yes, but unfortunately that isn't a cargo flight. We had several plans ready, but your sensational escape has made them worthless, I'm afraid. Let me talk to the brains and see what they can come up with. I'll call you back as soon as I know something."

"Yes, ma'am," Noah said, but the line was dead before he even got it out.

Sarah had walked over to stand beside him while he spoke to Allison and heard most of what Allison had to say. Monica looked up at them.

"I take it she wasn't fond of the idea?"

"It's the photos they took when we were arrested," Noah said. "Between facial recognition and SVR and FSB holding our pictures and looking for us, we don't think there's a terrific chance that we'd be able to make it onto the plane. I'm trying to think of something that would make it feasible to get us on without us being seen, but I don't have a clue what it would be at this point."

Neil was sitting at the table with his computer. "I heard you mention disguise," he said. "I could do an overprint on our photos, on the IDs of passports, I mean. I can change hair color, eye color, add whiskers or whatever, but it probably still wouldn't fool facial recognition."

"No, I'm sure it wouldn't. The Dragon Lady is going to talk to the brains, which means Molly and Wally, I'm sure, and see what they can come up with. She will call us back when she has something to tell us, so all we can do is wait until then."

"I know something else we could do," Neil said. "We could get something to eat around here. I don't know if anybody else has noticed, but when you have eleven people in one little bitty house, the groceries go pretty fast. I'm hungry, and there's nothing here to eat."

"I'll fetch," Catherine said. "There's really not much for me to do at any road, at the moment. Anybody want to give me a list?"

Everybody had a suggestion or two, so it was almost 20 minutes later when Catherine left to go and find a grocery store. Noah suggested she pick up something ready-to-eat on the way back.

Sarah took hold of Noah's hand and pulled him toward the bedroom they shared, and they lay down on the bed together. "I heard what you said about me and Neil getting on the plane ahead of you," Sarah said. "I would think you'd know by now that's not going to happen. I'm not leaving without you, Noah. If it means we have to live the rest of our lives right here in Moscow, I'm not leaving without you."

"Unfortunately, the rest of our lives wouldn't be very long if we don't get out of here sometime soon. Sooner or later, one of us is going to run into some situation that's going to get FSB on us, and we won't be able to bluff our way out of it. Somehow, I don't think they're going to risk trying to lock us up again. We would probably end up against a wall somewhere in the middle of nowhere."

Sarah was quiet for several seconds, then looked at him with eyes that were almost moist enough for tears. "At least we'd be together," she said.

"That's not an option," Noah said. "Just be patient, let's wait for Molly and Wally. With any luck, they'll come up with an idea that can work. Until then, we can just stay here and play house for a while."

"WHAT HAPPENED TO THE Cessna?" Molly asked. "I thought that was the plan all along."

"Not after a number of high-profile assassinations," Jefferson said. "The Russian Air Force will be patrolling the borders, looking for low-flying aircraft and anything else that's out of place. There's just not much hope that Noah could fly it out without being spotted, not when the whole country is on high alert."

"Monica's Gulfstream IV is sitting at Sheremetyevo," Allison said, "but we need to figure out how to get them on it. There's going to be security all over that airport and they'll be looking for our people. Disguises aren't going to help, their facial recognition is just too good. They'd be spotted by the distance between the pupils in their eyes, other little crap like that. The only hope we've got for getting them onto that plane is to find a way to make them completely unrecognizable, and even then we'll have to have a reason that makes sense for them to be getting on the plane. Monica came in alone with just a flight crew. They're going to be wondering why she's taking a bunch of other people out with her."

"That's a good point," Molly said. "Since she's not a Russian, anybody she takes out of the country is going to have to go through extra scrutiny, I'm sure. Has anyone talked to Wally?"

"I have," Allison said, "but he's coming up empty on this one. If they were here, we could probably find some way to disguise them enough that the computers couldn't spot them, but there's just no way to do it over there."

"Damn," Molly said. "There's got to be something we can do. What about getting them out of Moscow, to some other part of the country where they might not be recognized?"

Jefferson shook his head. "Facial recognition systems work off of the central database, and their photos are in it. With time, some of our best hackers might be able to get in there and get them out, but not when security levels are so high. We've got to figure something else out, because we are simply not going to give up Camelot and Cinderella. That's not going to happen."

"What about—no, that wouldn't work," Molly said. "Hey, they've got a British agent working with them, right? What about getting them out on a British diplomatic flight?"

"Same problem," Allison said. "How to get them onto the plane without being seen. You weren't with us the last time we had this problem, but there were SVR agents actually shooting at them as they boarded a diplomatic flight. Neil was wounded that time, shot through the leg. Ever since that happened, you can bet they've got cameras and armed security watching the charter and diplomatic tarmac areas. If they were spotted, they'd never make it onto the plane either way."

Molly shook her head. "There has to be an answer," she said. "There simply has to be."

CATHERINE RETURNED with the food, and they gathered around the living room area to chow down on pizza. Noah chose that time to explain to everyone that the experts back home were working on a way to get them out of the country, which led to some humorous, if impractical, suggestions. Tony VanHorn, who had been terribly quiet since they arrived at the house, came up with the idea of putting them all into coffins and trying to ship them out as dead bodies, while Catherine herself suggested that they take all of the pizza boxes they had and glue them together into a big one, then ship them out as the world's largest pepperoni and cheese.

"I actually toyed with the idea," Monica said, "of trying to pack you all into boxes from my beauty product line, but it would look awfully unusual for me to be taking cases and cases of it home by air. Besides, the biggest boxes we've got would be too small even for me, let alone one of you."

"Okay, that won't work," Neil said, "but what about packing us into a shipping container? I'm sure we could manage to survive a few days, maybe the couple of weeks it would take to ship us back to the states."

"No, sorry," Monica said. "Customs and export regulations require every shipping container to be opened and thoroughly searched before it leaves port. They find us, and we'd all be dead."

"Well, I'm trying," Neil said.

"Could it be," Catherine asked, "that you're looking at this from the wrong direction? What about taking it from the angle of what kind of things are allowed to leave the country? I mean, surely there are certain things that can be sent out without too much bother."

"I'm not sure what they would be," Monica said. "Neil? Any ideas?"

"I'm looking," Neil said. "There are certain things that can be classified as noninterference, meaning they don't get searched or hassled in any way. Unfortunately, those only include shipments from the Russian government, humanitarian flights carrying terminally or seriously ill or wounded patients to doctors in other parts of the world, diplomatic flights or vessels... Yeah, that's about it. Any of that sound like an idea that might work?"

"Nothing I heard," Jenny said. She reached out and rubbed Neil's back. "Don't worry, baby," she said, "I've got confidence in you. You'll figure it out, you always do."

Neil shook his head. "I'm trying," he said. "I really don't think there's much chance of convincing the government to ship us home, and none of us could pass for someone who was dying or so sick they had to leave the country to survive. We can't make it to a diplomatic flight, we already established that. I just..."

"Wait a minute," Monica said. "You mentioned two things that caught my attention. The first is getting the government to ship you home. It's actually possible that I might be able to make that happen. Barring that, I was thinking about what you said about humanitarian flights. What if I, a wealthy American businessperson, were to offer to take several sick or injured people back to the States for medical treatment? We could put all of you on stretchers and have you carried right onto the plane. If you're all wrapped up in blankets and so sick you can't even talk, we might just get away with that."

"You know," Neil said, "that just might actually be possible. What I want to hear about, though, is what you meant about getting the Russian government to send us home. Are you talking about in body bags, or what?"

"No," Monica said, "no. I'm actually thinking of a way for President Feodor to maybe avoid an extremely embarrassing situation." She checked her phone and saw the time, then mumbled about time zones. "I can't even attempt it till morning, but if we haven't come up with something by then, I think it's worth a shot."

Noah looked at her. "Explain it to me in detail," he said, "before you try it. I want to run it past Allison first."

Monica grinned at him. "Okay, look at it like this," she said. "If you get arrested trying to leave the country, especially at a very visible place like Sheremetyevo Airport, the news services are going to be all over you. While the Russian government does have some censorship powers, they've also got a population with cell phones and Facebook accounts. No matter how they may bully the news services, the story is going to make it onto the Internet, and then some of the news organizations would run it anyway. You guys are the famous sleeper agents; the president would find it extremely embarrassing if you suddenly turned up dead, simply because it was because of you that the government found out about the whole Committee for restoring the Soviet whatever. Right?"

"I'm not sure he'd find it all that embarrassing," Noah said. "To be honest, I'd think he'd find it a relief if we suddenly died. There'd be no one to answer the questions that are bound to be asked, whether they get us or not."

"Okay, maybe if you want to look at it from a cynical point of view, that makes sense. But how about this: what if we could change the story again? You know, there's a story floating around now that you were rescued from that place by Russian military, right? What if the story got out that those soldiers were ordered there by the president himself, because the truth of the matter is that you were all double agents who were actually working for the president in order to expose this conspiracy?"

"All he'd have to do is deny it," Sarah said. "I can't imagine he'd want to go along with it."

"He would if it makes him a hero. What if we got the story out that President Feodor actually learned from some high-placed aide to the prime minister about the conspiracy, and about the plan to assassinate what's-his-name, the one that you were charged with killing? What if we said that you were really supposed to kill him, the president, but instead, you went after that minister because he was part of the whole conspiracy? If you did that to protect the president, and then helped him expose what was really going on, you'd be heroes, and then if you got killed, it would be a serious embarrassment."

"I could do it," Neil said suddenly. "Same way I put out the story about you in the prison. Inside of three hours, I could have that story screaming around the world."

"Okay, I can see where that could change a few things," Noah said. "The problem then would be that, if we were supposed to be heroes, wouldn't the president want to keep us close? Maybe parade us in front of the TV cameras? That's the last thing we would want."

"On the contrary," Monica said. "I know how the Russian mind thinks. I can get a message to him that would convince him the best possible situation would be to claim that those agents were sent back into deep cover, not in America, but somewhere else. That way, he can justify calling off the search for all of you. If he does that, all I've got to do is walk you right on that airplane and we are out of here!"

Noah thought through the idea and slowly nodded his head. "You're thinking of Boris, right? The guy who worked for the prime minister?"

"Yes. I'll guarantee you, he'll do whatever I tell him to do. If I tell him to go to the president and say that the only way he can avoid a scandal over having you all killed secretly is by declaring you all to be heroes of the Russian Federation and issuing a statement that you are continuing to serve good old Mother Russia, he's going to deliver that message. Feodor is no fool; since we already know that the U.S. ambassador has been crawling up his ass, this gives him a believable backstory on how he learned about the conspiracy and brought it to its knees. I'm telling you, the Russian people would hail him as a hero and the border states would probably join right in. The same ones that are arming their borders right now would be begging for a peaceful partnership with Russia within days, and that would probably save this whole country from falling completely apart right now."

Noah looked at her for a long moment and then he took out his phone. When he got Allison on the line, he explained the whole plan and even let Monica take the phone for a few minutes to answer questions. Thirty minutes later, he looked at Neil and said, "Do it."

BORIS PETROSKI WOKE to the sound of his phone ringing and groggily picked it up and forced his eyes to focus on the screen. The number was one that he recognized, and it brought him instantly awake.

"Yes?"

"Boris, I have something for you to do." The distorted voice he knew so well always sent a shiver down his spine.

Monica spent almost an hour going over the plan with Boris, and finally had to make him get on his computer and look at the stories that were already circulating around the world. The president was a hero because he had learned about the conspiracy and turned it against itself. The president was told of the conspiracy by a high-ranking official in the prime minister's office, a man who would remain anonymous despite being greatly rewarded. The infamous "sleeper agents" were of such great importance to the president that he had decided to keep their identities a secret, and they were comfortably placed in positions where they could maintain that anonymity until they were needed again.

"Now, Boris," Monica said at last, "do you understand what you must do?"

"I understand," he said. "I am simply trying to think of a way to get the president to see me. Everyone in Petrov's office is under suspension at this time."

"Oh, come now, Boris. Someone in the position you held would have a number of people who would prefer you not reveal something you know. Use that to your advantage. Call on those you know who have the ear of the president and tell them that getting you an audience with him will guarantee that you remain their friend from now on. That way, you have not made a threat, but they will understand."

Boris hesitated. "Well, yes," he said cautiously. "There is one man..."

Five minutes later, Boris made another call. "Vasily," he said. "This is Boris Petroski. I need your help." He listened for a moment and then a sly smile stole across his face. "Vasily, all of us have friends, don't we? Some of us have friends we would prefer not to let others know about. Incidentally, do you know Mr. Wilkerson at the American Embassy?" He listened again and the smile became wider. "And this is why you and I are such good friends, Vasily. There are times when we each need something from the other, is that not correct?" The smile became beatific and Boris closed his eyes in delight as he listened to his friend Vasily. "Vasily, I need to speak with the president, and I need to speak with him right away. I know that you can make this happen, and it will ensure to you my continued friendship—and silence—forever if you do so."

THE GULFSTREAM LANDED at Kirtland Airport and nine weary travelers disembarked. They made their way across the tarmac to the parking lot, where they all climbed into a big Hummer. One of them was dropped at a hotel, four others were dropped at their own various homes, and then the Hummer made its way to Temple Lake Road and eventually to Noah's house.

Two of the four remaining passengers staggered inside the house and made it to the bedroom. They dropped their bags on the floor and stripped out of their clothes, then crawled into the bed and were asleep in seconds.

The other two drove the Hummer across the yard to Neil's house trailer and went inside. Like Noah and Sarah, they headed straight to the bedroom, got out of their clothes and lay down. Neil wrapped his arms around Jenny and held her close, kissing her gently once.

He realized that she was shaking, and he opened his eyes to look at her. Tears were streaming down her face as she looked up at him, and he asked her what was wrong.

"Nothing," she said. "There's absolutely nothing wrong. Actually, everything is absolutely wonderful."

Neil's eyes narrowed as he looked at her. "Baby, are you okay?"

Suddenly she wrapped her arms around him and held herself as close as she could. She kissed his cheek several times, then whispered in his ear, "You came after me."

SPECIAL OFFER

B uilding a relationship with my readers is the ultimate goal with writing. At least, it should be. Without you guys, us writers would just be making up stories for ourselves...which would be weird. That's why I like to connect with my readers in a way many big name authors don't.

I occasionally send newsletters with details on new releases, special offers and other bits of news relating to Sam Prichard, Noah Wolf, and the other varies series and stand alone novels that I write.

And if you sign up to the mailing list today, I'll send you this free content:

- A free copy of the first Sam Prichard novella, FALLBACK (plus the audiobook version)

- A free copy of the first Noah Wolf novella, THE WAY OF THE WOLF (plus the audiobook version)

- Exclusive content and pricing to my mailing list – you can't get this anywhere else. Every book launch I set a discounted price for my mailing list for a couple days. This is exclusive to my list *only*, and something that isn't publicized anywhere else.

You can get the novella's, the audiobook's, and the exclusive discounted pricing **for free,** by at: www.davidarcherbooks.com/vip

NOTE FROM THE AUTHOR

I f you enjoyed this adventure, would you please consider taking a moment and leaving your thoughts for others who might also enjoy this book?

It takes only a handful of seconds to leave a review, but can literally make or break a self published career. Please don't feel any obligation to do so, but if you had fun, or perhaps enjoyed yourself at all, then I'd sincerely appreciate it!

Thanks so much,

David Archer